Salabhanjika

Salabhanjika

Indramani Jena

Edited by:
Raju Samal

ବ୍ଲାକ୍ ଇଗଲ୍ ବୁକ୍ସ

ଭୁବନେଶ୍ୱର, ଓଡ଼ିଶା

BLACK EAGLE BOOKS
Dublin, USA

BLACK EAGLE BOOKS

USA address:
7464 Wisdom Lane
Dublin, OH 43016

India address:
E/312, Trident Galaxy, Kalinga Nagar,
Bhubaneswar-751003, Odisha, India

E-mail: info@blackeaglebooks.org
Website: www.blackeaglebooks.org

First International Edition Published by
BLACK EAGLE BOOKS, 2022

SALABHANJIKA
by **Indramani Jena**

Edited by: **Raju Samal**

Copyright © **Indramani Jena**

Cover Art: **Tanuj**

ISBN- 978-1-64560-325-2 (Paperback)
Library of Congress Control Number: 2022948122

Printed in the United States of America

Dedicated to *Siddha Saints* for their blessings on today's deranged humanity

Author

Acknowledgement

Author expresses his gratitude to a host of personalities for transforming the contents of the proposed story into the present format. Such self-less help has been rendered by: Dr. Gourahari Das, Prof. A.C. Sahoo, Prof. P.K. Mishra, Prof. M. Simanchal Rao, Prof. Swarnamayee Tripathy, Prof. Padip Kumar Samantaray, Mr. Kahnu Charan Sahu, Dr. Sujata Priyadarsini, Dr. Tanaya Jena and Priyanka Priyadarshini . I thank the artists who have portrayed the figures of some important characters from rock-art, particularly Mr. Sunaram Singh deserves the most.

The author expresses his deep gratitude to the Editor of the book Mr. Raju Samal who had spent long hours of his valuable time in bringing this book to its present form. Special thanks to him as he is an amazing editor the author could ever imagine.

Author

Prologue

Kumarigiri, the first maiden hill of ancient Kalinga looks graceful with ancient architectural embellishments. The faded and decaying art not only attracts historians and archeologists but also reflects the ancient society in decorative details.

The British got back Orissa from Marahattas in the year 1803 and started archeological survey of temple town Bhubaneswar and hills of Khandagiri, Udayagiri and Dhauli. In 1837, the Hathigumpha inscription was copied and made available to the most adept decipherers of the nation. It took fifty long years to get some literal interpretation.

The year 1885 witnessed the publication of the encoded old Brahmi script of the inscription that provided the identity and limits of erstwhile *Kalinga*. It authenticated the historical record of brave *Kalinga* vs. *Piyadarsi* Ashok in the thirteenth rock edict. Written documents from Sri Lanka and Far East had the nomenclature of *'Holing'* or *'Kling'* Chinese and Malaysian documents too were deciphered. The evidences confirmed that Odisha was then, the Kalinga with *Ayur Mahameghavahana Kharavela*, the Emperor of *Kalinga* and the architecture of *Kumarigiri* lauded the supremacy of his power and strength. Decoding of the *Hathigumpha* inscription maintain the temporal flow chart of ancient Indian history and uncovers a dark period to a great extent.

After a thorough study it was conceived that *Kumarigiri* and *Kumaragiri* were much more than mere shelters for Jain monks. If somebody would ask about the existence of a massive educational institution of religious nature about 2300 years from now, it was here on these hills where the heart of kingdom of Kalinga throbbed. *Kumarigiri* and a lot of women figures in the caves sway our thought in the direction of emphasis on women's education, arts, crafts, dance and drama in those times.

The rock is ornately carved in a special manner to form beautiful caves which leads many secret pathways. Plenty of rare gems are believed to be hidden in the interiors of the cave. It is said that the British, after deciphering the *Hathigumpha* inscription could get a clue that the hills had hosted the wealthiest rulers of *Kalinga*. With the hope of hidden treasure, with dynamite.they blasted one cave closed from all sides They could not trace any wealth but to their astonishment, they found the closed cavity of the cave had elaborately been embellished with sculptural friezes. This folktale has continued for generations and specifically the octogenarian people of the village have mouthed it.

This *Salabhanjika* is inscribed on the eastern door of Jaya-Bijaya cave at the entrance of the Udayagiri hill, erstwhile Kumarigiri. She appears quite graceful with half-closed eyes and depicts the whole history of Kharavela in twelve moon lighted midnights during centenary celebration of *Kalinga Samaroh*. The events occur in full moon nights with a mystic spell of light and shadow made by *Dishidharikas*, the lamp bearers of the rock-cut art.

The remnants of Hathigumpha Inscription which reminds us of that epoch show that the drooping tree is destined to put forth new leaves under archeological survey. Growth of its wings had a birds' eye view of the facts and figures, arts and architectural focus to visualize the society and leadership in that golden period of history. For everyone who is conversant with evidences of Kharavela's time will easily discern by what author or from which inscription or rock-art the minor details have been derived and I am not interested to interrupt the narrative course of the book and spoil the pleasure of a large class of readers. The romantic traits which I have attributed to Emperor Kharavela are a cosmic power for a decade, a histrionic talent manifestation for two decades and a cultural icon throughout millennia. One of the arduous tasks I have ever set myself on was to construct his wave of romance within his own self, an ocean of love. The social and cultural petroglyphs upon the maiden hill speak volume for the sake of brevity and to impress the reader, the narrative flows straight from my heart.

Through the episodes narrated, I strongly believe that the readers will vicariously experience the presence of Emperor Kharavela the moment they go through the book.

Indramani Jena,
Samaroh, 128, Dumuduma (A),
Khandagiri, Bhubaneswar-30
Mobile – 9438007509

C o n t e n t s

Characters in this Novel:

1. *Kalingadhipati* (Emperor of Kalinga) – Kharavela,
2. Chief Queen of Kalinga – Dhusi (Dhruti)
3. Second Queen of Kalinga – Sindhula
4. Prince (son of the Emperor) – Kudapasari (Kandarpashree)
5. Son of Prince Kandarpashree – Vaduka,
6. *Mahamat* (Chief Minister) – Nakiya,
7. *Padamulika* (Personal Assistant of the Emperor) – Kusuma,
8. *Kama* (Works Minister) – Kama (Khina, wife of Kama),
9. *Nagara Akhandansh* (The City Judge) – Bhuti,
10. Queen of Paithan – Nayanika,
11. Magadharaj (King of Magadha) – Bruhaspati Mitra,
12. Pandya King, Naga Kinga,
13. *Salabhanjika*(the stony girl) – Pallabi Puspita,
14. *Dwarapalika* (the woman door keeper) – Suka Swagatika,
15. *Dishidharika* (the Lamp Bearer woman) – Jyotsna Dhabalika, Deepa Rasmita,
16. Assisting Characters – Alashpadma, Malati, Patara, Nandika, Sagarika, Lahari, Mohini, Binita,
17. Acharya and Religious Characters – Jatnasila, Gyanalokananda, Priyambada, Bicharapada, Kalingodbhaba, Brahmaputra, Siddhasampada, Kebalakalpa, Aparimeyananda, Kalpabigyani,
19. *Mahasenani* (Chief of Army) – Biraprasastha,
20. *Senapati* (General in Army) – Ranaprabara, Singhanandana, Manthansrestha, Ranatunga, Ranabhairaba,
21. Other Characters – Pandya King – Pandyan; Chola King – Utiyachera; Nagaraj – Nagaswarupa; King of Tamraparni – Ranachakra, Toshalisuta – Ekamraka, King of South Kalinga – Sagara Singha
22. Three Youth Invitees – Aparti, Abhirama and Pranabandhu

Chapter – 1

Beginning at Midnight

Three friends belonged to the same village at the foothills of present Khandagiri and Udayagiri. The twin hills with surrounding forest have tremendous influence on lifestyle of the residents. Even twelve years after independence these three friends, Aparti from Samal family, Pranabandhu from Samantray family and Abhiram from Barik family are unable to find employment after completing college education.

Even after graduation the trio was engaged in playful activity, amused themselves in a way characteristic of children and they spent most of the time playing cards at the village community centre. Seasons changed, so were the forests and they, like children, went after wild and tasteful berries. They liked *nirash,* a pleasant and tasteful berry from the hard plants of the hills. When eaten, these blue berries produce a thick blue coating over the tongue which remains stuck up at least for a day. They had the habit of catching fish from the depthless stream of water overflowing from the village pond. They were fond of stories told by Chintamani, the principal story teller of the village and the universal grandpa. No one knew when Chintamani, the outsider, first landed in their village but it was certain that he had been accepted as a permanent resident and was affectionately known as everyone's grandpa.

One day Chintamani said, "Oh three youngmen, why don't you all search the herb Bhanrmari (that attracts and kills wasps) available in the vegetation of the hill? There are two leprosy cases in our village. Every treatment has failed. There has been no cure for this cursed disease. I am afraid, the disease may spread to many in the village. But there is a solution. The twin hills contain this rare herb that can cure leprosy."

Aparti asked, "Grandpa, can you exactly trace the location on the hill where we will search for this herb? How can we identify it?"

Grandpa answered, "It is a small bush with creeper appearance that pulls in bees and wasps in large numbers. These insects are found dead around it in morning everyday. Identify, cut it sparing six inches from ground. I will prepare patent medicinal liniment out of it."

Abhirama queried, "Grandpa, we have been playing at every nook and corner of the hills and are well conversant with the berry plants of each type. I do not remember to have ever come across such a peculiar plant."

Grandpa informed, "You must have heard how three guys of our village spend whole nights scouting over the hills in search of gold *Yakkha*. You must be knowing , the rolling gold ball is like a living creature created from huge mass of gold buried somewhere for a very long time. They had completed ten years of their nocturnal tour and now speak confidently that they have got trace of it and it will be netted soon. You must remember, in the five villages that surround the hills, one can't have much of wealth from any other trade. The only way anybody becomes rich overnight is from such mysterious gold ball."

Aparti added, "Grandpa, we have also heard the brother of milkman Madan Behera who disclosed some secrets confided to him by the ascetics and was punished with sudden death."

"These auspicious hills are full of such myths. Their tranquil atmosphere attracts so many ascetics even now. We know that Mahima Gosain was enlightened from this soil. Great happenings in the past might not have been limited to Jainas and the Emperor Kharavela alone. Nowadays, any tourist coming here takes interest only in the sculptural works related to Kharavela. But local residents feel proud of believing that Kharavela is still landing at full-moon nights in a decorated spacecraft and many tourists also observe some unknown ascetics, with wooden sandals and water pot moving along the forest tracks of Khandagiri." The information accidentally leaked from grandpa.

Pranabandhu interfered, "Grandpa, whether these are true or fabricated?"

Grandpa replied, "I don't believe all this. But I am afraid of one thing these hills harbour is 'Danshani', the flying poisonous snake. I dare not go to the hills unless it is midday. Some say they have seen it but nobody can give a vivid description of the serpent. Many pretend to have seen it. There is no evidence of deaths from such snakebite."

All the three uttered simultaneously, "Grandpa, will there be any danger if we go to the hilltop at midnight? Will there be any problem from the ghosts and wild animals?"

Grandpa jokingly remarked, "You three are the robust youths of the village. So many people roam about in the hill in search of the hidden treasure. It is a shame that you are afraid of ghosts and spirits. This place is consecrated and set apart for some sacred purpose. If you encounter someone, he will be none other than an ascetic in meditation. Last year the archeological department dug out a step pattern in front of Hathigumpha that was buried under the earth. That way many mysteries have remained hidden here. Even though the Hathigumpha inscription reveals many things, many more remain unrevealed. Why don't you, the dynamic three, do something which has never been done before?"

Now fearless and determined, the three agreed to go to the hill at night to get the herb for leprosy cure. In addition they will observe the nocturnal happenings. They decided to go there at midnight without informing anybody. They would start right from the community centre where they sleep at night. They will quietly return to their place of sleep after completing the mission. They may carry some equipment with them for safety.

It was Buddha Purnima in the month of May. The full moon was almost in the centre of the sky. They noticed their shadows, almost glued to their foot steps. The ambience was silent and windless. The trees and vegetation were in the lap of deep sleep like the people in village. The shadows of the trees were motionless. Abhirama, the most courageous among them, whispered to hold the hands of one another and move in a concerted manner. This will ward off their fear and give them courage and confidence.

They reached the Udayagiri hill and climbed up the short stairs leading to the courtyard in front of Hathigumpha. It was early summer midnight. A gentle breeze was blowing. Swaying bushes welcomed the breeze with dance of delight. All of a sudden the trio sensed a sweet fragrance wafting in the breeze. They looked up at the stone cave which was without any vegetation. But the fragrance was of wild jasmine. The sense of olfaction perturbed their mind in apprehension. Grip of their enlaced palms became firm.

But their heart shuddered and they could feel the tremour of their fingers. They apprehended that something very dreadful was imminent. They were looking everywhere with fear in their eyes.

Two shadows of human shape suddenly appeared and got transformed into damsels, neatly dressed and fabulously ornamented. Gradually their limbs started movement and their faces became clearly visible.

This was quite unexpected. They were about to collapse. There was no way to escape. They never expected such an encounter on the lonely hill.

Of the two girls, one with a lamp was standing nearer to the cave. All of a sudden the lamp lit up. It illuminated the field of vision like daylight. The three youngmen were taken aback. They held each other's hands firmly to muster up courage to face the mysterious human forms.

Now the second girl smiled and indicated that they are quite friendly and happy to have their presence. Without waiting for any reply she said, "Dear guests, we are not new to you, you have seen both of us earlier. In this tensed situation you may not be able to recollect that."

She continued, "I am in my ambulatory shape emerging from the sculpture, *Salabhanjika*, the sculpture from right entrance pillar of Jaya-Vijaya cave just below. My real name is Pallabi Puspita. The lamp-bearer accompanying me is *Dishidharika*, the sculpture on the middle column of Ganesh cave just behind us. We came to know about your arrival and hurried to welcome you to our function.

"Our function is the 'Centenary Celebration of Kalinga Function by Emperor Kharavela'. You might be knowing that Mahameghavahana Kharavela established Agrajina Risabhanatha on this Kumarigiri hill above Hathigumpha, rescuing him from Magadha. He also inscribed a brief history of his times with the help of best stone inscribers and erudite Jaina scholars available in the then India. This was dedicated to inhabitants of Kalinga on a day of great festival known as Kalinga Kumarigiri Inaugural Festival. Lord Risabhanatha had graced the occasion for which that function is retrieved as original show once in every hundred years. It has a time specification, twelve full moon nights of the year, starting at midnight and ending before the day dawns.

"All sculptural beings come out alive from their stone forms to play their role, as they did in the first inaugural ceremony. All the episodes of the golden era under Kharavela are reenacted sequentially in the moon lighted night. It is led by Kalingadhipati Kharavela. All the events of history may be forgotten but the association of Mahameghavahana Kharavela with Kumarigiri hill will be remembered for ever. The relationship is as permanent as the engraved inscription on facades of Hathigumpha.

"Although confined in the stone sculptures we have been celebrating this Kalinga Festival for the last twenty two centuries. In course of time our spoken language has transformed to yours due to our continued contact with you. We invite you for all our future celebrations in these full moon nights. You will have the opportunity of seeing your glorious past.

"Although we are stone-girls in the guise of *Salabhanjika, Dishidharika, Dwarapalika, Banshibadika, Swagatika, Nrutyarata* in real life we were the representative pattern of the model our primary artisan had in his mind. Along with all stone sculptures, Kumarigiri and Kumaragiri hills will be rejuvenated to life in this ceremony as hosts. People of Kalinga who were present in the primary ceremony will be seen coming to life in this centenary celebration.

"Kumarigiri and Kumaragiri harbour so many types of sculptural characters. They are *Kama, Mahamat, Mahasenani, Nagara Akhandash, Padamulika, Dwarapala, Dwarapalika, Salabhanjika* and innumerable *Gandharba, Apsara, Yakkha, Kinnara*. You humans move in a corporeal plane, but we move in an aerial plane. Neither you can touch us nor can we touch you. You need not be afraid of such elated gatherings and high-spirited events."

The comforting statement of *Salabhanjika* assured the trio. Their fear disappeared. They consoled themselves with the belief that there was nothing to fear. None of them had courage to speak to Puspita. Then they looked around and noticed that the configuration of the hills had changed. Caves appeared new and decorated. The stones of the hill were not soiled and discoloured but looked white and sandy. The traditional thick leaved *nirash* bushes had changed to decorative floral plants. It was no more the hill they had climbed up, its physical appearance had changed to its past form.

Pranabandhu guessed, "Is the vegetation we see now is of Kharavela's period?"

Aparti noticed that *Salabhanjika* receding to her Jaya-Vijay cave below. *Dishidharika* was returning to be in Ganesh Cave with her lamp. It was enough for the first day of the centenary celebration.

Pranabandhu started prompting with a steady voice after the girls left the courtyard, "Don't think of any more function tonight. Whatever we have seen must be accepted as truth and nothing but the truth. We have been invited, no question of danger in future. We have a chance to see something unbelievable and precious. We three will make a promise now to keep this matter a top secret and will not allow it to be leaked out."

Raising his right index finger Abhiram said, "We are lucky that we got this great opportunity. I feel delighted to have seen some glorious events of our ancestors. We should be hopeful of getting glimpses of the location of the Emperor's treasure."

Pranabandhu replied, "Don't expect too much. True tales of the past are more precious than gold and silver. We are fortunate enough to relive the golden era of our land."

Three of them had the same thought in their mind, "We postpone our search for leprosy cure, we may fix it sometime later."

They descended from the foothill of Udayagiri. Now they begin to feel relaxed by the dawn light. The version of the *Salabhanjika* was trustworthy. The memory of experiencing some glorious past delighted them.

Safely three perplexed minds returned to their place of rest with the sweet memory of having seen the damsels of the past.

Chapter – 2

Maidens of Kalinga

The trio was frightened and could not accept the invitation easily. They thought that they had heard so many stories of ghosts and spirits like this. It could be a spirit that would have caused such an episode. But for reasons unknown, they had to trust *Salabhanjika* for her authentic voice and affectionate invitation. Ghosts, if at all there, have no place in the sacred abode of ascetics. Gradually their doubts faded away giving place to eagerness to accept the invitation and move forward.

Aparti told assertively, "I feel to be invited to such celebration is a great opportunity for us. I do not smell a rat on this issue. Why we should lose such a chance?"

Abhirama confirmed, "There is no going back on this. Prepare how we will reach the venue in time. But let me remind you the whole thing be confined to us three only."

At midnight they reached the base of the hill. Within moments the place got crowded. The *Salabhanjikas, Dwarapalikas, Swagatikas* were part of the crowd. The lamp bearing *Dishidharikas* illuminated the hill to the level of daylight.

The *Salabhanjika* of Jaya Vijaya cave, who had given invitation to these three friends spotted them at foothills and rushed down to welcome them. She accompanied them to seats for Aparti and Abhirama in the courtyard of

Hathigumpha and sent Pranabandhu with an escort to have a seat in the opposite Kumaragiri.

The *Salabhanjikas* and the *Swagatikas* are quite elegant. They are well dressed, courteous and are best suited for guest management. They managed to have people evenly distributed in witness stands of both the hills facing each other. It is with the grace of Lord Risabhanatha, the twin host hills will be rejuvenated to deliver the key note address. All are eagerly waiting to listen to them. They are waiting for some auspicious indication from the sky, not visible at the moment in the full moon night.

The sky turned blue like the clear sky of the day. Kumaragiri shaped himself as a person clad with olive green flora. He is the prince of this natural kingdom born of nature. He is a disciple of Lord Rama. Temperamentally peaceful, judicious and considerate, the prince is about to stand up to put forth his presentation. Kumarigiri is the princess of this royal house, sitting beside his brother to assist him during this address.

All of a sudden the place became dim as the *Dishidharikas* dimmed heir lamps. The moon too, was dimmed by a vagabond cloud floating by. A small nocturnal bird flew to the west with faint noise arousing attention of the audience.

Gracefully Kumaragiri said, "Attention my audience, I am enlightened by grace of Lord Risabhanatha to deliver this keynote address, that has been delivered twenty one times earlier for which I express my gratitude to Him. Ancient Kalinga is part of Jambudvipa since Purana times. Life in Kalinga began from jungles, man was feeling his sociality within himself but society had not evolved. Mahabharata was yet to happen, Mahavir and Gautama Buddha were still farther in future. At this juncture civil life was awaited and family life was not regular. Society needed social discipline and higher consciousness. Few great people could attain this to enhance the quality of intuitive judgment to give insight to the vision of mankind.

"Society formation was the target of Lord Risabhanatha established at hill top of Kumarigiri as you all feel today. He is the first of twenty four Tirthankars in Jain principles. He had laid the foundation of a moral society. He was managing the humanitarian and religious motives of residents of hinterlands of Kalinga through his school of disciples. Thus a religion of compassion started by him much before *Dwapara Yuga* and earlier than the Vedas appeared which is rightly mentioned in the Rig Veda.

Thus Risabhanath dedicated himself to form a society from nomadic and barbaric life of man. He created the custom of marriage and concept of family by getting married himself. This was an enlightened revolution out of polygamous and polyandrous chaos. The religious trend he set was sourced from a humanitarian concept which later on became *Sanatana Dharma*. The timing of this endeavour was between the Harappan civilisation and the Mahabharata. Man became capable of distinguishing food from poisonous and taste from distaste. There existed neither any festival nor ritual. Vision of man was limited to what was visible with no insightful capability of thinking ahead. It was the kingdom of the wild ruled by the law of anarchy.

A few insightful men had the concept of man's ability of being human which could be the social cohesion for the society. They outlined the aim of human life that differs from that of the animals and instructed on the lifestyle of a superior animal called man. The most prominent among such mystics was Risabhanatha, who is acclaimed as an ideal man of his time confirming to the ultimate standard of excellence. He initiated the society with humane temperament. A society without education had no choice of profession. He had to distinguish professional attitudes as of sword bearers, writers, educationist, agriculturists, traders and craftsmen. No matter what one's choice was but he would be an expert in corresponding trade in the long run.

He discovered seventy two scientific components for males and sixty four components for females like fire, cooking and many more skills of living. Groups of his disciples dedicated their lives for the upliftment of society. They travelled down to the unapproachable areas of human settlements. They preached civilised principles of Adijina. The course of education comprised dress codes, manners and spiritual knowledge. They were called *Anagrahis* or *Nirgranthas*.

Thus dawned the human civilisation. Birds in the tree tops have started chirping. Men were given religious discourses on non-violence and non-stealing. The society began to overflow with compassion of great ascetics and developed with classes based on economic principles. Better standard of living transformed the society from rural to urban settlements.

At this stage, a resourceful kingdom could be located on the east coast of Jambudvipa. Guarded by deep forests and river streams, it was not approachable from outside. But its residents were self sufficient with food, clothing and had a pastime of maritime trade. Its military capability was amazing. Its economy, culture and language were magnificent. It was the kingdom of Kalinga.

The King was more interested in showering benevolence on his subjects, not in rolling in the luxury of the crown or in constant engagement in retention of the crown. People were spiritual and believed in truth and God. The king had internalised the benevolent essence of Jainism and practiced it in life. Jain *Arhats* and *Nirgranthas* traversed through remote areas for the purpose of inculcating the spiritual and socio-cultural behaviour into the lives of people."

When the speaker paused for breath, there was the polite intervention by Kumarigiri who was anxious to learn about role of Kalinga in the great war of Mahabharata. Kumarigiri is the hill aptly given the name Kumarigiri or Kalinga Kumari (maiden of Kalinga), a loving daughter. She appealed Kumaragiri to take a pause and elaborate on the heroic achievements of Kalingan military in Kurukshetra.

Mahabharata records excellent military capability of Kalinga. Srutayudha, the king of Kalinga was a General of Military Forces of Kauravas gathered for war. He happened to be a marital relation of Kauravas as Duryodhan had married to his sister. Kalinga's participation in the war was quite emphatic. A huge battalion of elephantry, cavalry, chariots and infantry was dispatched along with a special ardent Nishad Sena, led by Bhanumat, son of Srutayudha. This Nishad Sena was well equipped tribal division of Kalinga with agile and fierce temperament in the battle field. General Srutayudha with his two sons, Bhanumat and Sakradev was in Kurukshetra with ten thousand robust black war elephants from Kalinga.

Then Kumarigiri interrupted her brother Kumaragiri when he talked about 'black elephants' of Kalinga and said, "Dear brother, give the detailed description of Kalinga military forces waging war. How did the black elephants of this area play a major role?"

Kumaragiri replied, "The moment Lord Krishna blew

his Panchajanya conch and the war began. Pandavs fought with a few relatives whereas the whole of India's prominent kings sided with Duryodhan."

At the outset, at the very sight of Bhima, Duryodhan decided to deploy Kalinga elephantry. Instantly Srutayudha arrived with his squad of Kalinga elephants and Nishadraj Bhanumat with his skilled Nishad Sena. They encountered mighty Bhima and Chedi royal forces. Fierce attack of Kalinga forces could ward off Chedi militants; Chedis were scared and they retreated in order to save themselves exposing Bhima to face the force of Kalinga alone. He started with his bow and made a torrential flow of arrows.

Sakradev, son of Kalinga king Srutayudha shattered the wheel of Bhîma's chariot. Bhima dropped to the ground. Furious Bhima got up, lifted the crushed wheel and hurled it at Sakradev and quieted him into eternal silence. Srutayudha and Bhanumat rushed in rage to confront Bhima. They shot a huge number of arrows but Bhima smashed each one of them and sroared like a lion. With a sword Bhima rose up to the elephant of Bhanumat and killed him, with difficulty though. Finally riding on a new chariot he confronted Srutayudha and struggled a lot to overpower him, ultimately depriving him of his precious life.

Furious Kalinga generals and forces fiercely attacked Bhima and surrounded him. Anticipating danger to Bhima, Judhistira, Sikhandi and Dhrustadyumna came to his rescue. This was the first day of Mahabharata with glorious Kalinga Generals and black elephants fighting against Pandavas by exhibiting their utmost capability. They lost to Bhima, not because they were less brave and less courageous but because Dharma was on the side of Bhima.

Kalingakumari Kumarigiri became quite emotional

now. She was grief-stricken as the Kalinga elephants were on the side of Duryodhan while the grace of divinity was with the Pandavas. She consoled herself as each of the elephants and warriors have fought to their full potentiality without any retreat. This was Kalinga principle. Such type of bravery had been very rare.

'Well done, Kalinga!' She sighed consoling herself. After depicting the bravery and heroic performance of Kalinga in the Mahabharata war Kumaragiri said, "At the time Mahabharata War, twenty one Jaina Tirthankars including Risabhanatha had completed their tenure, the twenty second Tirthankara happened to be the relative of Lord Krishna.

He was Neminath. It is said that he had relinquished his home due to animal slaughter in the celebration of his marriage ceremony. He took sanyasa and never returned. His insightful bride also followed him as a sanyasini. Thus Jainism has a long line of twenty two Tirthankars till Mahabharata period. The society, then, was indulging in animal slaughter and idolatry. The Nirgranthas of earlier Jain sect kept persuading people to be non-violent and truthful.

Now the twenty third Jain Tirthankara appeared twelve generations after the Mahabharata war. In the contemporary period Karakandu, the wise ascetic occupied the throne of Kalinga. He had realised the difficulties of Jain Arhats during the rain months. He could notice that few of them have opted natural caves of Kumarigiri for shelter. On the instruction from Rajarsi Karakandu, some more caves were carved as shelter of the ascetics. In rains both Kumarigiri and Kumaragiri evolved to be the sanctum sanctorum of meditation illuminated with enlightened saints.

Kalingakumari felt proud of sheltering monks during hard times of the year. It is due to them that people of Kalinga were non-violent, truthful and maintained discipline by following Jain way of life.

Politely Kumaragiri intervened and said, "I am quite proud of twenty-third Tirthankara, whose existence was historical compared to earlier twenty two who were mythical. He was Parsvanath. He visited Kalinga and Kumarigiri on the invitation of Rajarsi Karakandu. While in his place at Kashi, Parsvanath was aware that Kalinga was a favourite place of Jains and a Jain saint was the ruler of Kalinga. He was curious to visit my location, the site of Kumarigiri that was the abode of innumerable Jain Mendicants.

"He honoured Karakandu's royal invitation but with a condition. He had prefer to stay in the Jain caves and not in the royal palace. Karakandu agreed and excavated a bigger cave for accommodating him in the front row of the caves here. His stay was for more than a month, there was heavy rush of devotees to get the blessings of the spiritual leader. Devotees came from far off places of India.

"I was proud of his visit. He was a saint with a broader outlook. Every morning he would be murmuring, 'this hill is great and pure. It had a sacred element in its creation. That is why only mendicants are attracted to inhabit it.'

Three centuries had passed after Parsvanath. The last Tirthankara, twenty-fourth in the row was Mahavir Jin, born at Vaisali. He was quite popular in Anga, Banga and Kalinga. Contemporary Kalinga was unique among neighbouring states. It was far advanced in trade, specifically in maritime trade. Major fraction of its trading population was either in transit or in Far Eastern Asiatic

Islands. The capital of Kalinga was at Pitrunda Metropolis in east coast of the sea. The name of the sea to east of Kalinga was Kalingodra. Pithunda port was famous international port to travel to Champa, the modern Vietnam in Far East. The port was very near to the south of Chilika lake which too had a huge ship building yard.

King of Kalinga then was a staunch Jain. As a religious principle, he had dedicated the state capital to Adijina Risabhanatha and had his statue installed. The territory of Kalinga was extended from the Ganges in the north to river Godavari in the south. State capital was changing its position between Rajpur and Dantapur, administrative and military headquarters were alternating between north and south locations.

The idol of Risabhanatha was made of metal with a special crown. This idol was declared as Kalinga Jina, the icon of Kalinga, mark of sanctity and gravity of the state prestige on religious grounds.

Mahavir Jain had heard of Kalinga as a genuine centre of Jainism in India. He was aware that the state was flourishing with Jainism and the ruler was a Jaina king. People of Kalinga had the expertise in maritime trade, possessed knowledge about the ebb and tide of the sea and the impact of the north and the south winds. They too specialized in the dynamics of boat movement. On the military front, they were not aggressive to invade neighbouring states, rather kept their defense battle ready against the imperialist and expansionist Magadha. Kalinga people were designated as 'Kalingah Sahasikah' meaning 'Kalingas the Brave.'

Father of Mahavir Jain, King of Vaisali happened to be a friend of the king of Kalinga. Mahavir expressed his eagerness to pay a visit to Kalinga. He had travelled all the way from Vaisali to Bardhaman in Banga, then entered Kalinga through Kupari in Balasore and reached Kumarigiri. He was received by Kalinga administration and kept moving in a chariot.

Mahavir could not believe such places like Kumarigiri and Kumaragiri existed anywhere in the world. Nature was sparse in the beginning but Kings of Kalinga had added so many caves for Jain ascetics. Decorative arrangements were made to receive Mahavir here, in Kumarigiri. In the peak moment of his tour, he reached the top of Hathigumpha and from there announced all principles of Jainism, *Dharma Chakra Pravartana*.

He elaborated his love for Kalinga and was emotional about the acceptance of the religion as heart and soul of the people here. The great distance between Vaisali and Kumarigiri could not stand as a geographical barrier against his will to visit this adorable site. He was happy to see the manner and sincerity with which the hermitage of the *arhats* and ascetics were maintained. He expressed his emotions in his speech, "I announce my feelings and love for this twin hills, specifically for Kumarigiri as gracious, capacious and accommodative. I ascribe her title, 'the eternal Princess of Kalinga'."

The second attraction of Mahavir during his Kalinga tour was to pay a tribute to Adijina at Pithunda. He travelled all the way from Kumarigiri hill to the sea coast port town. He was amazed to behold the grand statue of Adijina Risabhanatha. He exclaimed when he saw the beautiful crown adorning Adijina, "It is befitting because he is none other than Kalinga Jina!"

The name of Risabhanatha in Kalinga had been Kalinga Jina. The glorious Kalinga!

Mahavir could not confine himself only to the

activities of religion. He wished to visit the Pithunda harbour. He was astonished at Kalingans making it an international port with direct voyage to Champa, now modern Vietnam. All ships from the whole of the east coast listed all the Champa bound passengers here. The city had a good port market with wide variety of materials obtained from foreign lands.

Kalinga's prosperity and joy lasted for centuries, when Mahapadma Nanda, expansionist of Magadha brutally attacked Kalinga which the latter had not expected. This Nanda attack had been quite lethal to the warrior class of Kalinga, unprecedented and treacherous. As a mark of victory Nanda carried away Kalinga Jina with his crown to Magadha. Kalinga had no way to recover the deity in such devastated post-war times.

Then followed the Great Kalinga War by Ashok Vardhan Maurya who had inflicted the worst inhuman attack on Kalinga. Lakhs of Kalingans were massacred. More than that got injured and equal number were taken as captives. Since then Dhauli Giri, where the bloody battle was fought had been voiceless spectre.

Power of any king on earth is on his time zone. So it was with Mauryas. The last Maurya was assassinated in an easy way. Every time Magadha takes on Kalinga, the latter tactfully escapes from its yolk as early as possible. But Kalinga had always been obsessed with the Kalinga Jina captived at Magadha. Kalinga had always been a renewable economy by virtue of its maritime trade while Magadha had no sea route to compete. No doubt desperately Kalinga was in search of an opportunity to get back Kalinga Jina.

Today, Kalinga has given birth to a mighty son, a rising star. He is none other than our present Kalingadhipati, the sole Chakravarti Emperor, and the great protector of mankind who was instrumental in formation of Vibrant Kalinga stretching from the Ganges to Godavari. He has decorated me with beauty and splendour while organising this grand function as a memorial of his achievements.

Every civilisation faces decay and degeneration. The achievements of Kharavela would have vanished after next few generations. But we two hills have preserved them to get a meaningful interpretation for all time to come.

Now let us wait to see what comes next.

All of a sudden the lamps of the *Dishidharikas* went off and noisy atmosphere of the hills settled down to early morning tranquility. The hill stood revealed as Udayagiri in the first light of the day.

Three friends so far lost in the past, shook their heads to get adjusted to their own world.

Chapter-3

Giving up the Throne

The full moon night was only two days away. Aparti called upon his friends to plan for the show.

Abhirama started in a calculated manner, pointing his right index finger, "Of what use is gold *Yakkha* to us? What we had seen last night would be immeasurable in value. Possibly the reign of Kharavela in Kalinga was the golden era in our ancient history!"

Pranabandhu responded, "Tonight we will enjoy the show better than the earlier occasions. Of course, we can ask for clarification when we fail to follow any event. We can ask the *Salabhanjika* to guide us. She is eager to help us. Although aerial in existence she had confirm that she can converse in our language. We will feel free to communicate with her. The milieu of the hills on full moon night is captivating. The configuration changes with each show; the vegetation changed altogether and the trees and bushes transform into strange shapes. We had never expected the hilltop would be such an adorned garden. The trees were also well organised as if somebody had deliberately planted them decades back. We walked on ancient Kumarigiri, not the present Udayagiri. For all this we are thankful to *Salabhanjika* Puspita."

Abhirama said, "Today is the Debashnana Purnima, a great function of Lord Jagannath at Puri. In the neighbouring room of our community hall there is the small temple of Radha Krishna. The deities will be carried in a *Biman* to the village pond for rituals of Snana Purnima. The moon is also worshiped by many people. So the village will be awake at mid night. Are you aware of this?"

Pranakrushna replied, "Nothing to worry, each one will be busy in his own way. We can easily escape unnoticed."

They started in time and reached the foothill. Moon in the sky was ready with fullness of light. The ground was neatly visible. The surrounding was well illuminated.

The hills had assumed their ancient shape. The berry bushes had turned to tall leafy plants. Many mango and jackfruit trees were laden with fruits imparting pleasant fragrance. The slope of Kumarigiri was starting to be crowded. Puspita emerged from the small crowd and whispered, "We have to wait here".

She was looking gloomy and desolate. Eyes were full of tears like a flooded river. She was unmindful about her dress and hairstyle. Haste and anxiety perturbed her. Her hands were tremulous. She was moving with an element of anguish in her heart. Her seeming poise and postures were not perfectly coordinated as if she was in a sleepy state.

Dwarapalika Suka Swagatika, the chief receptionist of Kumarigiri was standing beside Puspita. She happened to be her cave mate in Jaya Bijaya cave. She was a beautiful tall lady clad in a silk sari. Her hairstyle was extraordinary and a pair of gorgeous earrings ornamented her ears. It enhanced the glamour of her smile and grace of her speech. She had a live parrot seated on her right shoulder uttering 'welcome' to every newcomer. But she too looked also grief stricken.

Both *Salabhanjika* and the *Dwarapalika* had something in common: they felt themselves as direct relatives of Emperor Kharavela. Tourists to the hills were treated with such hospitality that they would remember them for long. This job was offered to two most efficient girls. During the spell of serial victories, the Emperor visited so many places and came across beautiful sculptures. He could employ many of artisans in Kumarigiri to carve out beautiful damsels that are called in different names. But the sculptures are carved out in the image of only one model. Indeed, Kalingadhipati wanted talking statues in the caves of Kumarigiri. It was for his artistic bent of mind and his financial abundance, he could get rock carving artisans from North West of India to train local sculptors. Thus local artisans would erect women dominated cave architecture, women outnumbering men.

Abhirama asked Puspita, "Why do you seem to be aggrieved today?"

Puspita replied, "The future scene is coming to my mind accumulated from last twenty one episodes. You are going to see it yourselves a few moments from now. Let me see how you would control your tears."

Some woeful voices came from behind. They turned back to the foothill road and were speechless gazing at the foot hill area which they had just traversed through moments back. That road had been converted into a palace, where a procession had arrived and halted. The three companions recollected the folktale of their village that a procession arrived at the foothill at dead of night. They got convinced that folktales are not always fabricated. The statement of people that the procession comes from the east was right. It was from the direction of Kalinganagari, the then capital of Kalinga, now identified as Sisupalagada about twelve kilometers away.

The palace was crowded with royal family and

noblemen. A healthy tall person seated at the centre was removing his crown and royal robe and placing them on the table. There was no doubt that the tall healthy person was none other than Emperor Kharavela, whose figure had been carved at many places in the caves of Kumarigiri. His appearance was a visible symbol of compassion. The posture, gesture, ear rings, necklace and the crown were revealing the greatness of the Emperor.

Puspita aroused them from deep thought and puzzle they were brooding over. She whispered to them, "See, how Emperor Kharavela is going to relinquish his throne. He has hardly completed thirteen years of his reign and is quite young at thirty eight. It is strange, with victory reverberations all around, administration at its best, he wishes to step down to lead an ascetic life in these two sacred hills!"

The three friends were quite astounded. They never expected to behold such ancient scene of more than two thousand years old. Quite curious in their mind, they thanked Puspita and the Kumarigiri hill that retained such memory. Benevolent Kharavela becoming a Jain monk was a tragic event in the history, but was as important as Ashok becoming Dharmashok.

Some proceedings were going on in the palace. One King seated next to Emperor Kharavela had introduced himself as the King from Pandya State. He had travelled to Kalinga by the sea with shiploads of jewels, valuable stones for the construction of a great religious institution in Kumarigiri. Pandyan was quite famous. He is always cited as having good relationship with Julius Caesar, the Monarch of Rome.

Two years ago Pandya Kingdom was conquered by Kharavela after a fierce fight with Tamil Confederacy led by Pandya. Pandyan was not granted permission to meet Kalingadhipati. Afterwards he was permitted to meet the Emperor of Kalinga with one hundred thousand pearls, precious stones and many other things. Pandyan, then a staunch Jain, was religiously related to Kharavela and he had been excused. In fact, it was a critical period of Indian political disorder and Pandya was next to Kalinga in power equation. When Kalinga was trading in Far East, Pandya excelled in its maritime activity in West extending from Arab to Rome.

Pandyan had strong diplomatic and military opposition to Kharavela during his invasion of south India. But after his surrender he was inclined to Kalinga. He appreciated the benevolence of Kharavela. In the deeper layers of his mind he had a special attachment to Kumarigiri. It is because this hill had natural caves that invited Jainism for its growth.

In the crowd Kharavela looked exhausted but he was firm in his decision. Nobody understood why he had decided to quit the Crown. He had established himself as the invincible Emperor of India. What would be the reason of such decision he had taken overnight?

It was a surprise for the audience; they thought the action of the Emperor was a joke; they eagerly waited to listen if the Emperor would reverse his decision in a dramatic style. They were family members of Kharavela, all his teachers, the spiritual and religious personalities associated with him,

Sri Mahameghavahana Kharavela! Had he ever changed his version? Anyone may feel that he had little attraction for his crown and wealth. Someone might doubt that he was embarrassed with the shackles of administration. It was a puzzle for the audience there. One day Sakyamuni renounced the world. This day was witnessing the abnegation of the throne by the mighty Kharavela.

He was surrounded by the group of people who were staring at him. He was the centre of focus for all the eyes there. The Pandya king was seated to his left; Chief Queen Dhruti, Second Queen Sindhula, eight-year-old son Kandarpashree were behind him. All the family members were grief striken. They could not believe how Emperor was going to sleep on the stone bed of caves leaving behind his royal bed of roses!

Row of royal authorities was on his left. The Chief Minister, The Chief Justice, the Works Minister, the Deputy Minister of Works, his Personal Assistant, the Military Chiefs and so many other royal employees were present. They all assembled there in uniform as per the emergency call from palace. Everyone turned mute. The Chief Minister was staring at the face of the Emperor in despair. The Emperor was speechless and expressionless. He was firm on his declaration and had no regrets. Neither did he give any hint of his wish nor did he expose his future course of action. Each one of Kalinga administration was very intimately associated with him. None, even the queen could guess what was going on in his mind. His decision had disheartened everyone. They could hardly believe that such a great misfortune had befallen the kingdom of Kalinga.

The Chief Minister Nakiya expressed in a shivering voice, "Kindly excuse us Your Majesty! We will never bother you. Let not Your Highness make us helpless orphans by quitting the throne! Can Kalinga ever thrive without you? Can our neighbours spare us?"

The Emperor was critical on Nakiya's statement. He did not express anything, but his grimace indicated that he was not pleased with Nakiya's appeal to reverse his decision. His future course of action wouldn't invite any such apprehension. Kalinga was firm and unshakable with a secured future. Kharavela was calm and unmoved as Sakyamuni Gautama in deep meditation. Then queen Dhruti attempted to speak something. Her voice was feeble and had lost all its grace. She was sobbing. Kandarpashree, his son could not follow what was going on there. But the gravity of situation forced him to presume that something was wrong with his father and others. He was viewing the faces of his parents and bursting into tears at intervals. Dhruti then requested the Emperor to look at the face of their son who was his greatest weakness. He was born seven years after his coronation. He had just completed eight years on that day.

The king was not moved by such emotional prayer, as if his being separated from Kalinganagari would not make any difference in the palace! The momentum that had accumulated during his tenure would lead the Mahameghavahana dynasty longways.

All the royal teachers who were in charge of Kharavela's education thirty years back were looking at him with openmouthed astonishment. This clever student of theirs had achieved the title of Chakravarti. But they were unable to unravel the cause of his relinquishment. Young Kharavela was brilliant in all branches of his education. He had been crowned with success due to effective application of his knowledge. His abrupt decision to relinquish the throne even after reaching the peak of success had forced out from each one of them a stare of amazement.

This royal group of teachers was inseparable part of the palace. They were drawn from diverse subjects. Chetaraj, father of Kharavela had capable teachers in respective fields appointed as royal teachers. He had recruited highly educated Gyanalokananda who had obtained his education from Kashi and has done in depth studies in Sanskrit. He was a student of Taksasila University and had specialised in administration and management of State affairs. Most of the subjects of his study covered the works of Kautilya School of Economics.

Gyanalokananda who had education in Taksasila with experience of Kasi was enlightened to a great extent and he was in charge of young prince Kharavela. The young student had completed his ninth birthday. He had promised King Chetaraj to impart the best education to the prince.

All the experienced and retired teachers of Kharavel adjudged him as an intelligent student with a great sense of humour; he would compete in all fields of education and would excel in his life as per the desire of his father. The young prince took interest in the study of human behaviour. He observed the subjects of Kalinga and expected many things that they would undertake in useful professions, enriching language and fields of art and craft. He had heard people have to suppress their natural tendency of singing a song or dancing with the tune of nature. They had been subdued by the rigorous Maurya administration since the days of Ashoka. They were prohibited from performing dance, drama, public functions, *Utsab* and *Samaj*. They had tremendous fear of Maurya royal authorities. Inhabitants of Kalinga were naturally fond of dance, drama and music. They had surreptitious live performances in the interiors of the province to escape detection by Maurya officials. Administration was strictly carried on in populous cities like Toshali, Samapa, Lalitagiri and Tamluk of Kalinga. But that had not percolated down to micro level to villages. This

Maurya period of one century could restrict *Utsab* and *Samaj* in urban Kalinga, but the interior was not bereft of such socio-cultural performances. Rural dominant Kalinga did not dance to the tune of cities. The colonial officials were not many enough to impose all their prohibitions in remote and tribal areas.

Open environment was the platform of Kalinga. Heart of each subject here was pulsating with the waves of Kalingodra sea. The inner mind was painted green like the greenery of nature and their soul was as pure as the free air breathed by birds. Feeling of the heart had penetrative capability of torrential rains. The melodious tones of the girls of Kalinga were audible in dense forests. Those melodies filled the mind with streaks of joy and hopes which were conducive to a successful social and conjugal life. Heavy rainfall attracted the peacocks to dance spreading their rainbow wings stimulating human hearts to be creative and enjoy nature. Kalinga maiden enjoyed this natural creativity. She could spread wings in her dreams and fly to achieve them in reality.

Young girls with bangles and armlets looked beautiful. Their expectant faces look elegant with the glittering necklaces which enchanted the heart of young lovers. They possessed the glamour of the sky and the rhythm of the larking birds. The girdle of their waist swung with their slow dancing gait and their natural coiffure had all fascination for onlookers.

Kalinga had worst days under Nanda and Maurya. Natural calamities did frequently ravage the state; the populace experienced stronger oppressions and deprivations under them. The subjects were in deep agony. Magadha had the punitive attitude to these nature driven people!

One day, prince Kharavela asked Gyanalokananda, "People of Kalinga are peace loving by nature, they struggle in the adversities of nature even if they take the risk of maritime business for their survival. Why then this Kalinga had been eyesore of Magadha?"

Teacher replied, "Really there is a geographical factor ensuring security of our state Kalinga. When India is terrorized by western invaders, the *Yavanas* in the West, Kalinga is safe due to its distant location and its geographical position.

"Three hundred years ago, Alexander, the all powerful emperor of Greece achieved wonders in all battle fields on his way to India. After entry into this land, all his hopes melted away like ice in a hot desert. He could not anticipate that elephants would be so competently deployed in the battle! It would dishearten any warrior in the field of war. When he reached the west bank of river Jhelum, he noted how troops of Pallav king Puru were ready with swords on the eastern bank. All elephants and horses of Puru were peeping at the new enemy from the west. The depth of the stream did not allow the enemy to enter and once somebody enters the opposite shore, he will be slain on the spot instantly. Alexander lost his hope of winning Puru in direct face to face battle. He advised his most capable General not to undertake the risk of direct war with Puru's battle ready army.

"Alexander opted for a tactical war, the war with pretence; not one, so many Alexanders were visible along the western bank of the river. Puru's men were concentrating on them pointedly, whereas the original Alexander with a small troop travelled far up to a place where he could cross the river easily. Strangely he attacked Puru from north and conquered his kingdom. It is centuries old history. Alexander had respect for the brave. He did not kill Puru, but asked him, "What sort of treatment do you expect from me?"

Puru stood with his head erect and replied bravely, "A king should be treated like a king."

Alexander was pleased and he appointed him as his Governor for the kingdom. What a right decision! But the Nanda and Maurya attacked Kalinga on two occasions, once the Nanda killed the whole warrior class; second, Ashok butchered millions in Kalinga War. Their attitude for the enemy was utterly brutal and barbarous.

Alexander had in his mind to attack the main part of India. He heard from Puru and others that they can proceed up to the Ganges. The broad and deep river and elephant force of Nanda were difficult factors to tide over. His Generals did not agree to advance farther and they had to return from there. The aspiration of Alexander to conquer the world came to an abrupt end.

Gyanalokananda continued, "Here for your Kalinga, there is natural security by the Ganges and Godavari streams through dense forests. Over and above, here the king is guarded fulltime by seventy thousand infantry, one thousand cavalry and seven hundred elephantry. No doubt enemy will automatically be driven back.

The teacher observed some positive impact of this story on the young prince.

The prince asked with a smile, "If I were Alexander!"

Gyanalokananda queried, "Then what would you have done?"

The prince replied, "I would have Kalinga elephants. Why would I be scared like him?" The teacher could get glimpses of his greatness in that answer.

One fine morning, both the teacher and the pupil had a walk to the nearby Dhauli hill, just three miles distant to the south of Kalinganagari. The great cyclone that had affected the area had made a mess of things with trees uprooted everywhere. But the flowing water of the river Daya emitted the loud cry of desperate humans. The noise of commotion and lamentation of the wounded was disturbing to the prince.

The prince asked, "Why noises of outcry are being heard when there is no one around the river? The sound tells us something terrible that had happened here. It was so horrible that the noise has overstayed. Don't you not hearing the sound?"

Gyanalokananda replied, "Yes, this noise had been disturbing me since I came here two decades back. Today I have knowingly got you here to make you aware of it. Your father had warned all teachers not to bring you here where the great battle was fought. Warm stream of human blood from Kalinga warriors kept flowing in the river due to the ruthless massacre by Ashok the Black. He had employed hired cannibals from Africa to eat away strong warriors of Kalinga who fought gallantly. Patriotic people of Kalinga did not surrender to the Magadha king, but fought unto their death. Ananta Padmanav the King of Kalinga was killed. Innocent people in the villages were butchered and the residential settlements with harvest ready rice fields were set on fire. Kalinga was ruined. It all happened two centuries ago. But Ashok the Black could not smash Kalinga to ashes. It got resurrected from the same soil with renewed vigour. It is now with Mahameghavahana power.

Continued the teacher, "However, I am a submissive servant of your father, Chetaraj. His apprehension was to keep you away from that black period of our history. Otherwise it would be frustrating for you to know the horror of that massacre. But my logic is quite simple. The prince is now shaping his military establishment. He is planning to restructure all the four wings of Kalingan military forces. He has been provided with diplomats and spies to get vital information from biggest power structures of the country at Magadha and Satavahana kingdoms. In this context, the information about Kalinga War is very important as it can add to the rejuvenation of our forces.

"This is a field of life versus freedom of Kalinga. Emperor Ashok had the biggest military power on the earth. But Kalinga did not surrender despite his perilous forewarnings. It fought until the last drop of its blood recruiting civilians, children and the old people when the military forces got exhausted."

The young prince was silent for a while and then burst into tears. His body was trembling and hands were tremulous. Goosebumps appeared on his skin. After sometime he wiped off his tears and muttered to himself, "Our courage has to be reinforced and bravery reinvigorated. Yes it is a must."

The prince was overflowing with the emotion of intense dislike for Magadha and Emperor Ashok. He was consoling himself that history will never forgive him for such cowardly genocide.

The prince and his teacher proceeded to the lonely Dhauli Giri. The prince could notice the stone statue of Kalinga elephant half emerging from a stone wall. The rear portion of the elephant still merged with the stone. He suspected that this stone sculpture must have been carved out by Magadha administrators. Magadha could not impress him on humanity grounds. He was irritated and told his teacher, "Dear sir, what sort of construction is it? I am so fond of the tail of the elephant, Magadha king could not get it out?"

The teacher replied, "This elephant is an insignia of religious attitude of Magadharaj Ashok. He could conquer Kalinga that was unconquerable by Magadha for three generations. Kalinga War was deadlier than the Mahabharata War. Mahabharata War was fought on some war principles, but Kalinga War was unleased terror. No principle ever governed it. Recruitment to Magadha side was from hired inhuman giant *Yavana* troops. Ashok Vardhan, no doubt, won the war, but lost on moral grounds being portrayed as most inhuman among humans. He had no alternative but to adopt Buddhism in the battle field itself.

"The prince who murdered six of his brothers brutally for the throne was composed of savage stuff. It is irony that his edicts gave him the identity to the world as 'beloved of Gods'. A man who decapitated one whole race could write on stones that he liked them as sons was a hipocrite. After all his victory was not total. The tribal tracts of Atavika and Vidyadhar units created tremendous fear in his mind by targeting him with arrows from their hideouts. They belonged to undivided Kalinga and their retaliation was anticipated at anytime."

Gyanalokananda recollected so many stories of past three decades. Once on their tour to west from Kalinganagari, they came across a number of dilapidated *stupas* made of stone. Kharavela stood beside one of them and asked his teacher, "Are these constructions by Emperor Ashok? The stones must have been carried away from Kumaragiri hills. People in charge of stone cutting must have been a terror to Jain monks inhabiting the hill since time immemorial. Kharavela was reviving the past history of the ascetics during Kalinga War. They could not have avail royal alms no doubt, but direct atrocity by huge number of Magadha soldiers must have been a menace to them. Magadharaj begged apology to the saints and *sramans* no doubt, but it was too little and too late."

Kharavela could envision the horror of the Kalinga War and disliked to utter the very name of Ashok Vardhan once more. He did not reveal his emotion to his teacher but analysed in the depth of his mind the evidences to designate him as an impostor. Why did Ashok opt for Buddhism and not for Jainism? His father and grandfather were Jains, but he would not have preferred such a rigorous food habit, austere life style and attitudinal adjustment. Really, even in his 'Piyadarsi days' he had issued circular of giving up animal killing but he had not given up taking peacock meat in his royal food. The fact that Ashok, a man of deceitful pretence was an eternal enemy of Kalinga got implanted in young Kharavel's mind.

The naval teacher of Kharavela standing in the row of teachers was puzzled as to why he was taking such a hasty decision to relinquish the throne? The prince was a master in all fields and had shown his extraordinary naval skills in a Kalingodra maritime guard issue just two years ago. He was ill at ease about his getting down from the throne.

Chetaraj was quite particular about naval education of his son. He selected Kalingodbhaba, the best naval expert as his teacher. Kalinga was the home of maritime trade since time immemorial. Kharavela must gain knowledge and skill of oceanology, maritime travel, trade and maritime commerce. When kings and their administrators of Kalinga were busy with administration, the shipyards of Chilika lake went on building ships and boats with methods invented and reinvented year after year by experienced seamen. Kalinga searched for treasures from *Suvarna dvipa* or Gold Islands of Far East through the sea. It was said in Kalinga that sea was the father of Laxmi, the Goddess of wealth. All this speaks volumes on the maritime trade of that age.

Chanakya had detailed description of sea trade and state taxation on such trade in his *Arthasastra*. But sea trade during Maurya administration was confined to western side, *Ratnakara* or the Arabian Sea. That was only for merchandise. There were no passenger ships. Passenger ships were there, they were from Kalinga coasts of Tamralipti, Paloura, Dantapura and Pitrunda Metropolis. Pandya and Keralaputra had their naval direction to west. Kalinga traded with Suvarna Dvipa: Java, Sumatra, Bali and Champa. Kalinga was emotionally attached to Bali Islands for reasons not known. But it is said this island is named after Bali who was a Kalinga king.

Ashok took keen interest in navy and maritime trade. But the problem with native Magadha was that it had no coast. The west coast under the Maurya was a narrow strip. Out of utter jealousy he had employed one representative to count Kalinga bound ships. For ages, different sizes of vessels, ships and cargo ships were sailing from Kalingan coast. Kalinga dominated at Tamralipti, the major harbour of India at the northern end of Kalingan coast. Magadha possessed strong military power, but had to manage with the rules of commerce imposed at the port of Kalinga. Magadha had wished to own at least Tamralipti for a thoroughfare in the Kalinga Ocean.

A province in the interior of a country was deprived of a sea coast. When geography of a kingdom is unfavourable, how long will it wage war to engulf a coastal province for maritime trade? Kalinga was the eyesore of Magadha and was invaded so many times by Nandas and Mauryas. But each time, it slipped away from their clutches.

Kalingodbhaba came to his senses. He was among the crowd sympathising with the Emperor. Kharavela was very clever and wouldn't be guided by anybody. He was decisive from his very birth. He remembered one instance when Kharavela risked his life to prove his sailing ability. He was learning how to sail in Nanigaun small port at Puri. He left the shore and sailed into deep sea in a small vessel beyond safety zone. The teacher was alarmed at his attempt and was praying God for his safe return. On arrival at the coast, his teacher had a sigh of relief that Kharavela had returned. But he was asked many troublesome questions about the problems faced by Kalinga sailors here in Kalingodra and there in foreign lands. The Pandya and Keralaputra probably indulged in sea piracy against Kalinga bound ships. This had to be solved by coast guard ships. It was the demand of the sailors which could be perceived by young Kharavela. Immediate communication to his father could end in a decision of appointing coast guards to check it.

Young Kharavela mused, "Can I reach the foreign lands? I wish to see how my motherland looks from there, how green and resourceful."

Hardly had Kharavela completed twelve years in the throne of Kalinga, when he blotted out piracy from Kalinga coasts. No more the Pandya or Keralaputra caused obstacles to merchandise or passenger vessels of Kalinga. On land and sea, he had succeeded in breaking the hagemony of Tamil confederacy.

It was the strong capability of Kharavela who has converted king Pandyan, his arch enemy into one of his close friends and had invited him to this celebration. Kalingodbhaba looked at the face of Pandya king and became attentive to the proceedings.

The dance and music teacher of Kharavel, Priyambad was lost in analyzing the activities of Kharavela, his favourite student decades back. He expressed his satisfaction that music and dance not only gained prominence but also made India a throbbing site of these aesthetic fine arts. Often Priyambad was afraid, Ashok's prohibition of 'No Utsab and no Samaj' was very much working in this direction. This prohibition was broken by social revolution of prince Kharavela. He himself was an artist of *tauryatrika*, master of dance, drama and music; he nurtured these elements in the people and mostly the women folk who were zealous practitioners of this art. Kalinga had her own set of musical instruments like drum, harp, flute, conches, mardal, and dundubhi. There were some village level folk songs which were sung in small recreational functions.

Highly trained Priyambad was designated as Gandharba Guru by Chetaraj. Gandharba Guru had noticed some fascinating trait of the young prince in mimicking. He did not hesitate in manifesting such histrionic talent. He was a singer by instinct. He was a resident of the palace of Kalinganagari but had no inhibition in mimicking the mannerisms of remote rural people arriving at the capital metropolis. Young prince was famous in Kalinga for his melodious songs. He was quite proficient in speaking for hours in perfect spoken language of Kalinga while convincing groups of people.

Prince Kharavela liked all types of musical instruments. The original village equipment for music and dance were drum, the mrudala, harp and flute. The native dance of Kalinga had a special character. The whole body of the dancer would move in tune with music, the dancer's limbs seamlessl melting into it. He liked and accompanied his Gandharba Guru to village settlements to spread this Gandharba art.

Gandharba Guru could not ascertain what had happened to Kharavela. After triumphs in every field why he wanted to give up the throne! If the Emperor had in his mind to spend the rest of his life with music and drama, he would not welcome it. The State and administration were the harbinger of treasure and prosperity of the country. In comparison dance and drama are less important. It would naturally follow the wellbeing of populace at large. Priyambad became thoughtful with a blank expression staring at the face of the Emperor.

Jatnasila, a favourite tutor of Kharavela, had seen Kharavela from very childhood and had noticed the temperament and inquisitiveness of the toddler. Jatnasila had experienced the joy of Mahameghavahana family when this little baby was born. The royal astrologer indicated the name and fame waiting for the newborn. He forecasted thebrilliant and charismatic character of the prince; one day he would be the Chakravarti, the unconquerable one. He had all good signs with him and was vested with tremendous divine energy to conquer Magadha. On attaining youth, all his capabilities would multiply and he would be a well-wisher of people and the society. None on earth would surpass him in military power.

Jatnasila had noticed the joy of Kharavela's grandfather, Mahameghavahana. He burst into laughter when he learnt from the astrologer that a mighty prince would glorify the Chedi dynasty. He had in mind the hidden agony Magadha had inflicted on Kalinga and breathed a sigh of relief at the favourable forecast of the astrologer. Rays of hope flooded his imagination. Father Chetaraj too had the optimistic vision as foreseen by the grandfather. But Chetaraj was hopeful about the third generation of the Mahameghavahana dynasty on military strength and administrative capability. The seeds that had been sown on elephantry earlier must yield its result at the right time.

Waves of joy were inundating the Kalingan mind far and wide beyond the Kalinganagari and Toshali. A good number of well-wishers, priests, astrologers, Brahmins, *Arhats*, Buddhist monks queued up to bless the new born prince and the royal family. Grahacharya, the royal astrologer had already analysed the future of the prince and aired it all around. Since the birth of prince Kharavela, Mahameghavahana had kept in mind to appoint an ideal tutor for his grandson and Jatnasila was the choicest of all choices.

Jatnasila had noticed uncommon qualities of the young prince from his very childhood. The young Kharavela would bloom with joy when he heard the victory of the brave and triumph of the truth. He did not enjoy when the wrong man or thought won the race. He was a different child, not so egoistic, but had his mind glued to wider sphere of social welfare. He was happy when his family achieved political and social glory. Jatnasila had to adjust himself with the mood of the young prince.

Whenever there was any problem in the mind of the prince defying solution, Jatnasila was reliably entrusted with the query. Once the prince insisted that Jatnasila must tell him the story of the glorious achievement of a Kalinga youth. Jatnasila, after thinking for a while, found a powerful story with a strong moral and answered, "Yes my dear prince, we will now listen the story of a great boy Vijoy related to Kalinga. You will appreciate his achievements."

Jatnasila narrated the story of Sri Vijoy, a relative of the royal family. This story dated back to the time of Budddha's Mahanirvana. The prince was silent and attentive. He was looking at Jatnasila.

Jatnasila narrated, "Sri Vijoy happened to be the grandson of a Kalingan grandmother, who hailed from

Kalinga royal family. She married in Banga royal family and King Sighabahu was her son. The story might be of Gautama Buddha's time. Sri Vijoy had gene inherited from two powerful dynasties. For his royal abandon and lavish character he had hundreds of follower friends. They all had created nuisance in Banga kingdom. The nuisance was of such magnitude that he along with his friends was driven out of Banga and Kalinga kingdoms. Along with his seven hundred followers they were thrown into the Kalinga Sea."

Kharavel was curious. He asked, "How could Vijoy overcome such a punishment?"

Jatnasila continued, "They all got into a big Kalinga ship and started rowing it with oars in a direction away from Banga and Kalinga coasts. Days passed but they could not get to land, nor did they find any passer-by to trace the location. Luckily they reached an island. That island was none other than Tamraparni, the Sri Lanka of Ramayana Epic. They reached the shore, kissed the sandy ground of the sea shore. They hoisted a yellow flag with the figure of a lion at the centre. They named this island as Tamraparni."

Young Kharavela exclaimed, "Hurrah! They could find a way. Sir, please continue."

Jatnasila continued, "Prince, you will be astonished to know what the day was when Sri Vijoy arrived at Tamraparni. It was the last day of Lord Buddha."

Young Kharavel remarked, "Tamraparni was born, when Lord Buddha breathed his last!"

Jatnasila continued, "When they entered the island, there was no king in Tamraparni. Vijoy could obtain the throne with help of the Kuveni, the queen of the place. She expected to become the wife of Vijoy, but that could not happen. Sri Vijoy and his friends could get rid of *Yakkhas*, *Kinners* and *Asuras*.

Kalingan maritime trade had extended to Tamraparni and beyond the Far East. It is told, elephants of Kalinga were carried in ship to Tamraparni. Even much before Sri Vijoy could establish Tamraparni, sailors of Kalinga had reached this island in search of the golden treasure. They might have been enchanted by the natural beauty of the island. It was irresistible passion of Kalinga sailors to cruise to distant waters. Kalingan maritime drive had been initiated earlier than boundaries assigned to kingdoms and ownership to adjacent seas.

Sri Vijoy could be a favourite of Pandya king, the great grandfather of Pandyan, now seated beside Mahameghavahana Kharavela. He could marry the princess of Pandya. His seven hundred friends also got married to beautiful Pandya girls. This initiated tripartite sea trade among Kalinga, Tamraparni and Pandya.

Jatnasila very lucidly narrated this story of *Mahavasma* Buddhist epic that happened in Sri Lanka when Buddha was taking his last meal at the potter's home and developed illness lying between two Sal trees with Ananda, his attendant at the time of Mahanirvana.

Prince Kharavela was disturbed for some time when his caretaker asked, "Dear prince, how do you appreciate Sri Vijoy's role?"

Young prince replied, "Sri Vijoy might have committed some crime in his paternal kingdom, but his achievements would earn him rich tribute. He is a worthy son of Kalinga soil, had imprinted his name with Tamraparni in golden letters. Bravo Sri Vijoy!"

The prince jumped to the next interrelated question, "The achievements of Sri Vijoy were legendary. What was the status of Magadha and how did Magadha appreciate this event?"

Jatnasila noted the depth of the Prince's attraction for Kalinga. Prince believed in east or west, Kalinga was and is the best for all times. He was eager for a comparative statement of two neighbouring geographical boundaries. Jatnasila knew his limits. He had simple knowledge on folklores but was unaware of what happened five centuries ago. He pondered over how to answer the prince. He was afraid that he would be exposed before Chetaraj on this issue.

Jatnasila arrived at some conclusion. He knew Jainism thrived in Kalinga since time immemorial. Jainism was widely accepted in the kingdom of Kalinga much before Mahabharata War. Jain *arhats* ascetics believe this Kumaragiri and Kumarigiri as seats of achievement. These ascetics were so dedicated that they would sit in meditation like Valmiki until they turned into anthills. A sacred ascetic was the treasure of the society. He was akin to a consecrated place, so termed a Tirthankara. Jatnasila knew one of the Jain ascetics who very often visited Kalinganagari for alms. He was Bicharapada, a popular representative of Jain sect of the hills. Often he undertook the pains to cover the distance of sixteen furlongs to reach Kalinganagari. He was an erudite scholar with experience of his visit to many lands including Magadha, Anga, Banga and Mathura. It would be appropriate to put forth this question of the prince to Bicharapada for an answer.

Bicharapada recounted the tale of past five hundred years to prince Kharavela. It depicted Mahavir's Jain concept, Gautama Budddha's long meditation and the small state or Janapada-Mahajanapada formation of north India and many things about socio-cultural upheaval. His discussion laid emphasis on hegemony of Magadha engulfing its incompatible neighbouring states. But contemporary

Kalinga was a naturally protected province; it had geographical barriers to arrest north Indian dominance. Its subjects never bothered about castes. Kalinga extended from the Ganges to Godavari north-south and Kalinga Sea to Amarakantak in east-west directions. Three divisions of Kalinga were prominent, division with Ganges at north, Kalinga proper in middle and Macco Kalinga as southern part. Kalinga identified its residents on professional basis. Kalinga has been depicted as a great Janapada in Buddhist documents. Magadha was once Jarasandha's kingdom in Mahabharata, Anga belonged to Karna. But by Buddha's time, Bimbisar was the king of Magadha. In Jain language he was called as Srenika. Based on a conflict between Bhatiya, father of Bimbisara and king of Anga, Bhatiya was humiliated. It was the crafty Bimbisar, who through unfair means killed the king of Anga by deploying *Vish Kanya* or poisonous girls. Magadha was centrally located in India, prosperous but very hagemonic to swallow up neighbouring states. It might be a king of Nanda dynasty or the Maurya dynasty and his sole characteristic was expansion and dominance. Bimbisara married the princess of Koshala kingdom and got Kashi as dowry, again married the princess of Vaisali and had great influence over Vaisali. It might be the time when Mahavir Jain attained his nirvana.

This story of expansionist Magadha had so many aspects on religious side. Bimbisara constructed his capital initially at Rajagriha. Pataliputra was built next. He was the contemporary of Buddha. He was a staunch Jain, yet invited Buddha to the harem to bless the queens. The queens had been blessed with Buddha's nail and strands of hair to construct a *Stupa* in the harem. Bimbisar was amazed at the simple character of Tathagata Buddha, the enlightened one.

This narration of Bicharapada enhanced the outlook and understanding of prince Kharavela. He analysed that Mahavir was the only prince of India who had some mental inclination to give up the material life. As prince, Mahavir left Vaisali kingdom, so also Gautama Buddha relinquished his family and kingdom. Society became the victim of selfish ideology and subjects of kingdoms became a prey to annexable hunger of kings. Kharavela appreciated the truth obtained by Mahavir and Gautam through meditation but in his consideration this truth could have been attained without relinquishing the family and society. He considered himself too small to comment on the vastness of the issue.

Kharavela pondered and seriously put forth a question to Bicharapada, "Can a prince get rid of sorrow, hunger or disease by relinquishing the family or kingdom?"

Bicharapada could grasp to what dizzy heights could Kharavel's mind leap. He had to reply him in simple terms so that the young prince would understand. He told, "Gautama Buddha was quite compassionate from his birth. His father wanted to keep him indoors so that he would not come across social maladies to which he was the most vulnerable. He arranged an early marriage for him in order to divert him to conjugal pleasures. But nothing could prevent him from relinquishing everything and spending over a period of six years in search of truth."

Young Kharavela added, "What was the truth discovered by Gautam? It is the same old story of every one's life. Buddha claimed his ideals as absolute new facts and he became very popular and rose above kings and emperors. Desire is the cause of sorrow. By destroying desire, we can destroy our sorrow. But desire is an aspiration."

Bicharapada remained silent. But he studied the

strong material aspect of young prince against a spiritual background. Bicharapada continued, "Exactly one century before Gautama Buddha, Mahavir was overwhelmed with grief at the sight of human violence and savagery and this prompted him to relinquish family and society both; he gave himself free to meditation, and finally, when enlightened, preached about life presenting it from all possible perspectives. People at that time did not hesitate to tell a lie or to steal something from others. They committed violence and killed animals, birds and even fellow human beings. His instructions of truthfulness, non-stealing or *asteya* and non-violence or *ahimsa* are significant for social behaviour of man. Educated princes like Parsvanath, Mahavir and Gautama Buddha could feel the suffering of man. So they gave up social life and opted for spiritual life.

Bicharapada turned the discussion to the life of Lord Parsvanath, the Jain Tirthankara. Parsvanath had faced enmity of Kamatha, life after life. A story of approximately one thousand years ago: Aswasen was the king of Varanasi. Son of Aswasen was prince Parsvakumar. There was a saint named Kamatha. He was an orphan and was brought up by unknown people. Kamatha was managing his life with much difficulty. In order to practise Panchagni, he lit a bundle of wood and as the flames leapt up, Parsvanath could see a large number of insects the flame lapped up. And he could also notice two snakes hidden in the bundle the fire would soon devour. Without waiting a moment, the prince asked him to refrain from such activity.

He asked Kamatha, "How would I grace your lordship?"

Kamatha replied in fury, "Prince, better you involve yourself in your comfortable life of a prince. You can't understand the life of a sage like me. How could you know some animal is going to be burnt in the pyre of wood meant for *Panchagni?"*

Parsvakumar exposed a half burnt snake from the burning pyre of wood. He chanted the Jain *Namokar* mantra. The snake died and was reborn as a serpent named Dharanendra. Kamatha was aggrieved. He took much care in his meditation and was born as Meghamali in his next birth.

Parsvakumar renounced the family and kingdom to become an ascetic at the age of thirty. His aim was to spend his life in quest of peace. He went deep into meditation. Then Meghamali could trace him and was revengeful by applying his spiritual forces in the guise of tiger, lion, elephant and snake. Torrential rain was set by Meghamali; Parsva was submerged in rain water up to his neck. But he was undisturbed in his meditation. At this juncture, Dharanedra appeared. He saved meditating Parsva supporting him from under his feet and spread his hood as an umbrella over his head. Dharanendra persuaded Meghamali to refrain from such sinful behaviour. Kamatha surrendered to Lord Parsva. These two stories depict his ninth and tenth rebirths of Parsvanath. Previous eight births are also based on such atrocious deed of Kamatha. But Kamatha representing violence yielded to the truth and non-violence at last. This story is the backbone of a sincere Jain's non-violent neutral character. Parsva preached four principles, *Ahimsa, Asteya, Achourya* and *Aparigraha*. Mahavir added later the fifth one, *Brahmacharya.*

Bicharapada impressed young Kharavela very much who pondered whether he would opt to be a Jain saint. His royal family had adopted Jainism and then he was strongly motivated to becom a Jain mendicant.

But Bicharapada came to his rescue. He had instructed

him to become a powerful Jain king. A married person of Jain principle is called *srabasth*. An ordinary person as a *srabasth* can achieve miracles in the grade of Jain religion. He cited one example of Mahavir's time. There was a commercial settlement with king Jitasatru. In this city, lived Ananda. Ananda possessed four million gold coins, huge number of silver coins and other assets. He owned four thousand cows. King Jitasatru also appreciated Ananda.

Ananda was inclined towards the twelve oaths elaborated by Mahavir Jain for *srabasth*. He followed the rituals of this principle for fourteen years. Then he wanted to renounce the world. After meditation for a long time, he could attain the truth and purity of mind. He also obtained the Jain attainment called *Abadhijnana*. Luckily Mahavir was passing through the town with his disciples. Mahavir's main disciple, Gautama Swami went to the town for alms and could hear that a *Srabasth* was claiming to have attained *Abadhijnana*. Ananda met Gautama Swami and saluted him and informed him about his attainment.

Gautama Swami asked, "It is not possible on the part of a *Srabasth* to attain *Abadhijnana*. You have told a lie. So you undertake penance for it."

Ananda claimed, "One who speaks the truth, will he repent for it?"

This matter went to Mahavir. Mahavir gave his decision. Ananda was right. He had attained *Abadhijnana*. He was astonished how Gautama Swami could not appreciate it he being his prime disciple. Gautama Swami could realize his mistake. He went to Ananda and begged apology. Ananda praised the truthfulness of Jainism in general and Lord Mahavir in particular. He exclaimed the genuine application of Jainism to ordinary men. Great sadhu like Gautama Swami too came to him to know the truth. Ananda was contented and immersed himself in Jainism.

Now, young Kharavela danced with joy. He appreciated the importance of this religion in the life of a man as an ideal way of living. Each individual without relinquishing family and society could lead a Jain way of life. He thought if all opted for giving up material life, the human population would be extinct from the earth. He was convinced that this religion did not require anyone to give up the worldly affairs and live the life of a sage. But an ordinary man can obtain the highest spiritual state as a disciplined *Srabasth*.

Kharavela had a great question stirring up in his mind. But he did not spell it at that instance. He had to wait until he became a Yubaraj to call upon Bicharapada to answer his reserved question.

He stated, "Sadhuji guide me, can religion be a serious obstacle in day-to-day political affairs. Punishment is an ordinary weapon of managing a kingdom which is nothing but violence, just opposite of non-violence which is the cardinal principle of Jainism. So kindly advise me how a staunch Jain king should manage the affairs of his kingdom."

Bicharapada's face lit up in joy. He replied in a cool voice, "It is very simple, dear prince. A king's life has two parts, one as a king and the other as a man. As a king, he has the entire responsibility of the kingdom. So he has to be meticulous in politics, diplomacy, economics and military, the necessary qualities for survival and prosperity of the kingdom. But in his personal life, he may follow Jain pattern of lifestyle. There has never been any instance of Jainism conflicting with kingship. This had been the history of Magadha, Vaisali or any other *Mahajanapada* in the northern parts of Bharatavarsa. No king had ever given up his personal religious pursuits nor the state administration had been implanted with pure religious principles."

Bicharapada continued, "The best example is Emperor Chandragupta Maurya, whose kingdom extended from Banga in the east to Pandya in the south, Kashmir in the north with Taksasila in the west. He was a Jain. His religion had neither prevented him from winning any territory nor going to war. He followed the strategic principles of Arthasastra by his Chief Minister Kautilya which contained all the military, diplomatic, political and economic principles.

"As the Emperor of India and General in the battle against Seleukos, the Macedonian General of Alexander, Chandragupta fought and could win the battle and was gifted with Helen, the daughter of Seleukos as wife. Jainism was not a barrier in any way."

The young and moralist Kharavela's heart revolted. Chandragupta's spirituality is absolutely flawed, he thought. His own dynasty would never follow such a vitiated path, come what may. "What was the nature of Chandragupta's marriage with Helen?" he asked himself. "Was it lust? Was it love, or was it diplomacy?" He got no answer. Bicharapada, however, ignored Kharavela's muttering. He continued, unmindful of what Kharavela murmured.

He affirmed his statement, "Chandragupta had applied the best of Kautilya's Arthasastra for good governance and he was successful. But he did not lose himself in royal duties. All of a sudden, he has relinquished throne and followed his religious teacher, Vadrabahu. He relinquished his family life to become an ascetic and led a life of Jain *arhat* at Shravanbelgola, the greatest Jain centre of the time. He never bothered how Magadha would run after he had quitted. He even opted for fasting unto death, the Salehan characteristic of Jains!"

Bicharapada could see in the mind of young Kharavela a better sense of history that changed the gloomy expression of his brows to that of a cheerful one. The prince appreciated the last decision of Chandragupta and was respectful to his Jain behaviour. He appreciated the idea of a Jain King relinquishing the throne at the height of his achievement.

Bicharapada recollected the event happened twenty three years back when Kharavela was coronated as Yubaraj of Kalinga. He corroborated the recent affair with Yubaraj's ideology.

He faced Emperor Kharavela and asked, "Kalingadhipati, the Great! Are you accepting a Jain ascetic life like Chandragupta?"

Kharavela became graceful, his face shone like enlightened Buddha's face. He replied, "Oh my spiritual teacher! You have instructed so many aspects of a Jain King, I have obeyed each one of your principles in my life. I had my aim of relinquishing the throne at the height of my achievement. Yesterday I did exactly that.

"I have completed my military victories all around. I had set two ideals to attain my target: I must conquer Magadha for the sake of my motherland and second, I must get back Agra Jina, Risabhanatha statue of Kalinga that the Nanda had lifted away."

"Chedi administration of Kalinga would continue. I will lead my spiritual life here in Kumarigiri hilltop. The Kalingan art and music will adorn the last phase of my life. But at this juncture, I promise, any Emperor of Kalinga, if consults me on any issue, I will suggest him the way I would handle it."

This statement of Kharavela dimmed the vision of

the palace. The royal family began weeping convulsively. Kharavela handed over his crown to his chief queen standing with son Kandarpashree and started climbing the stairs of Kumarigiri.

Suddenly a piece of dark cloud veiled the moon. The *Salabhanjika*, the *Dishidharika*, the *Dwarapalika* and all sculptural characters left the place with a heavy heart and flooded eyes. The vast crowd disappeared.

Three youngmen were dazed by the replay of this glorious history of Kalinga. They rushed back to their resting place.

Chapter-4

Princess of the Diamond Kingdom

In the night before full moon, the three friends were discussing the last episode on the hill. The cake of Gamha Purnima festival of the day couldn't charm them as much the replay of events to come next. They were delighted with the pomp and grandeur they could see in full moon nights. Their assumption that the society was primitive two thousand years ago was simply untrue.

Aparti was courageous to start, "Tonight I will ask *Salabhanjika* Puspita about her whereabouts. Her name is quite attractive and she is a fairy. Even if she is a stone-girl there must be some mystery around her creation. Nowadays we see different shades of *Salabhanjikas*. How do they get shape in stone art? It is quite strange, how did such stone artisans exist two thousand years ago?"

Abhiram replied, "Hey, are you in love with that girl? But how come? Your mom has given this name 'Aparti', meaning the child least like to survive, and she had to, because all her children born before you died. Now, you being the only survivor, you are too precious for her own life. How can you smash all her hopes and dreams by loving not a human but a woman shaped stone?"

Pranabandhu reconciled, "It is alright Abhi, do not talk like that. We are lucky enough today that we are able to see some past events live. In case Puspita replies to Aparti's query, we will know something more."

On the full moon night, they had some minor problems to get together. The clouds covered the moon. Luckily the clouds vanished before midnight. The three friends noticed Puspita getting down the stairs. A number of lamp-bearing *Dishidharikas* were illuminating the hills.

Puspita was looking fresh. Her eyes were no more drowsy. She looked wonderful with grace and elegance, clad in a sari with an ornamental girdle around her waist. She had a coiffure studded with jasmine and adorned with twig of Sal leaves. Smilingly she was getting down making the ambience pleasant with her dignified demeanour. At the foothill she received the guests.

The guests followed Pallabi. Aparti came closer to her and asked, "Madam, how come such innumerable agile stone-girls like you landed here on this hill. We are pleased and we accept it as the good fortune of our province, Kalinga"

Puspita replied briefly, probably some event was to unfold within a while, "Kalingadhipati Kharavela achieved innumerable victories and amassed huge amount of wealth, cavalry, trained elephants. But the most important of them all were the sculptors of Maurya and Sunga dynasties. Originally Macedonians and Persian stone art had arrived in India from the west, centuries earlier. Kharavela could motivate stone artisans and skilled masons to showcase their masterpiece in the background of caves of the twin hills. Our Emperor had often quoted that he had been attracted by the stone girls particularly *Salabhanjika*, one he saw at Sanchi and few others at Barhut of Magadha.

She continued, "Since you are interested, let me tell you the concept of how stone girls set into the environs of stone artisans and masons. A *Salabhanjika* is both sacred and profane, noticeable just outside the temple. A *Salabhanjika* is beautifully carved in stone; she is accepted as masterpiece of an artisan. As a mark of craftsmanship, the artisan works to his full potential to embellish her with jewellery and the finest of clothes. The artisan chooses a well carved headdress and matches the hairdo with conceivable zest.

"I am feeling ecstatic to tell you that stone artisans are mad after *Salabhanjika*. They beautify her with all ornaments, ornate her with qualities of high degree of excellence. They make her waist slim and her chest full breasted to enhance her sensuality. To convert a piece of stone to *Salabhanjika* for an artisan is to set an outstanding example of elegantly animating beauty and bliss in lifeless rock.

Puspita concluded her emotionality with a boast, "A *Salabhanjika* is in the stone sculpture of a buxom lady beneath a leafy plant or under a tree, at times holding it. Most often it is the Ashoka tree. Sometimes the trees they hold are laden with fruits. She may be seen in a tri-bent posture.(i.e. dance posture wherein the body bends at three different areas say, Ankle, waist and breast?)

All these elements are a composite art of expressing prosperity and fertility. Our artistic Emperor had made an indent of wish trees or *Kalpa Bata* from Mathura so that people can invoke it for any of their aspirations. Additional indent was *Salabhanjika* from north Indian stone sculpture to establish a brilliant, prosperous, fertile and green Kalinga."

Though she was in haste as some event was about to start, she added, "With same temperament the stone artisans and carpenters have carved all male and female statues, be it a *Gandharva*, *Vidyadhar* or *Kinnar* on the twin hills. At the entrance of Kumarigiri, the stand-up feminine door keeper, *Dwarapalika* is an embodiment of an affluent advanced contemporary Kalinga girl.

The youngmen were satisfied with her explaining and

they had no chance to ignore her as a mere stone stuff. She was not only an ornate stone masterpiece but also represented an affluent girl of her times in Kalinga.

Puspita informed them that the desired moment had arrived. They have to hurry up a little. They have to reach the nearby Manchapuri Cave.

Puspita stated, "Kharavela himself was an admirer of the stone art that carved how he was worshipping the Kalinga Jina with a priest. He had two queens behind him and the stone artisans had created a majestic spiritual ambience with all Gods, well wishers and supernatural forces enriching the cave of worship. The great aspirant Kalinga Emperor started his centenary celebration from this spiritual background. In this full moon night, he recalled into his memory all that he had dreamt and achieved. He may not have his corporeal body any more but his ideals and achievements survive the flow of time. The spirituality has never been an element to perish with time."

They had already reached the Manchapuri Cave by the time their conversation was over. The courtyard of the cave was crowded. One tall person with brown complexion was waiting there in a pensive mood. It could not be ascertained what was his worry: whether it was for some relatives inside the cave or for the deity inside. He was looking like the Lord of the kingdom, but the worry did not disturb any of his royal concerns.

A number of tourists were on visit. They were creating a little noise. They were talking in some language, not clearly understood by the three youngmen. But they felt as if the language they were listening to was of some remote rural region, meaning of which could be partly understood. The people seemed to be satisfied with worshipping the idol inside the cave.

The tall person had a drapery of transparent cloth and was waiting for somebody. He had a pair of pendants ornamenting his ears. His thick yellow metal necklace was dazzling in the moon light. He had sharp features. He had a peculiar ponytail hanging down at the back of his head, peculiar with the male drama artists. A long thread of gold extended from the left side of the neck to below his right arm. One would be mesmerized with such a presence. His body, gait and posture were quite distinct. He looked too simple. He had an inviting appearance to attract conversation. His face spoke of his interest for intimacy with outsiders. The two ear ornaments were keeping the spectator's vision fixed on them. The crown was an excellent match to his head, his glossy skin could lure the eyes of any inattentive person passing by. His appearance matched with somebody the three youngmen had seen earlier, but memory failed to identify him.

It is probably the Manchapuri Cave was dug years after Kalinga Jina was established on top of Hathigumpha. The Emperor of Kalinga had made this cave his shelter when he came from Kalinganagari to Kumarigiri. Stone artisans had carved a scene of worship of Kalinga Jina in a spiritual environment with heavenly creatures like flying *Gandharvas, Kinnars, Fairies* and *Elephants*. The Emperor along with the royal priest and two of his queens were on the site.

In the meantime, two queens of Kalinga had come out of the Manchapuri Cave. Both of them were tall, unparallel in beauty even in their late middle age. The chief queen was healthy, clad in a sari and was embellished with precious ornaments. She had the semblance of a deity. Sindhula, the second queen was an epitome of beauty. She was grave and possessed all qualities of mother earth. Her facial expression was radiating knowledge and intelligence.

Her attire was a colourful sari with magnificent pleats, her necklace and ear ornaments were of tastefully esoteric.

Salabhanjika Puspita who had revealed identity of Emperor and his two queens said, "Chief Queen of Kalinga is the mother of would be king of Kalinga, Mahameghavahana Kandarpashree. A time was there when Kharavela was waiting to marry in order to be eligible for ascending the throne of Kalinga. When Kharavela was fifteen years of age, his father Chetaraj relinquished the throne. Nine years passed in Kalinga without a king and the Yubaraj Kharavela had to marry in order to be eligible for the throne. Marriage according to Vedic rites was considered as a prerequisite for the ascent to the throne.

"Reminiscence of that period is thrilling even today. From the very childhood he was fond of song and dance. His creative mind would find a rhythm in every happening of nature including display of light, darkness and sound. His feet would assume the pose of rhythmical movements. He believed in original cultural heritage of Kalinga and was conscious of people's choice.

"He had completed his education in all fields befitting a king which included military training, politics and diplomacy writings, accountancy and public relations. He was a veteran in archery and had promised to be in forefront of every war against enemy as Commander. He had developed close understanding with a few Kalinga elephants and well-bred imported horses. These animals also had shown reciprocal dedication to their master. The prince had promised himself to help Kalinga emerge as the most powerful kingdom of the country. 'Might is right' was the order of the day. So military strength was of paramount importance. He made periodic evaluation of his army and trained them with the state of the art techniques.

Now Kharavela was recollecting his past activities. There was a time when he was going to complete ninth year of his princehood and the throne of Kalinga Empire was waiting for him. One delicate issue definitely delayed this ceremony. That was his marriage. Strangely, a prince qualified in all respects but there was no matching bride for him which turned to be a misfortune for the state. Chetaraj, father of Kharavel relinquished the throne and exposed the kingdom to neighbour's envious attack. Kalinga wanted an able military leader and was waiting when Kharavela would ascend the throne.

In that juncture, he had led a hunting expedition to the west as far as Vajiraghar, the diamond kingdom. These expeditions were considered as royal custom of the time. That particular expedition was a matter of chance to have the princess of Vajiraghar as queen of Kalinga. Kharavela became emotional when the incident of that expedition came to his memory. The scheduled time of the party was early in winter, the harvesting time which was suitable for hunting. The hunting excursion was conducted about fifteen years ago when he started to move to the west with some experts of archery, a few hunters and a small team of military forces. This was led by the best archer of Kalinga, Dhanukaguru, archery teacher of Kharavela.

They had travelled far to west, but could not get any prey. They came across the Suktel River identified by archery teacher, Dhanukaguru, who belonged to that area and was intimately acquainted with it. He informed that the river was a tributary of Chitrotpala River of coastal Kalinga. This area was once ruled by the forefathers of Mahameghavahana family. Jainism was promoted by the royal family in the past. Most of the residents of the tract were Jains. As resourceful leader, the Mahameghavahana could be Maurya representative of Kalinga and take over the charge of Toshali and administration of Maurya colony. Kalinga had noticed some humanitarian services since the rule of Samprati, a descendant of Maurya and a staunch Jain.

The hunting excursion team travelled further to the west. The forests there had new varieties of plants and vegetation. After a long arduous journey, a herd of deer could be sighted. The members of the team were scattered as they ran as animals, separated from the herd. The deer chased by prince Kharavela was tired and peculiarly took shelter under the shade of a tree. The prince got down from his horse and caught the deer alive.

The prince was astonished. It was not a wild deer but a doe, a hind, a female deer. It had a small musical bell around her neck. This indicated its domestication and existence of a nearby settlement. He fetched a handful of water for the doe from the stream nearby when three girls reached the spot. They were laughing aloud. They were silent on seeing the prince carrying water for the doe.

The doe was no more apprehensive. It walked to the most beautiful among the three and started licking her sari. The prince could realize that he mistook the doe to be a wild one and tried to hunt it down. Instead he felt himself hunted down by tender feelings. He was astonished to notice the saris worn by the women folks were costly Kalinga silk worn only by the ladies of the royal families. She was whispering at the doe, "Bhagyabati, you had left us three days ago. We had been searching you without taking any food."

The prince felt shy amidst the company of girls. He realized that the girls were in the forest in search of this doe. The second girl wearing a blue sari spoke in a low voice, "Thank you Arya Kumar, I am Mallika, a companion of Her Highness Bajraballi, the princess of Vajiraghar. I express our gratitude for getting us back our lost doe. May we know your identity?"

The Prince gave his identity courteously.

The three girls turned silent, felt shy and tried to veil themselves. Mallika whispered, "Is he the prince, the Kalinga Kumar. He is the dream of the King of Vajiraghar, Lalarka. He is the hero declared by the royal astrologer and would be the son-in-law of the kingdom"

Yubaraj was silent. He admired the Kalinga sari enhancing the beauty of princess of Vajiraghar. He felt himself proud as a Kalingan. In his thought he praised the professional weavers of his kingdom. Women in the dense forest also use Kalinga clothes and ornaments. They have beautiful hairdo. Who is the king here? How is he related to Kalinga.

Prince Kharavela was eager to learn about Vajiraghar and its king when a palanquin with four bearers arrived to take the guest as if Vajiraghar Palace was waiting to treat the Prince of Kalinga.

Prince Kharavela reached Vajiraghar palace. He respectfully greeted king Lalarka; bowed down before the royal deity, Parsvanath. The royal heritage was great. Lalarka was the grandson of famous Hastisimha, the leader of whole Vidyadhar kingdom. Kalinga happened to be their respectable neighbour. Overseas merchandise trade of Vidyadhar kingdom used to be transacted through Kalinga.

Prince Kharavela informed about his hunting expedition party. The group was invited to the palace and was offered royal hospitality. The king was satisfied with the state of affairs of Kalinga and Jain *arhats* of Kumarigiri. He invited the prince and his party for an overnight stay in the palace.

Prince did not feel Vajiraghar as an alien land, rather as intimate as Kalinga. The king and his subjects there were like those of his motherland. People did not consider him as an outsider, rather were talking to him like their own prince. It was a prosperous kingdom, where people were not only rich, but did care for life, be it an animal or a bird. He analysed the name of the kingdom, Vajiraghar, the abode of diamond. Principal profession of people here was collection of precious stones and diamond from river beds and mines. Despite affluence, people were simple and unassuming.

Yubaraj Kharavela could feel the hospitality offered to him was much more than he deserved. Why was he treated with so much grandeur! He had a soft corner for princess Bajraballi. Mallika, the mate of the princess, was not present there. But as the evening approached, Mallika arrived there with a lamp. The prince could identify her in lamp light and asked her, "Mallika, can you help me?"

Mallika replied, "Arya, are you feeling uncomfortable here!"

Kharavela replied, "No, not at all. But I am astonished at the nature of hospitality being offered to me and my men. What could be the reason?"

With a flicker of smile Mallika looked at the face of the prince, studied his curiosity and felt like revealing the secret.

She said, "His Highness King Lalarka was discussing about marriage possibilities of his daughter Bajraballi with Jain saint Brahmaputra, the best astrologer known in Vajiraghar. He had this prediction which is known to the public here that the princess will marry the prince of Kalinga. Her almanacs are fitting with that of Kalinga's prince and the best time will prevail in Kalinga after their marriage.

The prince will ascend the throne of Kalinga with grace of Jain community. He will be victorious in every battle he will fight during his life time. Bajraballi will give birth to the next Kalinga emperor."

Prince Kharavela was silent but delightful with the flow of pleasant thought in his mind. He knew the saint Brahmaputra. The saint often inhabited Kumarigiri and visited Kalinganagari palace and had discussions with Rajamata, his mother. This forecast of the saint here in Vajiraghar might have been the unexpressed will of his mother.

The prince responded with a smile, "The forecast of the saint is then the basis of such unexpected hospitality!"

Mallika was hesitating to comment on prince's appreciation. But her face expressed as if she muttered, "Arya, your welcome has not only been initiated by the doe Bhagyabati, but you have been the Sun here with your rays brightening the life of our princess Bajraballi* the sun flower of this kingdom. The warmth of the discussion between Mallika and prince Kharavela was being enjoyed by the princess Bajraballi waiting nearby to eavesdrop the conversation.

This emotional love story of prince Kharavela had gone to the past by more than a decade, he got married, ascended the throne and had achieved all his targets in life. The Omnipotent Time had wiped out the fragrance of memory in its slow wavy contours. Such faint waves often inundate the shores in the mental reserves of the Emperor standing alone before Manchapuri Cave. His emotional outburst had been on the decline when the second queen Sindhula was stepping down the cave. Sindhula was a highly educated, broad minded woman of secular concepts. She was the princess of Southern Kalinga. She could be

the second queen of Kharavela in course of the political
flow of events in the life of the great Emperor. She had
joined the Mahameghavahana family with her capacity of
inheriting the territory for greater Kalinga. She had been
entrusted with the spiritual assignment of looking after
Kumarigiri institution. She had been under the care of
Jainist Lalita Devi at Queen's Palace.

The Emperor looked thoughtful. He sat down on
the piece of big sandstone of the courtyards of the cave.
Doubts clouded his mind but ultimately were dispelled by
winds of change the next moment.

He had ascended the throne at the age of twenty four,
married just before the coronation. Rajamata consulted the
royal priest of Kalinga. She gave a new name to her daughter
in law and called her *Dhruti*, meaning 'the peaceful owner
of earth'. Dhruti fulfilled all the predictions made by saint
Brahmaputra,

As the events of the Kalinga *Utsava* were unfolding in the beams of moonlit night there was a momentary and unexpected interruption. Well, small piece of cloud could obstruct the moon and our vision but the light emitted by the *Dishidharikas* was adequate to clear it.

Kharavel's relinquishing the throne was not an abrupt issue. It was his sweet will to get out of the tedious administration after becoming victorious in everything he touched. He had been preparing himself for the last three years. He had decided the Kumarigiri hill as his abode in motherland, a spiritual home for later ages. His stone artisans and masons constructed a secret cave opposite Kumaragiri hill that can constantly gaze at the Hathigumpha and Risabhanatha temple overhead from there. The gate and frontal of the cave had parrots and garlands as insignia of the Emperor's residence with his aide, *Padamulika* Kusuma. *Padamulika* was in charge of this secret spiritual cave, Kusum's Lenam.

The *Salabhanjika* also hinted at Kumarigiri which had some experience with Kharavela's final years. The Queen's Palace was in the last stage of its construction. This two-storied cave palace was dedicated to saints of all religions of India. It was a costly palace with floors made up of precious stones. Even emerald was set in the pillars in the upper storey of the cave. A Jain *Stupa* over the Hathigumpha was completed and it was the place of worship of Agrajina Risabhanatha. Kumarigiri was virtually a residential colony of girls and ladies. Lalita Devi was the caretaker of the women folk of Kumarigiri. The hill was exclusively reserved for women. Few of the rigorous *Yapannapak* monks were resting in some of the caves during rains. The melody parties of Kumarigiri were consisting of only women. Men were seen least involved in music and dance. The socio-cultural framework of Kumarigiri fanned out from the settlements far and wide throughout Kalinga. There were revolutionary changes in ornaments for women. Life was extremely pleasant and kings from far off kingdoms admired Kalingan culture fabulously.

The *Salabhanjika* continued the story of Kharavela's Aide, Kusuma and his Cave that was built on Kumargiri by cave masons. It was standing as *Padamulika Kusuma's Lenam*. It was adorned with art of garlands and parrots at its frontals and decorated inside with carvings of king and queen and decorative arts. Kusuma expected the emperor may inhabit there during the ascetic stage of his life. Puspita continued that this cave bore immense importance sometime in the centenary celebration, the disclosure of which might spoil their inquisitiveness of the show.

The interruption created by the stray clouds ended, the place got lighted back with moonbeams and hills gained clear visibility. Puspita showed the three invitees how Kharavela was sad while leaving Kumarigiri and climbing the steps of Kumaragiri for his shelter. The memory of young Kandarpashree was disturbing his mind. The young boy preferred the bed of his parents for a peaceful sleep. Emperor's staunch religious heart was weeping for the loss of paternal love. He could console himself with the experience of his own childhood. His father left the family early when he was learning from his teachers. It was the custom of royal Jain family.

The Morning Star was peeping at the eastern horizon. The centenary episodes started fading away and within moments, the sculptural characters receded to their respective motionless positions. *Salabhanjika* Puspita was no more with her three guests. The *Dishidharikas* were receding to their locations and the *mashal* in their grip were getting feebler. The two hills also were merging with the remaining darkness of the night. Day was not far behind.

The three companions travelled back.

* Literal meaning of Bajraballi is sun flower

Chapter-5

The First Expedition of
Chaturanga Troops

Three friends were bit late in arriving at the appointed place this time. They climbed up the stairs of Kumarigiri. The hills were well lighted and luckily, *Salabhanjika* Puspita and *Dishidharika* were waiting for them. Abhirama apologized for the delay.

Puspita expressed, "Welcome dear guests, nothing to worry. No event has rolled down during this short delay. Today, we will wait here at Alakapuri Cave. There will be the display of first war preparedness of Emperor Kharavela as a military genius. I am sure you will be interested in it."

Three invitees followed the *Salabhanjika* to Alakapuri Cave situated at the foothill of Kumarigiri. They noticed a great change in the configuration of the cave. The dilapidated and damaged cave had beautifully been reshaped. It was modified to a decorated royal chamber.

They were astonished with the episode that followed. A healthy youngman reached the cave on horseback. His identity was clear from his crown. Five knights reached there, each of them was a swordsman. They stood on the right side of the Emperor. The scenic beauty of the place was unique. It was early morning, visibility extended far up to south-eastern horizon. An open space was extending quite far like an endless ocean. Few industrial settlements were visible at long distance in the north direction. There were carpentry and iron smith factories nearby and the military camps were in the west. The western camps were the training ground for new recruits.

It was clear, Kalingadhipati was in front of the Cave and there were five swordsmen in military dress. A huge number of swordsmen in rows were facing the king about twenty paces behind. Few more officials joined the king. They were the personal assistants of the king, the *Padamulika*, Kusuma; the Chief Minister, Nakiya; the Works Minister, *Kama* and *Nagar Akhandash*, the Chief Justice of Toshali, Bhuti.

The Kalinga military forces had four wings, *Chaturanga Senani*, consisting of Army, Charioteers, Cavalry and Elephantry. Chief of each wing was beside the king. Emperor Kharavela received the salute of each group one after another. This Army was not newly formed. Rather it has been better organised for the last ten years since the Yubaraj Kharavela took over the charge. After the grand reception, the king started his motivational speech.

"My dear warriors of Kalinga, I praise the organising capability of the four concerned wings of our military forces. It had rebuilt itself with immense courage since its macabre encounter with Mauryan imperialists. Simultaneously recruitment to warrior training had continued incessantly. We should feel proud that our coordination among the four divisions is of paramount importance for attacking any enemy base and driving away any invader.

"I have evidence available with me that good days are not far off. There is a secret division directly in touch with me which carry information from all corners of the country, specifically from military bases of those powerful kingdoms. What is clear after meticulous observation for a decade that there is decline in the military power of all the powerful states like Magadha, Satavahana including their vassal states. We can secretly constitute a huge military base, here in Kalinga. Our *Chaturanga*, divided into two or three units can proceed for expeditions in north, south and west simultaneously. Of course in the east is our mother sea, the Kalingodra, guarded by our naval power which is in rudimentary stage, compared to the four land divisions

In the north, Mauryan power was on the decline. The last Maurya king was assassinated by Pushyamitra Sunga who was his own General. The great traitor neither maintained his military strength nor political tradition but succumbed to the temptation of his caste rule. There was also the loud voice of Satakarni in the west. One day he may go against us and our allies, the Vidyadhar kingdoms. The notable confederation in India was the Tamil Confederacy consisting of Pandya, Cheru, Keralaputra and Tamraparni bonded together for the last thirteen hundred years. They had proved to be unconquerable to the mightiest Mauryas like Chandragupta and Ashok. The south is almost unknown to many. They trade very cautiously in all spheres.

"Let me reveal you the secret behind our military power. Nature has furnished our royal armory with the most powerful elephants on earth. A large number of black elephants have already been tamed and trained from the time we became detached from Magadha just three generations ago. We will organise our resources to subdue the mighty and the powerful."

The place was reverberated with a loud slogan of 'Triumphant Kalinga.'

The chief of army, *Mahasenani* addressed the gathering of soldiers, "We are now waiting for secret informations from our spies engaged in most of the capital towns of our

neighbours and distant provinces. Kalinga believes in one principle: that is how to win a conflict with the least bloodshed and loss of life. Our elephants will play a crucial role from the beginning to the end and thereafter. From each of our troops, a vibrant small group will emerge to execute the fast attacking strategy."

A lancer covered with black robe on a black horse had direct access to the Emperor. He was quite excited. The whole crowd was eagerly watching him with heightened attention. He started explaining to the Emperor, "Your Highness, Kalingadhipati, I happen to be Senior Intelligent Authority in charge of Asikanagara. You have entrusted me the task of submitting before you the power tally of three principal powers of the country. I have to go to Asikanagara in the disguise of a retail trader. Language was a serious obstacle in my way. However, I could gain mastery over language in a short spell of time. What I have heard from the public there is that Satakarni, the

Satavahana king has propagated a rumour that he is Dakshinadhipati, the Lord of the South. Satakarni's men have forcibly occupied the town and have started this rumour. We have to confront him. Otherwise one day he will designate himself as Kalingadhipati."

Prompt orders were given to *Mahasenani*, the Chief of Military to demolish the Asikanagara city situated between Godavari and Krishna rivers. He would carry half of the *Chaturanga* troops from here to execute the military action.

At this time a soft woolly cloud overlaid the moon. The lamp lights of the *Dishidharikas* got dimmed. The visibility around the Alakapuri Cave became below normal. It indicated momentary break in the scene. But the cloud soon passed and let the moonbeams inundate the whole place.

Nobody was there when light reappeared. In this interval, Aparti was describing in low voice, "It is a peculiar episode, as dramatic as in a theatre. All that is happening had been scripted in Hathigumpha inscription. This story is not imaginanary but real history replayed live in the form of a supernatural event. The grandeur of this episode is associated with this ancient hill. The sun rises here with such a scenery that we befittingly name the hill as Udayagiri. The moon brings back the memory. No science can indeed follow its spiritual significance. And no longer can explain this ceaseless theatrical performance in the moonbeams night after night. In the midst of midnight silence the picturesque golden past retrieves itself unbelievably. It is accepted by the village elders here as folktale that continues from generation to generation for anyone who had been a lucky witness of the events."

Abhirama supported the remark of Aparti. He recalled Bhagi Behera who offered milk to monks of a closed cave.

This kind of folk belief is quite unacceptable to any rational test. But we take into account the highest spiritual consciousness of the Jain monks and the way they had consecrated these wild forests and hills, we cannot but belief and assure ourselves that all that actually happened.

He continued, "I am tempted to say that with the help of the *Salabhanjika* we may hunt the hidden treasure in the vicinity. People of surrounding villages have the belief that vast treasure of a victorious Emperor had been buried somewhere here."

They were eagerly waiting for the moonbeams to brighten. The sky became clear and the facade of Alakapuri Cave returned with clear vision. Three lancers came to the front of the cave where Emperor Kharavela was seated in a chair. The Emperor offered them seats beside him. They had in sheath the swords fastened to their side. They were the Chiefs of military, *Mahasenani* Beeraprasastha and *Senapati* Ranaprabara. They had with them the Chief Minister, *Mahamat* Nakiya.

They had a meticulous plan for Asikanagara raid. The route of their attack was being mapped on the surface of slate by Beeraprasastha. They envisaged a problem. In order to reach Asikanagara they had to pass through Satavahana kingdom. It would be a great hurdle in front of them. Satakarni might not permit them when they have the intention to destroy Asikanagara which was his dependant vassal. They had to move with adequate power to tide over the resistance of Satakarni.

The Emperor was very attentive. The Military Chief continued, "Chief of our elephants had with him one thousands of new war elephants, well trained, tactful and battle ready waiting for any assignment. When new squad is added up to the existing elephantry strength it makes a total of five thousand. The chief of cavalry had constituted a new unit with chosen young trained horses of brown colour. Their colour merges with the natural surroundings and the enemy can't trace our course during our travel to the destination. The infantry of our state are prepared to taste the first fight during their life time."

Kalinga military forces had been organised by the Emperor himself. This is the first ever expedition out of their homeland. Earlier it had only defence functions. The last fight by their predecessors was with infiltrators in Kalinga War. During his nine years in the throne Emperor Kharavela has rejuvenated all the wings of the military. He had applied the principles of warfare outlined by Vishnugupta. The infantry of Kalinga consisted of young dedicated and motivated warriors irrespective of caste and profession. They had adequate assurance of family care on the event of any casualty. The advance party with vibrant fighters was appeased with this offer.

Young Kharavela was not able to foresee the fate of Asikanagara attack, he said, "I consider this sort of attack as an experimental model. Now we can ascertain how our Chaturanga military performs in the battle field. If we succeed, our Kalinga might not be confined to area within the Ganges and Godavari rivers, but we would bulge out beyond that."

He alarmed the *Mahasenani*, "Beware of Satakarni forces, don't underestimate them. He is on throne for last eight years with cumulative experience of twenty years of his father Srimukha and twenty two years of his uncle." The Emperor also cautioned *Mahasenani*, Beeraprasastha, "You are aware of what the value of courage and tactics in war is. The war within one's own geographical territory is easier to avail all supplies. But war in a faraway location invites so many problems. Keep in the mind to complete the war within a short period."

The king asked if any secret agent nearby was evesdropping the secrets. There was no chance of any spy there. So, he whispered, "Follow the principle of rapid attack on Asikanagara. Better divide your forces into two wings: attack from the east and south; Satakarni will come from north and will be busy with south in front. At this juncture, your eastern wing will attack from east to break the backbone of Satakarni military. In case Satakarni himself commands the war, he will be forced to abandon the battlefield and run away."

So the Kalinga military proceeded to west.

In the meantime, the king was busy with Chief Minister Nakiya with the administrative affairs of Kalinga. There was discussion on the heavy tax that common people had been paying since Mauryan days. Tax relaxation for some years followed by rate reduction was decided to be supplimented in Kalinga.

There was an interruption due to the passage of a procession of clouds moving lazily in the western sky. There was brief darkness. As soon as moon emerged from the clouds, uproar was audible from the west.

The victorious Kalinga troops had arrived. They were marching with slogans. *Mahasenani* reached the spot with a sword and symbol. He stamped the Flag of victory before the king and admired, "Your Highness! We operated on your laid down principles and succeeded fully. Emperor Satakarni did not join the war. But unfortunately, Dronabahu, the General of Satakarni was killed in this war. This is due to his attack on us from the rear side after we had become victorious. Our southern division had to exert all its force to devastate the whole town of Asikanagara."

The Emperor congratulated them and supported their action egainst Asikanagara. He declared an award for Beeraprasastha for his bravery. He declared, "This Alakapuri will wait to witness the event of victory of Kalinga over Satakarni in near future."

The moon went behind the clouds for a moment while descending down to western sky. *Dishidharikas* also dimmed their *mashal* light.

After a while illumination was restored again.

The three companions quietly observing the events noticed the smiling face of *Salabhanjika*. She was looking joyful with a fresh branch of Sal leaves in her neatly arranged hair adorned with two strands of fragrant jasmine of Kumarigiri. She was all good manners and pleasing etiquette.

Three friends presumed that some enjoyable events might follow.

Chapter-6

Dancing Damsels

Three friends were amused by the eloquent beauty of Puspita. She was a rare flower in full bloom emitting waves of pleasure for the onlookers.

She welcomed the three guests with a warmth, "Let us proceed to the Queen's Palace. The cultural pursuits of Kalingan society are being exhibited there. Really Kalinga is in celebratory mood, let us squeeze out every drop of pleasure."

They followed Puspita but suddenly stopped at the entrance to the Queen's Palace. They were apprehensive if their entry would disturb the show being organised there. The moon had dropped farther down to the west. The cave palace of Kalinga queen had its ground and first floor balconies packed with spectators. The Royal family of Kalinga and possibly Mahameghavahana family were there on the first floor. Some ascetics were also seated on southern part of the balcony.

An chamberlain was on the platform in front of the cave and announced in a loud voice, "The current year is the year of amusement for Kalinga. It has a number of reasons. The sky above is free from any cloud. Each of the Kalingan is as free as a bird in the sky. He had years of confinement inside the cage of the Magadha empire. What was suppressed in Kalinga could explode in the form of *tauryatrika* that includes dance, drama and music: three in one and all the three at a time. Our victorious Emperor Kharavela is an expert of Gandharba Veda. He is well versed in all sixty four components of Gandharba Vidya. He has achieved excellence in all branches of knowledge just before his coronation. He has fully renovated the Kalinganagari Fort and its gate that had been awfully damaged by the last violent storm. He has built the set of stone steps in the cool water tanks, ponds and streams of the settlements. The state is beautified with many royal gardens. Thirty five lakh silver coins from the Royal Treasury have been diverted for these public works. This year is the Year of Celebration in Kalinganagari and Cultural Festival in Kumarigiri.

"Today every arrangement has been made for the daughters of Kalinga to showcase their talents in *tauryatrika*. Dance, drama and music have received Royal patronage for the last two decades to flourish with surpassing excellence. Making of musical instruments from small industries have increased manifold. The dancing girls of the dais are accompanied by musicians, *Mrudalabadika*, Flute of *Vanshibadika*; Trumpet and Harp players. Kalinga artists perform song and dance at the same instant. This is the specialty of Kalinga dancers. By synchronising simultaneous movement of many parts of their graceful body in a *tribhangi* pose, they create such fascinating charm that can mesmerise the novice and the dance lovers alike."

After the announcement is completed, the dancing Kalinga Kanya engraved in the Cave palace stepped out from her stony abode on to the cultural platform. She had with her the *Mrudalabadika*, *Veenabadika*, *Vansibadika* and the *Sankhabadika* - all the musicians of the concert party. The flute player had a special Kalinga flute with a lion head and added a mellifluous voice to the conerrt. The undulating notes of enchanting music wafted seductively trough the

forest, kissing and hugging its flora and fauna in swelling and swirling waves of ecstasy. The dancing girl's gestures and postures spurted the elegant founts of happiness and sorrow. The audience was spell bound. Even the moon became overwhelmed with the orchestra of the show. The coolness of the gentle moonbeams had added greatfulness to the show. The two stars accompanying the moon were dazzling in the overhead sky. At the climax of the concert the spectators were fully absorbed with the feeling as if an Apsara from heaven was performing the dance.

The dancing Kalinga Kanya was quite pleasing and alluring. She had excellent costume. Her special silk sari, her coiffure, necklace, waist girdle and armlets emitting refined quality of gracefulness and good taste. Her face was the mirror of her mind. She had the capability to swing from melancholy to ecstacy and from anxiety to bliss. Strands of hair danced in the wind with synchronous movement of her head.

Suddenly the music stopped. Slowly the dancing girl receded backward to assume her sculptural form.

Next episode was a tragedy, starting with the cry of Kumudabati. She was wife of a successful Kalinga sailor in maritime trade. The merchant had sailed to the Far East and was expected to be back in a year. He did not return and was untraceable for four years. She was lamenting in a pathetic tone. Language of the lady was not clear to the three invitees but they presumed it was one of the saddest songs ever sung. The wave of the music imparted such melancholy that tears welled up in their eyes.

The emotionally moved spectators who responded with tearful eyes. They could not tolerate the cruel separation of Kumudabati from her husband. By now the unfeeling heart of her husband in disguise had melted down to appear before his wife with tears in his eyes. He had returned to his place in time but doubted the fidelity of his wife which withheld him from uniting with family. He had misunderstood his wife, quite common with the sailor husbands. He had spent years in disguise of a lunatic. This song of tragedy could drive away all his suspicion and he vluntarily came forward to be united.

The union of the separated couple had transformed the music to an emotional concert of joy claiming heavy tears from the spectators.

Emperor Kharavela, the Gandharba Veda Buddha, the artist of all sixty four components was in the balcony with his family as a spectator and a cursory glance at the expression on his face would ascertain that he was conductor of the orchestra be it the dancing Kalinga Kanya or the crying Kumudabati.

A short intermission followed. The *Salabhanjika* Puspita hinted at the invitees, "Kumarigiri had witnessed such emotional scenes. This must be rejuvenating the drowsy hill. The soul of all these performances was Kharavela. He was trained with the sixty three thousand hymns of Gandharba Veda. He had applied many of the emotional components to appease the spectators through the *tauryatrika*: dance drama and music.

It was felt by spectators there that dance and drama were under feminine domain. But after the cultural functions by female folk, an army of men assembled on the dais. A patriotic song was presented in masculine voice. It transmitted a sort of cosmic energy that could warm up the cool beams of the moon. All attention turned to the west. All the warriors started chasing the enemy in the west. One of the actors in the role of Kharavela shouted at the enemy not to escape. This was his challenge to any secret force outside Kalinga to come forward and confront him.

After the end of this cultural function, the place looked deserted and earthly. A stray procession of grey clouds covered the moon. The *Dishidharikas* had already left the place. Only Puspita was there and she led them to Hathigumpha cave.

Chapter-7

The Hathigumpha Comedy

Salabhanjika Puspita asked the three guests, "Let us proceed to Hathigumpha to see the caricature of forest animals."

They had to wait for the show. In the meantime, Puspita informed, "In the fourth year of his reign, King Kharavela wanted to make Kalinganagari, his capital city free from danger. He arranged for maximum security as he had planned to command a long military expedition to the neighbourhood. The works minister and his deputy were in charge of new constructions. They had beautified the town."

The proposer of the comedy was the Chief Minister, Nakiya. One day when the Emperor was in a humorous mood, he proposed a dramatic work full of humour and laughter. This sort of episode would give immense pleasure to the spectators.

The Emperor accepted his proposal. He knew, in the field of music, dance and drama, a good deal of humour was necessary for the pleasure of the spectators and it was worthy to work on their choice. As *Mahamat* had pointed out, there must be some short plays. He analysed the importance of such programme and imagined that the comedy must fit into the natural setting. Someone would play the role of an elephant sitting on top of the

Hathigumpha. Others will sit on big stones around the cave. The contents of the comedy will be the wealth of the forest and the natural reserve of Kalinga's prosperity. He was sure in his mind that one day this natural cave will be remembered as a prominent tourist spot. The state should popularise it further. The role of wild animals must be given importance by the authorities of the state. This script had been written by the Emperor himself, the stage would be managed by the *Padamulika*.

Puspita had informed that the stage was ready. The *Padamulika* was managing the show. The Emperor had positioned himself on the top of Hathigumpha to play the role of elephant. The big piece of stone to the right of the cave was occupied by the city justice, the *Nagara Akhandansh*. Next to him in the row was Chief Minister Nakiya himself. The Works Minister and few others had taken their respective positions.

The master of the comedy, Emperor Kharavela opened the show. He was sitting calmly like an elephant. He asked the frog, the smallest animal, to start his speech.

The frog said, "Why should I be called small and weak in the animal kingdom? Nature had vested immense power in me. No rain will come until I croak loudly. No rain means famine and a natural calamity. But I am unlucky. People do not appreciate my important role in nature. They ridicule me. They kick me as soon as they see me. The snake always chases me as its prey. If the snake swallows up all of us and makes Kalinga frog-less this kingdom will be reduced to a big desert. I want public support against the atrocities of snakes. I want to live as a healthy participant in the country of all animals immersed in the rhythm of nature."

The Works minister, *Kama* had the role of a snake. He followed the speech of the frog, "Why should I be condemned as limb-less. Everybody is afraid of me because I can finish anybody at anytime. I am worthy to be present in this gathering. It is the nature of man to be fearful for which he creates idols of God. I always take my position in Parsvanath's hair.

"I am no religious symbol, Parsvanath doesn't need me for self protection; he is too divine to need such a thing. I am there in his head only to be highlighted as the Agent of Death; at least that's what the people want me to be. Hence my business is to be utterly secretive, treacherous by default. I hit without intimation and so I must be careful, circumspect. In this comedy, therefore I am here to teach you the qualities of alertness, carefulness everywhere in all your actions of life, in administrative affairs too. Otherwise Vish-kayas (poisonous women) will have you and snuff your lives out much before your time."

The king in his elephant role thanked the snake for his meaningful and justifiable speech. Then he turned his face towards the tiger. The role is being played by Justice of the city. In his judicial power he had to take a decision on what is right and what is wrong, who is innocent and who is not. He had been assigned the costume of a tiger. A tiger has little scope to be humane and no nerve to be judicious.

As tiger on stage the actor roared, "I am the mighty son of God. I pose myself as the most powerful animal in the forest. I had been denied presence in these twin hills on religious grounds, my presence today is only by invitation from his Highness King Kharavela. Since time immemorial, the twin hills were accepted as rains retreats of Yapannapak monks, Jain mendicants, tigers were salivating at their sight. But one mendicant, well versed with our animal language explained the main principle of Jainism, *Ahimsa*. So many of our predecessors were killed as they adhered to this principle. On the verge of being extinct, another mendicant instructed us to be cooperative to this hilltop life only but not to give up the natural instinct in dense forests. The rule of non-violence is in vogue over these two sacred hills since then."

The audience expressed joy over the statement of Bhuti as tiger. These two hills were sacred land and tiger or any other wild animal did no harm as people believed. So judicious was the Justice of Toshali that his statement was appreciated by one and all.

Now Kharavela in his elephant role, looked to his extreme right, he pointed out to *Mahamat* Nakiya clad ina grey dress. He had isolated himself on his remote seat. Kharavela told him with a smile, "Dear Bear, Are you sick? You shiver as Jambaban on Thursdays does. But today is not a Thursday."

The actor in place of wild bear replied, "Excuse us honourable Ayur Mahameghavahana Kharavela, I have allowed space in front of me for the frog and snake. They are small but now can see from the front easily. I am next

to brother tiger in the list of wild animals in the forest. We have intimate relationship with men on the one hand and with the Kumarigiri hill on the other. As a token of respect to this pair of sacred hills, we have adopted *Ahimsa* and adjusted ourselves to non-violence."

The emperor as elephant was shouting, "Animals are afraid of me due to my gigantic shape but I am not wild and do not intend to kill anyone until I am hurt. I am contented if the forest turns to be leafy and lush green. But my journey from Kalinganagari to Kumarigiri is one *yojana* with the Emperor on my back and then I relax looking to the south sky in this cave. We find our way back on completion of my master's visit."

With the elephant role, Kharavela climbed down from top of the cave to its interior and continued, "Our Kalinga is very fortunate. We have here a valuable resource of black powerful elephants. Once this natural resource is utilised appropriately, we will be the master on earth. God has shown us the way. Pointing to the cave he said, with the natural cave like this, let us be powerful and utilise the natural force of the elephants for political and boundary expansion."

The comedy show was nearing its end.

The *Salabhanjika* explained to the guests, "In order to make this eternal comedy, the Emperor had ordered to the chief architect to utilize the piece of stone occupied by Bhuti as tiger in preparing a wide gaping mouth of a tiger. Snake, Frog and Bear should be carved out in respective stone pieces. After the construction is over, these are to be dedicated to Kalinga as tourist spot.

Emperor Kharavela had informed the audience in his learned analysis, "Look to south-eastern direction from here. The inscription of killer Magadharaj Ashok is visible from here. The butcher, who killed thousands and thousands of Kalingans, is addressing himself as their father. I reserve the broad frontal area of this cave for inscription with facts of Kalinga which will be obtained from all mystics, philosophers, astrologers and erudite scholars of the whole country. Some memorable artisan masons of repute will be employed to carve it as a poem. These will stand unchanged to the ravages of time. Language may change, cultural behaviour of people may change, but people can decipher it to understand the way we lived in Kalinga and the philosophy we adopted. The Hathigumpha will remain as an eternal emblem for the posterity."

The speech of Kalingadhipati was meaningful. After the speech, there was the strong echo of what he recited loudly. As if the mountains were incessantly repeating, "Kalinga, Kalinga and Kalinga".

Overwhelmed with joy the Morning Star looked upon the stage to end the show. In the faded darkness three friends ambled back to their resting place.

Chapter- 8

The Second Expedition

Kumar Purnima is the full moon night in the lunar month of *Aswina,* usually falls in October. This day is observed by girls as a festive occasion and they spend the initial hours of moonlit night in amusement of song and group dance.

The three friends managed to reach the foothills of Kumarigiri without being noticed by village folks. The *Salabhanjika* and her companion *Dishidharika* were there to receive them. The hosts were looking nervous and anxious. They were not meticulous about their make-up and took no care of their dress. Even the fresh Ashoka twig was not properly set in their hairdo. Women are soft hearted and are emotionally moved by war scenes. It could be easily anticipated that some war event might be the story of the moment.

Suddenly Puspita started her speech, "We will see a war within a moment. This is not the scene of Kumarigiri but it is the glimpses of Pratisthan victory of Kalingadhipati Kharavela. Kharavela preferred to be the Commander-in-Chief of Kalinga Army and led the forces from the front. It was the fourth year of his reign and he was young and aggressive. It was his first war against Satavahana kingdom."

Both the hills and the surroundings were lighted with

blue rays. It was noticed that Kalingadhipati was present in front of Alakapuri Cave. The drifting clouds were at times cutting off the moon light. During the semi-darkness, Kharavela was seen having clandestine discussions with the Kalinga spies who had returned from their targeted kingdoms. That was a matter concerning the Satavahana king.

Paithan was situated near Nasik of Maharashtra. The route to this capital town of Satavahan kingdom from Kalinga was to reach Ujjayini in west, then to proceed to south. Linear military distance of Paithan from Kalinganagari was around 125 yojanas, maybe 1600 kilometers. When counted from war point of view, it is much less from Atavika, an ally of Kalinga.

The Satavahana king, Satakarni was seriously ailing. He was confined to bed. Treatment even for a long period had proved futile. Paithan had given up the hope of his survival. Her two sons being infants, queen Nayanika was regent, somehow managing the day-to-day administration. Maharathi Tranakair Kalalaya, the father of Queen Nayanika and king of Rathika kingdom was the chief advisor to the queen. He was allured by the territory of Kalinga. He dreamt of conquering Kalinga so that Ratnakar, the sea to the west of Paithan could be one with the Kalinga Sea in the east. It would be the Great Satavahan Empire of his dream!

Kharavela listened to the details calmly. He said that the illness of Satavahana king was known to him from others. Had it not been a fact, the fall of Asikanagara would not have been executed by them so easily two years ago. It is a misfortune of that kingdom. He had hardly completed 8 years of his reign when he fell ill.

The Kalinga spies whispered, "The expectation of

Tranakair is too much. He had also motivated the Bhojaka king, an ally of Satavahana to join his Kalinga expedition.

Kharavela sat down calmly, recollected his memory of Paithan. He had a dream in his youth to tour all sacred Jain places of the country and worship all the 24 *Tirthankaras*. Paithan harbored 20th Tirthankara, sand image of Munisubrat. This sacred place was visited by Lord Sri Rama in *Tretaya Yuga*. Each tourist experienced some miracle there. A miracle had happened to him just three years before his coronation.

A three year old child had unknowingly left his home and entered the Jain temple. He was crying and trembling in fear. Prince Kharavela was unable to assess his condition. He could presume that the child must be of an affluent family and was separated from his parents. He comforted the child and accompanied him to his place. He could know that the child was Vedasri, the son of Satakarni. The royal couple thanked him unaware of his identity. He was just a tourist for them.

Kharavela was very enthusiastic and was attracted by Satavahana kingdom. The Satavahanas proudly proclaimed themselves as descendants of Sun God, representing the seven spectrums of sunshine. Their kingdom was situated to the west of Avanti, consisted of area adjoining origin of Godavari river and Asika. It was established by Srimukha who was beheaded by his younger brother Kanha and Kanha ruled the kingdom for twenty years. In course of time, Satakarni, son of Srimukha was crowned as the third generation of the dynasty.

Satavahana dynasty had some link with Magadha after Sunga dynasty came into power. Pusyamitra Sunga was a Maurya army official who had assassinated Bruhadrath, the last of Maurya kings. Satavahanas were anxious to annex Magadha in north and Kalinga in east. This fact was known to Kharavela. In the consultation with Mahabhojaka of Bhojaka and Maharathi of Rathika vassal states, Satakarni proclaimed himself as the 'The Lord of the South'.

When Kharavela got the death message of Satakarni, he had profound sympathy for the widow queen and two orphan princes. He did not want to disgrace himself by attacking such a powerful kingdom in its distressed state. He knew queen Nayanika earlier and had profound compassion for the bereaved family. But hardly one year after the death of Satakarni what sort of decision was taken by Maharathi on behalf of the Satavahanas? That he would occupy Kalinga within one year. Chetaraj had left administration over ten years ago and his descendant Kharavela might not be able to withstand the joint power of Satavahana, Rathika and Bhojaka. He decided first to attack the neighbouring Vidyadhar States, the allies of Kalinga.

King Kharavela had keen interest in geography and the cultural heritage of the whole of India. He was sure the eighteen Vidyadhar states to the west of coastal Kalinga belonged to Kalinga itself. This had been the reality since the beginning of civilisation and much before the formation of Mahajanapada in India. Kalinga had mighty military forces who had fought bravely in Mahabharata and Kalinga Wars. The Nishad Sena of Kalinga or the Archers of Atavika had originated from these tribal tracts. Atavika was one of the Vidyadhar kingdoms very famous for archery. It was said, even a layman of Atavika was a Ekalabya of Mahabharata. The Kusumbi warriors of Mushika Vidyadhar state had immense combat experience. There were eighty-one towns in eighteen Vidyadhar states. Strictly speaking, Vidyadhar states were not vassals of Kalinga but in all practical matters were part of Kalinga. Vidyadhar states had also commercial line up with Kalinga. They provided shiploads of cottage industry products for maritime trade. They were producers of good quality cloth, wood products and were acquainted with iron smith's products for domestic use which were qualitatively very high. They had a good collection of precious metals and diamonds.

Kharavela was worried for these small Vidyadhar kingdoms. He was afraid that the Satavahanas might attack them. He ordered the head of intelligence to be vigilant to the state of affairs of Paithan. He was concerned at this juncture for the decline and eventual creation of a power vacuum in north India. Magadha, the mighty and powerful state of central India was crumbling down. This had allowed the entry of *Yavanas* from the west. Magadha was expected to regain its military power as a defence centre of India. He was in the process of perceiving the solidarity of India. Kharavel had two competent spies from his Yubaraj days, Nishithyaka and Nirantaka. He had sent the former to Atavika. Atapavishma, the ruler would prepare ten thousand of capable archers by the end of next rainy season. He must start production of war equipment like strong bows with metal edged arrows and strong strings.

Kalingadhipati passed orders for Nirantak, "You proceed to Kusumbi Vidyadhar tract, meet Kshyatikusumbha, the chief and pass on information of defending Kalinga and Vidyadhar tract from infiltrators. He must be ready with a contingent of ten thousand muscled swordsmen and five thousand well equipped agile tiger warriors. Never disclose our intention and preparation for attack and simply tell that we will pass through his way."

The ever alert Kharavela was constantly getting information from Uttarapath and Dakshinapatha kingdoms and about the movement of *Yavanas* from the west. He was sure that the belligerent Kalinga Chaturanga would explode one day and would unexpectedly shock not only the neighborhood but the whole of Bharatavarsa.

The two spies returned completing their assignments. Nisithyaka had returned from Taksasila and Nirantaka traversed the Dakshinapatha. They had noticed the sudden decline of power. There were constant invasions by western Persian and Bactrian plunderers and tyrants. They not only plundered the wealth but also dishonoured women. This was a matter of shame for the country. India must rise and fight back. The wrinkles on his forehead indicated his concern for the country. He couldn't remain at peace with a vulnerable western border.

He spoke in a soft voice, "Did you work as I explained in Vidyadhar states."

Kalingadhipati then called upon Beeraprasastha and collected information of the Chaturanga soldiers returning from Asikanagara. He commanded, "It is time to be ready with the other half of Kalingan soldiers who are waiting for orders for a western invasion. As a matter of principle, recruit more and more muscle-men into our army and make elephant tamers battle-ready for invasion of the west."

A momentary interruption!

Suddenly the lamps of the *Dishidharikas* lost their brightness and the three invitees looked up to the sky and noticed the faint cloud blurring the moon light. They surmised that this sort of interruption must be preplanned as part of centenary celebration. Nature plays a great role in this divine display.

Moments later the clouds dispersed. Alakapuri Cave

was neatly visible. with large number of elephants, horses, chariots and the infantry forces waiting for orders from the Emperor. This invading troops were headed by Emperor himself on a horseback. He was escorted by three elephants and five horse driven swift running chariots. Two of the chariots were loaded with flags of different colors as signals of the king's commands. The soldiers with their dress and war equipments created a dreadful environment. Mother Earth blessed them for success in the war.

The scene of war was visible all around. The loud sound of war trumpet was there with overwhelming loudness. The four-winged Chaturanga troops were proceeding to the west. The body language manifested their jubilant and aggressive temperament.

Within a fortnight, the troops added ten thousand archers from Atavika and ten thousand muscle-men from Kusumbi and left Kalinga to reach the border of Satavahana kingdom. They reached a junction near Nasik hills. Paithan was the capital of Satavahana kingdom in front. Rathika was to the south and the Bhojaka to the north. The three kingdoms were subjected to the pressure of a gallant troop with large number of elephants.

Queen Nayanika as regent of Satavahana kingdom was silent. Her father Maharathi Tranakair jumped down to the war as a capable defender. The queen could not grasp the gravity of the situation and the role of her father.

Maharathi could assess the size of the troop of Kalinga now stationed at the Vindhya Range of hills. There was another row standing at the base of the hill range. The size of the troop was too large. He was panic-stricken. He could foresee the aftermath of the attack. The life of his daughter and grand children of Satavahan royal family was in peril.

Within a short spell, both Rathika and Bhojaka felt

frustrated and helpless. Maharathi had no alternative but to retreat. He left the battle field and was untraceable. Kalinga troop in right command was chasing the retreating Maharathi and the left wing was inside Bhojaka kingdom.

Emperor Kharavela asked his military chief, "Satavahana kingdom is right in front of us. We are here for the last one month. Where is their defence against our attack? Why we will not accept it as surrender?"

So the winning Commander-in-Chief of the war, Emperor Kharavela entered Satavahana kingdom with an energetic troop of elephantry. The chief of Kalinga army had informed him that queen of Paithan was totally silent. She had no plan or arrangement for defence. Our intelligence gave useful information that Maharathi had appeased her daughter, the queen of Paithan that joint forces of Satavahana, Rathika and Bhojak would defeat Kalinga and she will be queen of the entire kingdom. But after his retreat, he had taken shelter in the Satavahana palace with Bhojak king.

"A clear surrender of Satavahana in this war!" exclaimed Kalingadhipati.

The massive elephant force of Kalinga accompanying Kharavel found no resistance from Satavahan forces. They could get around the enemy palace with effortless ease.

It was quite strange that Queen Sunayana along with king of Rathika, Maharathi Tranakair and king of Bhojaka was waiting at the main gate of the palace to welcome Emperor Kharavela.

Kharavela was about to proceed to accept the hospitality of Paithan. But he had to halt for a while until the Kalinga military escorted him and the military chief himself served as his personal aide.

Rathika king Maharathi was first to surrender by

placing down his crown. He reached with folded hands and begged apology for his ignorance and arrogance. He had to pour full contents of Rathika exchequer at the disposal of the the victor. He requested him for a guidance to the administration of Rathika kingdom.

Bhojaka King followed him. He relinquished himself, set aside his royal umbrella and surrendered the entire property and manpower of Bhojaka kingdom to Kalingadhipati.

The queen of Paithan, Sunayana surrendered herself as the ruler of Satavahana kingdom to Kharavela and was waiting for the orders from the victor.

Kharavel was not at all cheerful at his victory. He was so overwhelmed by the turn of events that he said that the three kingdoms were not mere vassals of Kalinga. Rather, they were states coordinate with, not subordinate to, Kalinga for purposes of administration. However, he left the Satavahana to decide the relationship themselves.

Kalingadhipati expressed his condolence over the sad demise of Satakarni.He showed his secular learnings subsuming Jain concepts and philosophy and Brahmanism of the Satavahanas. He addressed that a king must follow the rule of law in , ensure natural justice rather than let the parochial social practices like casteism, racism etc.

The queen promptly settled the administrative affairs under the supervision of Kalingan authorities and placed at the hands of victorious Kalinga Army chief the entire proceeds of three exchequers with some special horses and chariots from Satavahana stocks.

Now Kharavel could notice the two young sons of Satakarni there. The Emperor's face became gloomy on seeing the orphan princes. He visualized the risky life of a royal member, especifically that of a prince. The king enjoys the privileges in all normal times but had greatest risks at the time of war. He has the ever-present peril of the sword of Damocles hanging over his head. A war had so many uncertainties: win or defeat may come at any time. When the result of a war is uncertain, a king must be human. He must treat the vanquished side in the befitting manner that humanity deserves.

Kalinga's victorious men returned home.

Salabhanjika Puspita was explaining the arrival of victorious Chaturanga at foothills of Kumarigiri. The emperor of Kalinga was meeting the Mendicants to inform them and to have their blessings.

Moments after this ceremony, trespassing clouds covered the moon for a while yielding a hazy picture of the hills. The torch bearing *Dishidharikas* were also absent in the main side of Kumarigiri. In the darkness, Puspita asked, "Please wait for some time. We are going to have the Mathura expedition of Kalinga Chaturanga troops."

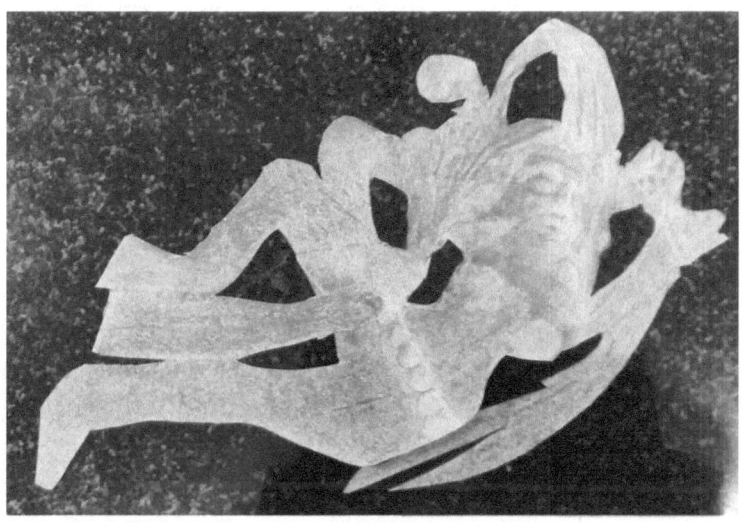

Chapter- 9

Dwarapalika

Puspita said, "I have to elaborate on this Jaya Vijaya cave. By now you are acquainted with this holy cave which is my birth place. It is the oldest man made cave of the hill. By planning his expeditions from this cave the Emperor has been victorious in every military action. He believes in the supernatural power of this cave. After completing expeditions he would employ outstanding sculptors to create rock-cut art having such quality that compels the tourist's attention. He had a strong desire to get two maidens engraved who would captivate all spectators with their charming spell and help them to receive pleasure from the wealth of rock architecture. They would be unparalleled in beauty and ideals of Kalingan folks: the *Dwarapalika* or Suka-Swagatika and the *Salabhanjika* or Pallabi Puspita.

The monumental carving of *Dwarapalika* was later guided by queen Dhruti when expert sculptors were entrusted with the job. She had requested Emperor Kharavela to install the sculpture of a *Dwarapalika* in Jaya-Vijaya cave, the entry point of Kumarigiri hill. The left pillar of the cave would have a *Dwarapala*, a stout male with a long spear as weapon in his hand, but the right pillar of the gate must be a representative of Kalinga maiden, the *Dwarapalika*.

A royal employee suggested Queen Dhruti who had

the desire of carving out a female guard, "With esteemed orders from your Highness, she would have a parrot on her right palm raised to the height of her shoulder with a welcoming face for the guests. She would be carved with such grade of elegance, hairstyle and choice of ornaments that would epitomise the beauty of the Kalinga woman."

"Right, dear Kusuma you are thinking one step ahead of me. It had been my dream to glorify Kumarigiri hill with feminine characteristics. Three years ago, when our son was born, the Emperor had consulted all the royal priests, astrologers and sacred *Yapannapak* Jain monks for naming the little prince based on numerology and birth star. After consulting sixty four components of *Gandharva Vidya*, the name Kandarpashree was finalised. I was most delighted with this name and was greatly satisfied. I was convinced that women are born with creative qualities of the Almighty. So my sole request to victorious Emperor was to beautify Kumarigiri by women statues with feminine grace."

The royal employee who gave some suggestions to the queen was Kusuma. The queen was overwhelmed with joy. Kusuma was closest to the Emperor among all royal employees. He received education from Sarabhanga institution situated on the bank of Godavari. He was the favourite of the Emperor from the day of his employment. Kharavela, the lover of natural beauty had his whims and fancies of beautifying the native land. The name of Kusuma meaning flower was quite attractive for the new recruit as the *Padamulika*. But how this delicate name had performed such wonderful administrative jobs right from the time of his appointment was a marvel to watch. Kusuma had the capability of satisfying one and all. He had his choicest and ambitious targets. Here stood the pinnacle of glory in selecting a model of Kalinga maiden at the entry point of reception. Her pleasant look, attire, gait and posture would be angelic in grace and elegant for attraction.

The sculptor who carved the image of *Dwarapalika* were briefed by Kusuma in minute details. When a parrot was set in her right palm, Kusuma addressed the image as *Suka Swagatika*. This *Dwarapalika* was an emblem of Kalinga woman in frontpart of a universal place housing innumerable saints, noblemen and scholars from all over Bharatavarsa.

The *Salabhanjika* concluded, "I am bit emotional on the sculptural components of the hill. I have narrated about me earlier and about *Swagatika* just now. I must inform you that the entire treasure which Kalingadhipati obtained from Paithan victory was processed here in Alakapuri cave and handed over to *Bhandagarika*, the treasurer of Kalinga.

"Now new events will be appearing here. You are welcome to see another interesting narrative."

The three invitees were keenly observing from a height. They were conscious of their shadows in the clear moon light but their shadows were confined to their feet area only. Of course they had gathered some experience by this time, their shadows should not interrupt the events of the occasion. Their presence must not affect the show in any way. The moon and clouds play providential role in regulating the show.

Their attention was diverted to some people coming from the north at medium speed. There was the arrival of two lancers in black robes on black horses. They were tall with robust physique and sharp features. They revealed their identity to the *Dwarapala* and produced their emblem as mark of identity of Kalinga intelligence and then were allowed inside. The authority behind the gate was waiting for them anxiously pacing up and down in the chamber with two lamp bearers illuminating the background.

After some time it was clear that they were secret agents on espionage arriving with vital information. Groups of them were on vigilance duty in powerful provinces of the country. They had gathered useful information of military and diplomatic nature. Despite so many principles of espionage laid down by Kautilya a separate equilibrium was prevalent among neighbouring states. The lancers revealed that they were in Mathura and had some emergency message for the Emperor.

Within moments, the Emperor arrived on horseback. He immediately asked them in. The intelligence agents appeared before His Highness with folded hands and one of them said, "Your Excellency, we rushed here to inform you that foreign invaders have reached our Bharatavarsa on horseback. They are tall, bulky *Yavanas* from western Persia, Bactria, Macedonia and Greece. They have unleashed terror. They plunder the kings and commoners alike and return with the loot. Some of them have started ruling small kingdoms.

The Emperor asked them, "Have you heard if the *Yavanas* had any elephant wing?"

Both the secret agents informed simultaneously, "No,

they only come in groups on horseback. They are dangerously armed with daggers, swords and arms of odd shapes. They aim at robbing treasure, precious metals and stones. Some of them abduct women. Mathura and its periphery are the worst victims of their raids. The queen of Mathura is the daughter of Magadha king, Bruhaspati Mitra. Magadha does not intend to rescue Mathura at all. It has lost its hegemony, it is no more the Magadha of Mauryas."

Kharavela was shocked and he muttered, "Sad that the power of India is at its worst decline. That is why *Yavanas* dare to come and raid. The king of Magadha does not have the courage to save his daughter and her royal family in Mathura. This is the fate of Sunga dynasty who assassinated Maurya ruler for power. Now this is the opportunity for us to trap the Yavans and the Sunga king in one go.

A whistle sound was heard from the background. It always heralded some important arrival.

Moments later, *Mahasenani*, the Commander in Chief arrived.

He informed thus, "My Lord, we have fifty thousand war elephants, twenty thousand cavalries and one lakh infantry at hand. Equal number can be ready within a short period. If we start towards Magadha in North, I don't anticipate any intrusion from west or from south during our absence here. The Satavahana are our vassals, but the Pandyas can't be trusted. All our neighbours are our perpetual enemies. We have all the evidence of invasion when we set out on an expedition. But now our internal security is strong enough to crush any intrusion during our absence."

The Emperor ordered, "Enhance our elephantry to double the strength. Move our quadruplet Chaturanga troops instantly to north. Our target is to conquer one kingdom that had been cause of our agony in the past. It had invaded Kalinga twice unleashing death and destruction. They confiscated our state deity as a mark of superior power. This is a perpetual challenge of Magadha to Kalinga for a war. Our target will be Mathura *en route* Magadha"

Moments later...

The troops of Kalinga had reached the gateway of Magadha, the Gorathagiri. It had been constructed by the Mauryas as a security measure against southern attacks. This gate was smashed by the Chaturanga troops of Kalinga. The security men of the post receded to the capital Pataliputra and signalled attack.

At the juncture Kalingan messenger from the west arrived with the most important message: the *Yavana* king was planning to attach Pataliputra from the west exactly when Kharavela would be invading it from the south. His strategy was to plunder Magadha treasury in the consequent mess. Demetrius, the *Yavana* king of Mathura had a plan most cunningly crafted. He thought Kharavela was an enemy of Magadha, so he would never resist if he, a Greek General, also attacked the kingdom. After all, both had their eyes on Magadha and it wealth. But unfortunately for Demetrius, Kharavela was made of a different stuff. He was a patriot at heart, and didn't subscribe to the principle of 'enemy's enemy' is a friend'. He decided to vanquish and chase the outsider out of the land.

He thought, "It would be ethical to fight and eliminate an invader first." He diverted his elephantry to the west to go after the *Yavana* chief.

The *Yavana* king could not believe how Emperor Kharavela rated him as an enemy number one. He did never expect to be attacked by the mighty elephantry of Kalinga.

The *Yavana* king was withdrawing his forces towards Mathura. He would save himself once he reached there. But he was caught by Kalingan forces on the border before his entry into Mathura. He was produced before Emperor Kharavela and was asked to explain why he attacked Magadha simultaneously when Kalinga was attacking from south?

The *Yavana* paused for a while and was alarmed by the massive power Kalinga was moving with. He replied, "I had been disappointed earlier as I couldn't lay our hands on the treasury of Magadha. But I expected to loot the whole treasury as Kalinga attacked it, so that I could fish out of trouble waters."

The second question was asked by the *Senapati* of Kalinga troops, "What punishment do you expect from the Emperor of Kalinga?"

There was expression of disappointment and disgust on the *Yavana* king. He requested, "Kindly allow me to go back to my place in Mathura. I solemnly pledge I will not attack any kingdom in future."

The commander ordered him in a crude voice, "You have no right to move to Mathura. Your surrender justifies you to leave this country right now. Disobedience of the order will result in capital punishment to you and your troops.."

This resulted in panicky dispersal of the *Yavana* troops from Bactria. But some of them were so much attached to the golden soil of India that they continued to live as Indian natives in disguise.

Before Kalingadhipati decided his return to Kalinga, he received an invitation from Mathura. He was received with great warmth and splendour. He was given a royal honour when welcomed to occupy the throne of Mathura he had recaptured from the Bactrian infiltrator. The King of Mathura in exile had come back. He expressed his gratitude to Emperor Kharavela for the indomitable courage and patriotism he had in his noble heart.

Emperor Kharavela was also felicitated as the 'Saviour of Mathura'. He visited the dilapidated Jain institution. It was one of the most prominent centres of the country years back, but suffered the worst during the *Yavana* rule. He asked for royal grant of the institution. He saluted the *arhats* and the *Yapannapak* saints. The Jain ascetics of Mathura blessed him. What can the Jain saints offer to this great benevolent Emperor! They offered the Kalpa plant (wish fulfillment tree) which will be the harbinger of health, wealth and happiness for people of Kalinga. Kharavela looked at the tree. He was aware that this tree of wonder was associated with Agrajina Risabhanatha and should be planted in every household of Kalinga.

During long the absence of Kharavela, the administration of Kalinga was carried on by Chief Minister Nakiya. The message of victory over Mathura had been communicated by the *lehaharaka*, the letter carrier. Nakiya arranged a grand receptions at Kalinga border in north and also at Kumarigiri, the sacred place of the Emperor. He would not enter Kalinganagari without expressing his gratitude to Jain mendicants at Kumarigiri.

On his return, the Emperor met the Jain saints and sought their blessings. He narrated the success of his expedition to Magadha. He could detect a sense of hopelessness among the Jain saints. He could know why they couldn't enjoy the victory over the *Yavana* so much. He could guess the reason. He asked forgiveness from them as it was expected that he must bring back Agrajina forcibly taken away by Nanda King three hundred years ago. He narrated the sequence of events that diverted his expedition from Magadha to Mathura. He had smashed Gorathagiri, the gateway of Magadha but was diverted to the *Yavana* who was about to attack Magadha from Mathura side. He had to apologize to Siddhasampada, the chief among the Jains of Kalinga for the inadvertent omission.

Kharavela narrated them to their pleasure the liberation of the age old Jain institutions of Mathura from the clutches of *Yavanas*. The *Yavana* king, Demetrius had tremendous impact on social and religious life of people there. Mathura was a place of all religions. The Jain monks and *Yapannapak* saints had blessed him for rescuing their pilgrimage. He had returned with Kalpa tree as benediction of Jaina monks of Mathura and as the seed of prosperity of motherland. He promised that he would get back Agrajina very shortly on his next expedition to north.

Siddhasampada was moved by these events. He apologized for hurting the sentiments of His Highness and congratulated the Emperor for the great humanitarian pursuits undertaken by him. He suggested for a grand reception on behalf of Kalinga administration to celebrate the victory of the Emperor at Kalinganagari metropolis.

A grand reception was awaiting the victorious Emperor at Kalinganagari. There was victory parade of the Chaturanga troops. The Emperor had the chance to offer glimpses of victory to his subjects. He argued in his statement that the victory belonged to entire Kalinga and so were the gains of the expedition which must reach everyone through suitable system. The priests would be deployed for such distribution. They are to distribute the wealth and Kalpa tree among the populace. This spectacle was thoroughly enjoyed by residents of the capital city. The city of Kalinganagari was then full of multistoried buildings and people were enjoying the celebration from their balconies ecstatically.

The Emperor declared the construction of a Victory Terminal or *Vijaya Prasada* near capital fort. The amount of money allocated for the purpose was thirty eight lakh of silver currency. The project was entrusted to *Kama*, the works minister.

At this juncture, *Salabhanjika* Puspita had asked the *Dwarapalika*, Suka Swagatika to narrate the events that followed in Kalinga after Kharavela's return from Magadha.

Swagatika was the greatest fan of the Emperor and his family. She added information about the Emperor's experience during the days that followed his Mathura expedition. He was a different man always thinking of diplomatic relationship among the states and the social and cultural elements that can enrich the living of life in a lucid way. His hobby was music, dance and drama. So he sat down in devising a new way of living before the return of his troops from Magadha.

The Emperor was very much concerned with the infiltration and infringement of religious life on Indian soil by the immoral *Yavanas*. The small kingdoms as fragments of the nation were victims of these foreigners who often invited them to settle scores. This was a matter of great concern.

Padamulika came close to the Emperor and whispered something in his ears. It could be assumed that some Southern *Tamil Mela* had vindictive attitude against Kalinga's old port town Pithunda. Numerous spies and pirates flooded the old capital. The *Pandyaraj* of Tamil State was intolerant to Kalinga's north Indian expedition and conquest. He was revengeful to Kalinga sailors and maritime traders.

The Emperor admitted, "Really we have overlooked our southern territory. A prompt disposal is the need of the hour."

There was a sudden silence and the hills returned to a state of shady darkness. The moon was about to disappear in the west and the Morning Star emerged from grey clouds which were turning crimson red in the eastern horizon. The three friends then felt that it was time to return. On their way they were discussing on how these past events were preordained and would not alter at all. It was the the grace of the *Salabhanjika* that they could re-live their glorious past.

Chapter - 10

Sindhula: the Princess of Intelligence

The three companions were very much amused with the midnight events, as if they were sailing in boundless ocean and the dome of the sky displayed those episodes. Every month the crescent moon kept expanding till fully illuminated on full moon night, so was their desire to see the centenary celebrations on the hill. Gradually they got addicted to their irresistible wish to see the show on midnight hills. They were amazed in the manner the retrieval of events was taking place. It was definitely incredible and celestial. These were neither dream nor real and the story of golden *Yakkha* heard from their villagers can't be laughed away as imaginary.

Sometimes each one of them was optimistic that the turn of the events may lead to gain of some unanticipated old treasure of the golden period. But the rolling out of the events was happening in such a charming manner no amount of wealth would match in terms of gratification.

One day Abhirama argued, "No one in the village can believe that Gopal Biswal of the hillside street had grown rich overnight by his own earnings. He had neither business nor the Government job to justify his wealth. His tall building and huge grocery shop did appear from a strange source which may have link with the rolling *Yakkha* story."

Aparti was nodding his head and spoke in support of

Abhirama, "Truly Abhirama these events shake our past belief. The visuals we have been seeing at night are just impossible to happen. Similarly the massive gain of wealth in a short period speaks of some supernatural source."

They were thinking themselves lucky. Aparti wished the Kalpa tree were implanted here on this hill by Emperor Kharavela. Only the lucky ones get to see the past come alive. He was also expectant for something material to come in near future.

Pranabandhu consoled himself, "Really, whatever we see appears to be true. We will never leak it out to anybody. In case we leak out these facts, people will think we have become insane. I am sure that the deity of Kharavela time must have blessed him for a retrieval of the occurrences in a temporal cycle. *Salabhanjika* too intimated it by a hint in our first meeting with her."

Aparti joyfully expressed, "Really we three are quite fortunate that we are allowed entry into those pages of history when the benevolent Emperor ruled Kalinga. After every episode, the pleasure of the past inspires us for a fortnight followed by a period of anxiety and apprehension until the arrival of the next full moon. The fear of cloud obliterating the full moon always haunts us like a nightmare. Of course the moon waxes to full size it boosts our confidence for next show like the high tides of the Kalinga Sea."

Exactly like the earlier episodes, there was sudden illumination of the hill. *Salabhanjika* reached there with two *Dishidharikas* of Ganesh Cave. Some *Swagatikas*, *Dwarapalaka* and *Dwarapalikas* in their smart but official attire were alert and watchful in their movement as security personnel.

Salabhanjika had adorned herself very beautifully. She

had a nice hairdo ornamented with a gold butterfly. There were two cute pendulous *kundals* swaying from her shapely ear lobes, matching with her necklace. She was no less than the Goddess of Beauty at whose arrival he Sal and Ashoka plants blossom out in respendence. She was a perennial source of prosperity for the country and harbinger of spirituality to this piece of humanity. Her drooping eyes indicated that she was conscious of her beauty and elegance. This model of excellence was designed for her to be at the entrance of Jaya Vijaya Cave. But now she looks sleek and agile, moves quickly to manage the show of the centenary celebrations.

The joyful mood of Puspita had emotional impact on the three youngmen. She was gifted with a charming look and languid charm of an *Alasakanya*. They were shy enough to air their soulful thoughts teasing their minds. They had always been just friends and would be a part of the eventless life, insignificant cogs in their insignificant lives. But even since they met *Salabhanjika* in real flesh and blood giving them company in those moon-blanched nights, there has been a sea change, a metamorphosis. To what end they didn't know, but, perhaps they would, some day they would.

Pranabandhu mustered up courage and asked, "Gracious lady, we assume today is something special in your life. We three congratulate you."

She was moved and a wave of smile overwhelmed her face. She gently replied, "There are reasons for my showing high-spirited merriment. It relates to some events of heart and soul of Emperor Kharavela that I am often reminded of. When he reached the climax of his achievement, he had intended to bring most of the good culture and manners from all over the country. The Tree deities and the beauty of plants studded with flowers and fruits graced his inner mind and satisfied his soul. He brought these components to his motherland.

"Sanchi and Barhut stone sculptures of Magadha had captivated his artistic mind. He was extremely engrossed with pendulous *Salabhanjika* at Sanchi. He was inquisitive. He came to know that this sculptural girl represented unimaginable beauty, chastity as she was never married. Image of *Salabhanjikas* in a religious medium magnifies the gravity. They stand at the walls of caves and temples. The souls of visitors get purified with glimpses of her at the entrance. With their very touch, trees bloom and bear fruits. They are the favourite of nature. They stimulate the feelings of mutual affection and consecrate the mind to a secure cosmic energy.

"Number of plans and proposals were occupying the Emperor's mind. He had almost spent his entire tenure in war. He had an extraordinary target to recover the statue of Agrajina from Magadha. That would restore the lost dignity of the province and the spiritual will of Jain monks and would make every Kalingan feel himself proud to be Kalingan. He would feel himself free from the vicious cycle of war and would live a normal life with rhythm of nature. A man can survive for one generation but information inscribed on the rock can continue for eternity. Kumarigiri and Kumaragiri of Kalinga had retained enough low height sandstone reserve to give form to his ideas. Anything of Kalingan society, culture and achievements can be carved out. Future might not favour Kalinga, Kalinga might lose its power and be a slave to an external power but a time will come when the rock inscriptions will be deciphered to confirm its identity of the golden period. They will continue to throw light on the victories and achievements of Emperor Kharavela and will make him immortal in history.

"Kharavel was quite enthusiastic to initiate the carving of a *Salabhanjika* at the Jaya Vijaya Cave. It would stand as the harbinger of success and prosperity of Kalinga. Of course, in course of time so many rock sculptures in shape of *Salabhanjika, Dwarapalika, Dishidharika, Gandharba, and Apsara* were carved out. But I got my life and vision on this day. The memory of the event creates ripples of joy in my heart. I was born this day. Although I am sculpted on a piece of rock, life courses through my stone form and I become a human throbbing with passion, thoughts and sensations. How did I get it all? Well, I hear it was from a virgin model of exquisite charm a citizen of the then Kalinga, who had a few sittings before the sculptor. Her warmth perhaps never left the artist's chisel strokes, and see, then I am today as his memento to posterity! Agrajina gifted me the human temperament and my birthday merriment stands as an open tale of Kalingan glory. Follow me. We will see the events right on Queen's Palace theatre platform."

It was the scene of a beautiful gracious lady talking to Emperor Kharavela. He was quite anxious and his royal attire was not in order. It was not clearly discernible from a distance but it implied that he was consoling the woman. The lady was speaking in a low voice and blushed her eyes downcast. Her gesture and posture did not match with Dhruti, the queen of Kalinga.

Who would be the lady? She was so shy that any onlooker could know the ocean of deep love in her. Her lips tremulous with self-consciousness. Sweat appeared on her forehead showing fear and apprehension.

Finally it was known that she was the princess of South Kalinga, the daughter of the ruling king from

Simhapatha. But why did the princess come down from her palace in such an odd hour to meet an outsider halting there for a day?

At the moment, Pandya was preparing for war against Kalinga. Emperor Kharavela had traversed huge distance to halt at the old palace of Kalinga in Pitrunda metropolis. Beeraprasastha, the *Mahasenani* was there with *Senapati* Ranaprabara. Kalinga had been crowned with victories against Asikanagara, Paithan and Mathura. Bharatavarsa was no more a consolidated Maurya kingdom under Chandragupta or Ashoka; it had disintegrated into small pieces again as it was like Mahajanapadas centuries ago.

Kalinga continued the *status quo* since Mahabharata War. Almost thirty two generations of kings had come and gone in Kalinga with Kalinganagari as capital of the empire but southern Kalinga, much smaller in size, had managed its kingdom with capital at Simhapatha. Simhapatha King was the monarch of the sea. All the marine routes ran to Simhapatha coasts. Virtually it was an ally of Kalinga, but its king was independent. Mutual relationship had continued as two parallel kingdoms. Sagar Singh, the king of Simhapatha was proud of his royal ancestors who took part in Great War. They had enjoyed pristine glory of the state equally.

Compassionate princess Sindhula happened to be the only daughter of Sagar Singh. She was proud of her soil, could not tolerate listening anything evil against Kalinga. She was shocked at some message she received from *Pratiharas* of the kingdom that the Pandya king was preparing for a war against main Kalinga. He had no courage to face the four winged Chaturanga troops of his opponent but opted for the cowardly attacks when Kharavela would lead his army beyond his territory.

Pandya was a small but powerful kingdom. Due to its strategic location it led the southern states of Jambudwipa. The conglomeration Tamil Confederacy had solid record of unity for thirteen hundred years consisted of Pandya, Chola, Cheru, Keralaputra and the Tamraparni island. Powerful Chandragupta Maurya could not acquire the southern part Jambudvipa and was confined to his Deccan quarters at Ujjayini. Third Maurya, the Great Ashok dared not wage a war against them but allied with them and acknowledged their might.

Pandyas were root cause of creating disturbance at its Kalinga border. Pandya's infiltrators created havoc in the social life of the Pitrunda metropolis. The administrative headquarters had shifted to further north to Simhapatha located near Puri. Pandya had been attempting to spoil the maritime trade of Kalinga. Every suspicion was pointing fingers at Pandya for its role of piracy in Kalinga Sea. Its failing trade in the golden islands of Far East, the *Suvarna Dvipa* was the reason for its anti-Kalinga propaganda. In fact, Pandya had its successful maritime drive in the western sea, the Persian Gulf or the *Ratnakar* extending to Arab, Africa, Greece and Rome but had a negative role in the eastern gulf. Pandya rovers had an intricate role in plundering away the home-bound vessels of Kalinga. The Kalinga Sadhav Association had appealed to Emperor Kharavela. The Emperor was convinced on the bases of intelligence reports.

Around the same time, the Princess of South Kalinga was in confidential conversation with the Emperor. Two of her confidantes, torch in hand, were in close range but out of hearing limits.

Kharavela, standing before this pretty young woman in the lurid glow of the torches, felt something sinister was brewing up in that black night. He could hear her saying, "Your Majesty, you want the friendly support of Simhapatha, and nothing else from my old father........."

He said nothing.

She went on, "The Nanda king invaded Kalinga, massacred the whole warrior clan of the king and took the Kalinga Jina. Well, they were *Shudra* by caste and had enmity with both royal and martial classes.

This time his eyebrows wrinkled. "Why is the woman telling all this?" he thought.

"When the north was basking in Aryan glory," the pride in her voice was palpable, "Kalinga was autonomous, powerful, culturally developed and quite peaceful as it had natural boundaries defending it. Kalinga didn't need to shift capital as the Pandyas. Kalinga, however, stood rock-like at one place, its capital Kalinganagari."

Swiftly changing the subject, she continued, "Ashoka massacred the Kalinga Army. Kalinga then was in three parts: the North part *Gangaridae* and Kalinga proper. Unfortunately these two segments were under control of Mauryas. The third segment *Macco Kalingae* had as its head, my father's ancestors. Kalinga had Vidyadhar kingdoms as its ally and Ashoka, the Magadha Emperor was terribly disturbed thinking of Vidyadhar archers."

Kharavela listened intently but at the back of his mind lurked a growing suspicion for the way the woman went on pouring praises on him.

"My father could never accept the way the third part was separated from Kalinga in respect of administration and political ties. He was so sad that he simply gave up his engagements with the affairs of the segment."

A little pause.

And she added: "Great Emperor, my father's sister

now is the queen consort of Tamraparni. My uncle and aunt both are disgusted with the Pandyas because of his highhandedness and brazen bravado, their intention to invade Kalinga and the way they are boasting of easily defeating Kalinga. When a great power as the great Chandragupta Maurya they did not care, Kalinga is too small to be of any importance, they bragged."

Kharavela's suspicion was gaining strength with every passing moment. Presently her face clouded in sorrow and she seemed to be cautious. She was blurting out, "forgive me, O king of kings, for I didn't want to let out these secrets and I was asked not to ...."

At this, he saw before his mind's eye the evil women haunting kings and emperors in the history of Anga and Magadha on diplomatic missions and they used to roam and trap men in power for their own kings. He felt more uncomfortable in her company in the darkness of night. He knew there were no *Vish Kanyas* (poison women) in Kalinga but still....." He could think no more.

Suddenly he recalled the Kalinga intelligence agent in Magadha, Nishithyaka, "We look every Magadha fairy with suspicion, we have to fear in our mind 'Still poison may be kept in the most beautiful vessels'.

He mused, "The maiden present had disclosed her identity and had erudite knowledge of state administration. She had reposed fidelity and integrity in me. The echoes of her speech are reverberating in my mind. She was simple, courteous and deserving of esteem and respect. The idea of suspecting her may be suicidal for Kalinga.

He realised that the Simhapatha princess had come in an odd hour in the interest of Kalinga. He could understand the depth of diplomatic affairs she was trading in. She proved this isolated part as a genuine part of Kalinga.

The information gathered by him from his astute spies moments back was known to the Simhapatha Princess much earlier. She revealed in her the deep love for Kalinga. She was all out to serve this kingdom. She rightly deserves our gratitude.

Courteously the Emperor responded, "Thank you princess, you are well acquainted with state affairs. I congratulate you for your love for Kalinga. We will always be grateful to well wishers like you."

The Princess replied, "Great Arya, I seek your permission for approval of one of my proposals. I feel embarrassed to interfere in other's affairs but then...."

Kharavela cut in, "You are favouring us by speaking from our point of view. Please say fearlessly what you have to say without hesitation. I welcome you."

Now princess revealed the secret. She proposed Tamraparni would attack Pandya from south when Pandya would be attacking Kalinga in Kalinga Sea. "How do you accept this secret proposal?", she asked.

Kharavela was amazed and speechless at the proposal put forth by the princess. He replied, "Princess, your capability is superb; in no way it is less than that of the ruler of a kingdom. A wise and scholarly woman like you, if continues to be involved in administration and foreign affairs, any country would prosper."

The princess was not in a state to be too gratified at this but was thoughtful to put forth another issue. The Emperor could grasp the situation and was attentive to her.

Pithunda city was busy with ship-load of passengers arriving at the port. It was headquarters of Kalinga one day. In course of time, it lost that glory but its port and commercial annexe continued to carry on its activity. Nights were turning to be lonelier than before. Only the few dim lights of the light house were there to guide the arriving vessels. Few port employees would be waiting for untimely arrivals from the *Suvarna Dvipa*, the golden islands. This was the story of yester years. Now Pithunda had been tremendously dominated by the southern states. Group of Pandya people had been involved in port business. They have a commercial centre adjacent to the old palace.

The Emperor had received a petition from Pithunda that there was growing Dravida dominance and antisocial activities by the new community. Finally the Emperor had to demolish the encroachers and plough the recovered land. He had to arrange donkeys to plough as in the auspicious land of Lord Risabhanatha bullocks were not yoked here to plough.

This coercive action of the Emperor did not evacuate the Pandya settlers from Pithunda, rather their antisocial attitude and espionage were enhanced.

The close discussion between Emperor and the princess was not free from risk. The enemy has eavesdroppers everywhere under the cover of darkness. The night makes a spy invisible. It is easier for them to overhear even without coming in disguise. Feeling such a contingency, the Princess did not want to make any delay. Moving closer to the Emperor she said, "Emperor, please send you convoy in sea route to Tamraparni. The king of Tamraparni is waiting for it. Your affirmation through the convoy will indicate them to move their naval war ship."

The Emperor was mute by the indomitable courage exhibited by the Princess. He had to appreciate her plans of diplomatic manouvres. In the process Princess Sindhula proved her education, ideology and administrative capabilities.

Kharavela questioned, "King of Tamraparni belongs

to the Dravida Mela, not to Kalinga. How do you believe that he will go against his own group relying on our spies?"

The princess explained, "The king of Tamraparni is the nephew of my father, being the son of my father's sister. He is our blood relation. He considers himself as kith and kin of Kalinga. Since the ancient days, Kalinga had been the sacred place of Tamraparni. There had been strong matrimonial alliances between the two royal families. Tamraparni vessels have been sailing to Ratnagiri *Sanghayana* on religious assignments since long. I have gathered from my father, Anuradhapura would definitely come forward in favour of Kalinga. I have come out at this juncture to intimate this message with two of my female security guards."

The Emperor looked at the princess gratefully. He was drawn in as much to the personality of the princess as to her brilliant tacts of management. She was as confident as a Commander in war, as decisive and alert as Captain of a sailing ship. Her foresight was well coordinated and accurate. Above all, she was elegant, refined and comely in appearance displaying an addictive charm.

The Emperor had never before tasted any such exaltation as he felt with the charms of the South Kalingan Princess. She was loving and intimate but the issue of military assistance was a pretention. So many thoughts were crisscrossing his mind like a tangled bunch cotton threads. The appetite of his soul was not satisfied and was asking for more and more of the Princess's presence.

The princess took leave and departed reluctantly though.

A few months passeed, the Emperor had not forgotten the evening with the Princess in Pitrunda metropolis. He could not keep off the memory of Princess Sindhula who had arrived with the courage of a lioness. She had created such an image of confidence in herself that it was unforgettable for the Emperor. Very few would have a ready wit. Very few will ask to strike the iron when it is hot. Nobody would have so much of tenderness, so much of intimacy and so much of fellow feeling. An appropriate and befitting award is what she deserves most.

Now the theatre platform of Queen's cave resumed illumination.

The Emperor could not be noticed. He had moved to southward as far as Pitrunda metropolis on hunting excursion. Pitrunda is an international port and the centre of all commercial activity. Every visitor buys a pearl necklace to prove his love for his loving wife. This proverbial pearl was imported from Vietnam and further exported to Babylon and Rome. The Macedonians had named the city as Parthalis. The city and its metro was no attraction for the Emperor who dreamt of the soft speaking Princess of Simhapatha, the cooling breeze for his soul.

King Sagara Singh had withered with his age but his royal instincts were intact. He concentrated more on the commercial aspect of the metropolis than on state administration. The visit of Emperor Kharavela had strengthened the confidence of people of Pithunda and its surrounding region. Kharavela stood as a symbol of saviour of humanity. He had subdued the intruding miscreants of south.

Sindhula might not have been his first love but she was the love that gave him added energy, new strength and freshness in life. On some pretext or other he kept coming to Simhapatha where the sweet speaking princess stayed. He is euphoric and felt contented recollecting the loving words of the Princess. Her whispering words would hum around him. She had acquired the administrative art from her father; she has the habit of getting elegantly dressed and coming with the musical sound of her anklet bells to whisper in his ears those words of infinite sweetness. Last time she had a valid reason to meet him in secret but what would be the plea for Sindhula this time.

He had reached the capital city, Simhapatha as a royal guest. Subjects of this place felt themselves proud for the presence of His Highness. The capital of south coastal Kalinga was in a joyous mood. Princess Sindhula was in charge of the hospitality of this Royal Guest. She had made all arrangements in the royal guest house inside the palace. The Royal guards were in charge of the security of the Emperor of Kalinga. Naval intelligence had been instructed to be alert.

The princess Sindhula, with her companions was perturbed when she got the information in the second quarter of the night that the royal guest was spending a sleepless night. She was restless. She rushed to the Emperor and asked, "Your majesty, excuse me. I got information that you are unable to sleep. I came here to find some ways, how the Emperor of Kalinga be comfortable to sleep. I am obedient to my father's instructions of taking care of you. Kindly show me the way."

The princess could not know why she was so worried for the Emperor. So also was the condition of the Emperor. In spite of his successful married life with queen Dhruti who was the soulmate ass the while suffusing him with her love, he was drawn to the Princess and her charm seemed to be irresistible.

Lay people had to manage their affairs with one wife. But kings and Emperors had been all along with many wives due to political and emotional reasons.The Emperor was perturbed on this thought. Queen Dhruti was there who had wholeheartedly poured all her love on him. How can he create another stream of conjugal love? It is just impossible, he thought.

Situations force the kings and emperors to marry many a time. Royal families extend their relationship with matrimonial relations irrespective of age or the number of wives. It was a formality of a defeated king to offer his daughter to the winner in marriage. There had been bright examples. The best cited instance was Chandragupta Maurya and Helen, the daughter of Seleukos.

Maharaja Sagara Singh and Princess Sindhula were rendering the hospitality to him very sincerely. Have them some self intent behind? The manner Princess Sindhula cared for the Kalinga Emperor was unparalleled and might be her heart's desire writ large for him to read and reciprocate.

Unmindful Emperor returned to his senses. He formally requested the Princess to sit for a while and asked why she, too, was spending a sleepless night?

Sindhula kept looking at the ground and avoided looking into the eyes of the Emperor. After a moment of thought, she replied, "We are highly elated as the mightiest Emperor on earth is here as our guest. If he is having a sleepless night who has the heart to tolerate this?"

The Emperor replied after a pause, "When the princess of his dreams is present right in front of him, why should someone cherish her in dreams?"

Sindhula blushed with her face expressing a sense of gratitude for the love that the Emperor had for her. She could not her eyes with his occasionally had brief glances of love. She was about to utter something but preferred silence to speak it all.

But the young Emperor had a sense of satisfaction. Sindhula could notice the joy of success on his face. After a moment, Sindhula put forth a proposal. Next morning His Highness would go for cruise in the sea if the Emperor has no objection to it. He would sail in the special royal ship, Sindhuja for an hour or two.

The Emperor accepted the invitation with joy that was reflected in his face. He reiterated that he would be happy if the princess accompanied him.

Sindhula expressed with a joy overflowing her face, "It is customary for the vessel to board Sindhula anytime for a sail and there is no instance if ever it had sailed without Sindhula."

She said "good night" to the Emperor and bade farewell for the rest of the night carrying the pain of momentary separation in her heartbeats.

Just before sunrise, the vessel left the shore of Simhapatha. That was a sunrise drive on Mahodadhi for an hour or so. It was a luxury royal vessel with a few apartments furnished as the sea castle of Simhapatha. The sailor's chamber was entirely segregated.

The morning sunshine, while welcoming two loving hearts in the sea got reflected from the face of the princess to paint the eastern sky with purple red. A new emotion arose in the throbbing hearts that sailed to see the sunrise together.

The princess came to her senses and broke the silence.

She asked curiously, "How do you feel at the sunrise, Emperor?"

"Superb! I had the rare chance of a voyage like this. This voyage immensely pleasurable in the presence of God's bounty, the sun with its red rays and the fairy Princess here who fills the heart with tides of joy. She is the Princess of the Mahodadhi, the Kalinga Sea. I am first to behold such a marine palace of Simhapatha. What makes it so special?"

Sindhula got amused at this query of the Emperor. She replied, "Sea and the ship are the assets of Kalinga. You will be astonished to know about this royal vessel Sindhuja. Its name almost matches with that of mine. Sindhuja and Sindhula. This vessel is my birth place. I was born on this sea and in this berth. This is the story of my mother. She dreamt of giving birth to her new born in sea only as a blessing of the god of the sea. In order to fulfil the cherished desire of his expectant queen my father brought her for a long maritime drive in the sea. Good luck, I was born. All the sailors renamed this ship as Sindhuja and my name as Sindhula. This lucky vessel had been adorned with all precious decorations."

The Emperor was enchanted. He would have the fragrance of fresh wild jasmine, the favourite essence of Kalinga. A reverence would rise in his mind to value the ship as the cradle of woman power. So many tall waves were inundating his mind with woman power and the Princess as the representative. Really she was great! The proud daughter of Simhapatha king and a daughter of mother Kalinga. She had accomplished excellence in all branches of education. Sagara Singha had appointed instructors of most available branches of education including administration, maritime trade, archery and swordsmanship to educate her. She was looked upon as a son, being the only royal offspring.

She had a great social circle in the cosmopolitan city of Pitrunda metropolis and was not confined to any single religion. She was inclined to Jainism, Buddhism, Brahmanism and many other religions that voyagers and seafarers belonged to. She was acquainted with that portion of religion which cared man as man and was based on humanitarian principles, neither parochial nor orthodox.

Being aware that the Emperor's family followed traditional Jainism, she queried, "Do you have full faith in Jainism?"

"I rightly respect the religion of my family. I have respect for all religions. I worship all idols with devotion, may it belong to any religion."

Suddenly a moderate marine whirlwind passed by the sea and the vessel swung as a pendulum. Sindhula was looking at the king during the conversation, lost her balance and landed in the lap of the Emperor. She could not move back to her original position. She got some relief by the soothing touch of the Emperor on her forehead. She thanked the Arya for the relief and sat down close to his left. Both the hearts throbbed like a single heart. The sea too echoed their serenity.

Sindhula rearranged her sari and disordered hair and was gazing at the waves. Her heart was throbbing like a turbulent sea wanting to disappear in the sky. She felt as if the sea was asking her, "Are you thinking to depart from me? I am your mother, I have taken pain for your birth here. I will feel myself blessed if you become the queen of Kalinga and unify this great empire."

It took some time for her to be free from her contemplation. She felt her father's dream was going to come true. She was happy as much as she was melancholic since she had to leave her birth place for ever after marriage.

The episodes of the Kalinga Sea disappeared from the courtyards of Queen's cave as if to bring an intermission to the flow of events. They were waiting for an instruction from *Salabhanjika*. She whispered, "You are at the right place. Some romantic events are going to happen now. No character is going out of the theatre platform and the stone palace. The sculptural figures will be on the stage after returning to life to perform the hunter scene of Emperor carved on the wall."

The episode of royal hunting expedition came to sight. The hunter was seen in a dense forest getting down from the horse clothed in finery and ornamental accessories. The hunter had his crown. The royal hunter shot one arrow at a deer which fell dead beneath a branching tree.

Coinciding with the hunting expedition, the scandalous abductor of a courageous woman had escaped to avoid the tough encounter. The abducted woman was left behind and was quite helpless under the tree where the prey of the royal hunter had fallen down. The kind hearted royal hunter gestured the assurance of safety.

A capacious Kalinganagari hosts the next episode. There was a hilarious event of matrimony. The Emperor of Kalinga was enjoying dance and music of a *tauryatrika* dance-drama-musical concert party in his royal chamber. The queen Dhruti was there in the chamber with her attendants. There were four ladies dancing in the middle of the chamber to the music concerts of different instruments. The woman, who was rescued from the forest was in the middle and this celebration was in honour of the new comer. Queen Dhruti was heartily enjoying the party.

All the spectators were eager to trace who was the lady treated with the party. To add to their curiosity, Gandharvas were flying all around like butterflies imparting a matrimonial ambience to the celebration. Emperor Kharavela was looking joyful. He was not sure if he had ever planned to rescue the woman in the hunting expedition. But the hand of Providence had dragged him to the jungle after two auspicious dreams he had the night before. One dream tempted him to annex one kingdom without any bloodshed. Second, he would prevent a great royal disaster by the hunting expedition.

In fact, the woman rescued from the forest was princess Sindhula of Simhapatha. She was abducted from her palace by the conspiracy of the Dravida Mela through one vassal military chief. To her good luck she was rescued by this hunting expedition of the Emperor. This shameful and embarrassing event prevented the entry of Pandya king to Kalinga.

This was followed by the episode of Emperor Kharavela and Queen Sindhula walking to the centre of the stage in civilian dress. It was their twelfth marriage anniversary and by this time Emperor Kharavela had already relinquished his throne and the construction of Queen's Palace had been completed. A team of very talented sculptors has carved out the real story of their marriage into rock-cut art.

While congratulating the team Queen Sindhula said, "Kalinga stone artisans, you are great. You have carved a vivid sketch of our life not only in words in Hathigumpha, but sculptured it on the stone wall of the hill with same details as I had faced in the dense jungle. I declare with applause that you have engraved the pictures on the stone wall that will stand the test of time for millennia to come."

A joyful Emperor said, "The stone carving on walls of Queen's Palace is a brilliant achievement of our native artisans. They had been assigned to immortalise the fact of history through stone carving. They had done it so beautifully. The dress they had adorned me with in the hunting expedition, the carving of the royal horse and accompanying royal employees distinguish me at once. The abduction story of princess Sindhula is no more the folktale of South Kalinga, but had been magnificently displayed. All that emerges from this artistic masterpiece is Queen's inherent courage and refined quality of gracefulness.

On this occasion, I felicitate the artisans of Kalinga for their sculptural excellence and insightful creativity. After relinquishing the throne, my aspiration to become a religious and *tauryatrika* researcher in an environment of this cultural university had been satisfactorily accomplished.

This would be a search-light for the posterity to rejoice proudly for that period of history when Kalinga had proved its complete hegemony."

Now the last episode is not yet over, the audience was stunned both with the abduction of the princess and the very idea of their Emperor having two queens which was considered immoral. Kharavela was a close friend of South Kalinga and the second marriage would have been performed with dignity and gravity. But it was conducted in a tribal manner not befitting a supreme ruler. At this juncture, Queen Dhruti appeared in her royal robes to convince that the marriage of the monarch had taken place as per the wishes of Lord of Matrimony in heaven in which the event happening by itself rather than as per any one's desire.

The show was over and stage of theatre lost its light and sound. The orchestra party was on their move. The audience was in the process of vacating the theatre. *Salabhanjika* was explaining to lamp bearer *Dishidharika*, "We will go to Jaya Vijaya cave from here and we will explain certain exigencies inherent in today's events. Our guest visitors have been puzzled at the sequence of events. The truth is not as skew as it seems but is realistic. They must be aware of the facts."

Three friends were guided to Jaya-Vijaya cave where the *Salabhanjika* explained the difficult situation of Kalinga when gracious princess Sindhula was being kidnapped to an undisclosed location. She said, "Kharavela was determined to build a formidable integrated Kalinga which was not possible in spite of winning territories after territories. The South Kalinga was a patch that was neither a vassal nor an integral part of main Kalinga and it continued for centuries as an autonomous state. Its integration by force was detrimental to maritime and internal affairs of Kalinga. There was no other way.

"The attitude of southern Indian states known as the Dravida Mela was quite vindictive and adverse to Kalinga from the days of Pithunda demolition. Southern states opposed Kalinga by sending their spies and miscreants to South Kalinga. They also stood as a hindrance to maritime trade. They planned the abduction of princess Sindhula for marriage with a king of the vassal state of Tamils and this was opposed by the Princess and her father, King Sagara Singha. Kharavel's intimacy with south Kalinga created a boiling point for the extremists of south.

"An incidence of divine nature happened; Kalingadhipati dreamt of a duty to proceed on hunting expedition. This could save the princess. Something concrete happened in Kalinga administrative machinery which was not disclosed to the public. After reaching Kalinganagari, the council of ministers was convened to take a decision on how to solve the issue of the rescuing the princess. The secrets of the abduction was discussed. But neither the chairman of the council of ministers nor the Emperor could reach the conclusion.

"But Queen Dhruti came forward to resolve the deadlock by suggesting to annex the emotional south Kalinga with mainland, thereby forming an integrated Kalinga stretching from the Ganges to Godavari. This was definitely the need of the hour for the Mahameghavahana family. Queen Dhruti welcomed the idea of the Emperor's marriage with princess Sindhula who was intelligent and elegant. Marriage of Sindhula was more of a political matrimony in the formation of invincible Kalinga kingdom.

After a brief silence, the Chief Minister of the council declared to carry out marriage ceremony with all grace and grandeur and to merge South Kalinga as the integral part of Kalinga with king Sagara Singha installed in the same position of his dignity and most importantly to disintegrate the Tamil Confederacy that has indulged in such heinous activity of kidnapping."

It was acceptable now to the three mute but interested companions to understand the compulsion, under which the Emperor was to marry again keeping the sanctity of his character intact at the same time.

Emperor's compulsion for second marriage was understood by the three.

They could finally assimilate the events deeply in their conscience. The live display from the stone pages of the caves came to an end.

The eastern horizon saw the appearance of the Morning Star. They could no more locate *Salabhanjika* and the *Dishidharika*. They had to hurry up to move to their place.

Chapter- 11

The Macedonian Soldier

It was full-moon December night of in the local month of *Margashira*. The clear blue sky was dispersing white jasmine of moon beams on earth. Three invited companions were marching with renewed vigour to the mysterious location. As usual *Salabhanjika* Puspita got down to the foothill to receive them with warmth. She was accompanied by Suka Swagatika. They began to proceed to the Queen's Palace.

Hardly had they traversed half way when they noticed many *Pratihars* and lamp bearing *Dishidharikas* rushing towards Queen's Palace. Puspita informed them, "A beautiful episode on a foreign national is going to be staged on the theatre of Queen's Palace. So many royal employees and lamp bearers are wanted there. The flow of events is about to start on the stage surrounded by spectators. Let us move fast."

The darkness of the night receded from the Queen's Palace. The two doorkeepers were focused. They were guarding at the entry of the northern gate of first floor, the eastern column is guarded by a local guard in a loin cloth but the western column is by a warrior wearing a long overcoat and boots.

The smart *Dwarapala* of western column slowly climbed down to the stage. He was tall and fair in complexion. His gait was extraordinary in the manner of rhythmic march past of a Macedonian infantry. His dress was different from that of all the sculptural characters of the hill. He had a stylish long coat reaching the knees. He had a pair of robust gum boots. He looked like hailing from a disciplined infantry battalion and got appointed as a guard at Queen's Palace.

The military door keeper reached the centre of the stage and was joined by a beautiful woman. Both of them moved closer to the cave and remained busy whispering sweet nothings.

The spectators could not imagine how this foreign soldier would be in love with an Indian woman.

While the show was on, the *Salabhanjika* whispered, "This Macedonian soldier got mixed up with the Kalinga army while the latter were going after the *Yavana* king at Magadha. He got an inferior posting as a gate keeper due to his love affairs. Follow the proceedings. You can see how this soldier was in love with an Indian woman, called *Nagarabadhu*, common bride in downtown of Mathura."

The stage got instantly converted to a bushy jungle with one soldier in brown military uniform hiding himself in a narrow space. He was surrounded by a troop of foreign infantry dressed in long overcoat, attic helmet, tall boots with rhythmical march, swords on right hand and a scabbard with sheath set in their dresses. They are combing the area, bush by bush to trace out their fugitive companion.

The solitary soldier hiding himself had escaped the search warrant. But then he was surrounded by a second team with elephants, horses and chariots. He discolored himself with back ashes. But he was caught by the new troop of vigilant warriors. He was produced before the local commander.

A Macedonian infantry soldier was standing before a mighty *Senapati* of Kalinga on its raid to the retreating *Yavana* Demetrius. Language had been the barrier of communication. He was about to be punished but all of a sudden a woman nicely dressed appeared in the scene. She addressed the *Senapati* of Kalinga, "You great Kalinga General, this *Yavana* soldier is endowed with human nature and temperament, different from the treacherous Indo-Scythian army that was to invade Magadha. He was sent from Bactria by Demetrius for barbaric rule of Mathura, but personally he disobeyed that Bactrian command and was in favour of Mathura populace."

The woman could communicate in Pali language the details of declining *Yavana* population. The *Yavana* General wanted to kill this man as he might reveal their secrets. Men of Demetrius wanted a thorough demolition of age old Hindu, Buddhist and Jain traditions of Mathura. The woman confirmed, "Andius standing before you, wanted to prevent them. Such noble efforts of this man are not known to anyone."

The *Senapati* of Kalinga was astonished when he learnt that Andius could achieve all this in a foreign land with language barrier. The woman pleading on his behalf felt embarassed for a while to reveal her identity, then she disclosed that she was Binita, the *Nagarabadhu* of North corner of Mathura. Andius was acquainted with her through a social contact. She became quite intimate with him to save the people of Mathura from the tyranny of Indo-Scythian rulers. Andius spent most of his time secretly with her. He was asked by his master to explain about his illicit affairs with her for an explanation from his master for keeping relation with her. Luckily, this Mathura expedition of Kalinga Chaturanga troops forced Demetrius to run away.

The *Senapati* of Kalinga was convinced. All of the Kalinga troops were aware of such evidence. This news had not yet reached the Emperor. No one dared reveal such silly matters to his Highness In Kalinga, a person was assessed by virtue of his moral excellence. The abnormal and unsocial relationship was not acceptable. Kharavela would never allow men to exploit women.

Finally the *Padamulika* could get the fact to the Emperor. He could convince the Emperor that the couple had decided to marry and spend their life as Jain *Srabastas* and practise non-violence.

Kharavela was interested to meet Andius and his wife. He wanted to know certain facts about *Yavana* land. He might have some unstated reservation on religion but was enthusiastic to learn about their culture and architectures. Man may belong to any but if he is living a simple and virtuous life, he deserves to be honourably acceptable. The people who do not practise non-violence and cow worship were *Yavanas*. But there would be no harm in getting information about their life style, culture and civilisation and way of life.

As Emperor Kharavela entered the theatre Andius bowed with bended knees and Binita showed her profound reverence with folded hands. She was to be there as a translator.

"What is your identity?" asked the Emperor.

"Your Highness, my Lord, I am in the Infantry Division of Demetrius. I belong to a separate land. They belong to Bactria who conduct horrible raids on India. I am a native of Macedonia, a heroic state of Athens, proud land of Alexander the Great. At the age of twenty I was recruited to Macedonian infantry from Pezhetairoi and subsequently got promoted as bodyguard of Queen Cleopatra at Alexandria, then a colony of the Macedonia. I had served her for 20 years. My life was in great danger when Queen committed suicide from snakebite at graveyards of Alexandria. I fled to Bactria in disguise and was instantaneously recruited to Demetrius's plundering army."

When Andius was taking a pause in his breathless narration, the Emperor was gazing at his face to determine his nature and inner quality. He was convinced that he was truthful, honest and trustworthy. It was on this ground that he was given important assignments.

Andius continued, "I had been running amuck to save myself with the sword of Damocles hanging on my head. Your Highness, you are my savior as your Mathura expedition released me from the shackles of Demetrius. I promise to dedicate my life for Your Majesty with my capability."

The Emperor assured to protect him and continued,

"From Pandya's maritime trade with Rome and our correspondent at Taksasila I am given to understand that Julius Caesar was assassinated in his homeland. The situation there is so chaotic that a ruler is exposed to the fury of an assassinator?"

Andius replied, "Your Highness, when the Sun of religion and morality was pouring its bright rays in the East, Egypt was in the grip of an evil star. The great empire built by Alexander the Great was about to collapse. Ptolemies obtained Egypt as their share of victory. The biggest port and capital was Alexandria. Egypt was ruled by Ptolemy dynasty of Macedonia for three centuries with no principle, no philanthropy and were only interested in the throne and power.

"Cleopatra came from the same dynasty. She ruled not only Egypt, but the entire Rome in a way for thirty years. She was not a woman, she was an Empress. An Empress wouldn't be a woman. Cleopatra had acquired the throne by immoral means. She got married to her own brother and gratified the sexual impulses of Julius Caesar. In a changing situation, she went to bed with Mark Antony. She was an Empress! But as a woman she was virtueless."

Apologetically, Andius explained to the Emperor in a low tone, "I had the misfortune of seeing Cleopatra committing suicide when she set a poisonous snake to her breast. She had the capability to possess all the kings and Emperors on earth by the charm of her beauty. She ruined the Roman Empire when Rome's declared to drag her on the streets of Rome victory celebration and when Mark Antony killed himself it forced her to end her life herself. In the midst of such deadly happenings, how I could save myself and escaped is a matter of miracle.

He was granted permission by Kalingadhipati. He had

great respect for the artistic temperament of the Emperor who had planned to instal his statue as *Dwarapala* at the northern gates Queen's Palace. His peculiar military dress with gum boot with a note of temper on his face had to be engraved by the sculptor.

The episode of Macedonian *Dwarapala* had come to end. Binita left the theatre stage and and Andius while receding to his architectural abode was congratulated by his friend at the eastern column of the northern gate for his successful presentation before the Emperor.

Chapter-12

Victory March over Bharatvarsa

The narrative presented by Andius astonished the three friends. Language and cultural differences were no barriers to foreigners. Even Andius could arrange a partner of life in a distant foreign land. Man is created with intrinsic instinct of adjusting to hostile circumstances.

Abhirama started, "When the principle of ethics dawned upon the earth, the East is the first to be imbibed with its light. It had to spread Westwards later. That may be the reason why nationals of Greece, Macedonia, Bactria and Persia were known as *Yavanas*. Whether it was Alexander or his general Seleukos, they believed in beastly principles of hegemony. They didn't bother about philanthropy. Alexander had gone for territorial expansion causing massive bloodshed. He had mercilessly killed the Zoroastrian priests. He had encountered an embarrassing question of Puru, the defeated king of west Punjab, "With plenty of food to eat and affluence for luxury why should a nation ever move to distant lands with evil intentions", to which Alexander had no answer.

Puspita and Swagatika had invited the Trio to Jaya-Vijaya cave. Puspita informed them, "Emperor had planned all his expeditions from this cave and ultimately became victorious. He was proud of Jaya-Vijaya and neighbouring Alakapuri caves. He formulated all his war strategies here in Jaya-Vijaya and was filling up Alakapuri with all his gains from victories. The plans got developed elaborately in Rainy season and were executed in Spring season.

"This cave was open only to spies and the military personnel who had uninterrupted entry to Jaya-Vijaya Cave, where many secret activities were scheduled. A number of fortes behind the twin hills were the recruitment and training centres for the military which extended up to river Prachi. There were barricade of huge stone pieces. The numbers of the war elephants and horses were beyond the estimation of anybody. The elephant and horse trainers had specific assignments for their job. On a call from the Emperor, thousands of war elephants could be ready at once."

Puspita had to cut short her narration. The illumination of the place was further brightened by *Dishidharikas*. The candle bearing maidens were adept in adjusting the wick of their lamps to enhance the intensity of light. Behind the shadows of nearby Alakapuri Cave some activity was going on.

Puspita spontaneously burst out, "Look at the ground floor of Alakapuri Cave. The light maybe feeble but you can clearly see what was going on there. The Emperor of Kalinga discussing something with two persons and two others are waiting outside for their turn. You can hear them from here. *Bhandagarika,* the treasurer, and the Accountant, *Ganaka,* are very much there. The Emperor is assessing the wealth of the royal treasury."

The *Ganaka*, the Chief Accountant had his record in palm leave document. He would meet the query of the Emperor regarding the perfect utilization of treasury. The *Ganaka* is apprising to the Emperor, "Your Highness, since your coronation, the assets of Kalinga has increased substantially. First year after ascending the throne, you have undertaken so much welfare activities like entrance gate repair of Kalinganagari, constructing the stone steps of ponds containing cool water, developing up so many gardens and fending orchards. The expenditure met from the exchequer is exactly 35 lakh coins. Our expenses for second year inclusive of expenses of war against Asikanagara and the cultural festival of Kalinganagari would be the same as our income of the State from all sources. But wealth seized from our victory over Satavahana, Rathika and Bhojaka are still accumulated in the Alakapuri Treasury, unpublished as per norms. It has met the welfare expenses of the state inclusive of irrigation projects. In addition, it has the balance equal to the revenue income of the state for the sixth year. Your Highness has generously declared the citizens of the state exempted from revenue tax. Your philanthropic attitude for your subjects has distinguished the State from other kingdoms. The whole of Kalinga is prosperous, joyful and is dancing in ecstacy."

The *Ganaka* took a pause, read out, "The gain from Mathura victory was huge and Your Majesty has distributed a sizeable part of it among your subjects through the priests and other mediators. A top secret, I have to expressly reveal that we have enhanced our royal treasury to five fold. Our benevolent Emperor has granted a sum of 38 lakh silver coins for construction of Victory Palace, which is not a big amount."

Expressing his happiness the Emperor said, "I am satisfied with performance of both of you. You have rightly applied the principles of Chanakya's *Arthasastra* to complete in future all welfare assignments in time. There is a big budget allocated for Kumarigiri. The preliminary job of training our native masons on carving is about to be

completed. They have learned to excavate caves and carving art on stone wall from the trainers of northern kingdoms. They are making their hammer, chisel, stone cutting and stone carving instruments in the local black smith's workshops. We have to restore Patalapuri and similar such caves from degeneration and give them new lease of life.

"A multistoried cave would be carved out as an ideal

secular religious emblem so that the initial rays of the Sun and the cool beams of the Moon would touch it first. The premier cave of Kumarigiri with a broad courtyard will be carved which will be a sign of the glory of Kalinga. All the stone works and architecture had been entrusted to *Kama* and *Chulakama* for timely construction."

Moments later, both *Bhandagarika* and *Ganaka* departed from Alakapuri and next in waiting *Mahasenani* Beeraprasastha and *Senapati* Ranaprabara got their entry. They were in their official robes. They reported that the the military forces were ready for an expedition. Without waiting for any command from the Emperor, they said, "Your Majesty, the troop of one lakh young agile elephants and cavalry is now battle ready. On this tenth year of your rule we are waiting for your orders for Bharatavarsa expedition."

With a smile the Emperor set aside his self-importance and said, "Is there no rest for Kalinga Chaturanga? Is it ever ready for any expedition? I support your idea of recruiting warriors of the Vidyadhar tracts as our military personnel. They have always proved to be mighty. Now there is a power vacuum in Bharatavarsa. There are no big kingdoms. All the small kingdoms are occupied by *Yavanas*. Governors and *Satraps* from west have inflicted intolerable misery into the life of people."

After a small pause the Emperor continued, "We must chase away the intruding *Yavanas* from Bharatavarsa. For that we have to travel westward to Ujjayini, then travel northwards in Dakshinapatha to reach Mathura. We shall march towards Yavan dominated *Mahajanapadas* to farther North West to Surasena and north Koshal. We may try to reach Taksasila, where the foreign invasion is in dominating state."

A piece of dark cloud veiled the moon down in western sky. *Dishidharikas* became feeble in the dim light *Salabhanjika* informed that the Emperor is on his expedition to Bharatavarsa. He will return after four months. But in our centenary celebration, the event of his return will be presented just after the dark clouds clear the sky.

The clouds receded and the hill came back to life. The chamberlain proclaimed, "Kalingadhipati had arrived now after his Bharatavarsa expedition. The military campaign with thousand young black elephants and one lakh soldiers had its march through Avanti, Mathura, Kasi, north Koshal, Kuru, Malla, Surasena, Matsya, Panchala, Vaji, Batsha and many *Mahajanapadas*. No kingdom had any courage to counter Kalinga's unconquerable Chaturanga but so many kings as fugitives had begged for help to recover their kingdoms from the *Yavanas*. The rapid action troops of Kalinga was effective in driving out the *Yavanas* to Bactria and Persia. Terrible winter interrupted his ambitions to the Taksasila University. During his return, huge swags of gains were poured on the expedition party by the restored kings."

Before the announcement ended the Morning Star in the east looked sad for being late. The events of the past ended and the hill got back its earthly shape.

On the way back, Aparti said that much of the huge wealth of the expedition must have been buried somewhere in this hill. He cited the example of his village cow boys getting some gold and silver coins from the foothills of Kumarigiri now preserved in museum as Jagamara coins. He expressed, "We too one day shall chance upon the hidden trove. I am very optimistic. One day we shall discover the hidden treasure of our victorious power."

Chapter-13

The Deccan Puzzle

Aparti, Abhirama and Pranakrushna calculated the number of full moon nights of the centenary celebration already over. The thought of its completion saddened them. Pranakrushna asked, "Do you remember the time line mentioned by *Salabhanjika*, Puspita?

"Yes, I remember; it is a spell of twelve shows. Do you remember how many more are left?" asked Aparti.

Abhirama replied, "Hardly two or three. This is not mere Kalinga Festival, but depicts the golden era of Kalinga. We noticed laborious inhabitants, brave warriors of Chaturanga troops, and prestige of motherland, prosperity in all respects and every Kalingan identified himself or herself with own profession. It is difficult to compare it with any other period of history and rule of any other emperor.

"During the last few full moon nights, the golden times that took Kalinga to the height of prosperity now were coming to end. I can't accept these twin golden hills to turn into stone again!"

Aparti consoled, "We have to confine ourselves to our fortune. *Salabhanjika* is right in her words. The function is limited to twelve full moon nights. It will have its next spell after a century. We neither can guess who all had witnessed this centenary events in the past, nor we can tell who will be fortunate to see them in future."

It was *Pousha Mash*, the English month of January. In Odisha it is said, 'Even grass does not grow in this month. The festive occasions are few. But moonlit night beautifies the village and brings bliss to the life of villagers. People are happy that they have harvested enough for the whole year.

But these three youngmen looked pensive waiting for the full moon to arrive.

On the appointed night they reached the site in time. *Salabhanjika* came down to receive them with three of her friends, all *Dishidharikas* with lamps. The place got crowded within seconds. The cause of such a sudden rush was not clear.

People in the crowd were robust but simple in nature. They had brought with them a group of dark skinned people tied with thick rope used in ships. The coast guards of Kalinga accompanied them. They arrived with huge commotion. It was not clear what really had happened.

Puspita started, "Whatever you have seen is the achievement of the Emperor in the last twelve years. Kalinga earned excellent reputation in internal and maritime trades. It might be a difficult venue for transportation on road, but it was possible to trade with hinterlands by waterways through which cargoes could pass to sea coasts and sea ports like Tamralipti, Dantapura, and Paloura. People of Kalinga had been well versed in maritime trade since time immemorial. Sea for them was as familiar as the back of their hands. Many of the sailors, too, took interest to colonise the new islands of the East.

"The Kalinga Sea was always quick moving with frequent sail of vessels carrying passengers and traders by experienced seamen. But in those days there had been frequent attacks on innocent trading vessels of Kalinga by southern states. The causes were many. But the chief cause might be the failure in their trade in *Suvarna Dvipa* and the other one could be the border disputes. Kalinga ships were subjected to piracy. There was no scope to identify the miscreants and trace them.

"Now Kalinga had been unified after Kharavela's marriage with Sindhula. The Chedi king had empowered state's naval power to enhance the coast guard activities and act of espionage over the pirates. The Dravida Mela was suspected for these nefarious designs but it was difficult to blame them without any concrete evidence of plunder. The Emperor of Kalinga had warned them time and again. He had strong suspicion that the confederacy was linked with forceful infiltration of Pitrunda metropolis and that was why it was demolished by Emperor Karavela. The Dravida Mela was involved in the failed abduction of princess Sindhula years back. The mischievous activities of the south puzzled the Emperor. Sweat appeared on the forehead of the Emperor resulting from increasing worry when he strongly suspected the Dravida Mela.

"The northern expeditions of Kharavela were conducted frequently. The Emperor was more interested in driving back the unknown batches of *Yavana* infiltrators from west than conquering the small kingdoms on the way. He took pleasure in the march of Chaturanga with veteran young elephants on *Uttarapath* stretching till Taksasila in west. But he was held back from his sincere intentions due to the conflicts raised by the south union. Only the Tamraparni Island was exception. It was aligned to Kalinga on royal matrimonial relationship and sea trade. Some secret information of south was coming out from that channel.

"The military power of the confederacy was huge, their power was immune to aggressive attack by Mauryas. Secretly the Emperor had fortified the military strength manifold to face them better."

Salabhanjika exhaled a deep breath and requested them to move to Jaya-Vijaya cave, a few pirates were being produced before the Emperor by coast guards, Spies and Security authorities of Tamralipti-Dantapura-Paloura port complexes. Let us listen to the proceedings of the case.

The Chief of Paloura port was the Secretary of Kalinga Traders' Union. He appealed, "Your Majesty, the traders and Sadhavas of Kalinga have incurred heavy losses. Despite high security alert on Kalinga Sea, piracy is continuing in full intensity.We request you to punish the confederacy to finish the atrocities in sea."

The Emperor consulted Kalinga naval chief *Manthanadakshya*, "Can you tell definitely that these people belong to the South? Generally we presume that piracy is a heinous work and occurs in the Arab Sea that too is done by foreign nationals. These people of south must not have indulged in such criminal activities. We must treat these guests in our military forts with hospitality.

But the Emperor whispered something to *Manthanadakshya*, the trading representative. It was quite acceptable to listeners there. *Manthanadakshya*, too, welcomed the decision of the king. It was an attempt of the king to extract some important information from the enemy by such exclusively friendly treatment. It was only he who could pull out the deepest secret by easier means.

After sometime, a few security personnel from Sarabhanga, the north coast of River Godavari dragged one soldier creating nuisance there. The king had a sarcastic laughter in a theatrical style and uttered, "Treat with careful hospitality in an isolated castle in the Southern commands here. We obtained two sets of people, those from waters and one from land. They have all secrets of Tamil. They must not be kept together.

They could succeed in extracting some information. A meeting consisting of all top officials of Kalinga was held, some decision emerged which was not given to public. Puspita decided to disclose the decisions to the three invitees, otherwise they won't follow the story any longer.

"The congregated troops of the south sector will be responsible for south expedition under command of the naval chief. This is for the waters of Kalinga Sea. Chaturanga has an assignment somewhere else, the expedition of remote north, the Uttarapath. That must be conducted in the right season. The southern expedition needs assembly of an alternative troop, many of them on their way back from last Bharatavarsa expedition.

The troops for Uttarapath expedition consisted of one lakh Chaturanga, i.e. five thousand elephants, four thousand horses, one thousand chariots, ten thousand *Kusumbi Khandayat*, some Kalinga Tiger forward troop with infantry. Kalingadhipati had entrusted *Mahasenani* to steadily assemble the second group for the south."

Dressed in black, a number of lancers entered directly to meet the Emperor inside Jaya-Vijaya cave. They could proceed inside without any interruption of the armed guards on security duty. The Emperor burst out in laughter after a brief discussion with the spies. Kalinga intelligence had got through the secrets of Tamil Confederacy.

Puspita again added something more to explain the discussion going inside the cave, "The series of laughter in the confidential meeting is indicative of the clue for expedition against the Tamil Confederacy. It had been rightly worked out. They could cleverly get through the secret of traversing the unapproachable Dravidian tracts. Kalinga spies had unraveled most of the hilly forts, hidden troops, strange troops those could inflict rapid massacre like that of Ravan's troops in Ramayana epic. The pirates of south who are in guest houses have already disclosed the secrets of past thirteen hundred years of Tamil Confederacy.

"In addition, the Emperor had declared to engage his personal precious horses, elephants, chariot and newly made military vessel for war against Tamil Confederacy. They would be instrumental for a win over south. Strangely, the leaders for each of the four-pronged land troops were not yet selected. The matter was left to be decided after obtaining Intelligence Report from southern wing of Kalinga. Everything would be completed shortly as the expedition will start within one month's time.

"Kalinga would arrange a sizeable marine and land troops that would attack from Tamraparni front. Tamraparni being a relative of Kalinga it would lend its support at the time of war. Now an active search was going on to locate a brave young General with aggressive character. He would be leading the troop with agile Tiger party with war elephants. The other three wings of Chaturanga will follow him.

"Despite this readiness the Kalinga intelligence did not pass on any favourable news. During long thirteen hundred years of closeness the five kingdoms continued to have unity unlike the northern kingdoms isolated and segregated by bouts of *Yavana* intrusion. There is a unitary defence troop namely, *Dravida Sena*. They were strong with elephants and infantry; the arms and armaments of the south were peculiar. No king of India had ever dared to fight against them for last thirteen hundred years. The Dravidas were shifted from north to peninsular south India. Since then south India had been unapproachable to Aryans who were the cause of their displacement. The *Dravida Sena* never accepted the principle of righteousness of war. They believed in immoral war with deployment of witchcraft, magic and treacherous attack from behind the back.

"In the Tamil Confederacy, the island Tamraparni was an exception. It was deeply related to Kalinga. Sanghamitra, daughter of Ashok had reached the isle two hundred years ago with eight families from Kalinga to settle there. Four hundred years ago, Tapasu and Vallik of Kalinga brought the holy strand of hair offered by Buddha to this island. Tamraparni was in a state of proper balance with both Kalinga and Tamil Union.

Salabhanjika continued after a pause, "The Emperor was worried with this intelligence information. He had to add this puzzles of in-land war to that which would come in the marine waters. The anticipated war was taken seriously by him.

" 'No', 'No', Tamil Mela can't go so far! Kalinga elephants have moved to west and to south so many times. They have experience of so many expeditions. Tamil Mela had no instance of aggression in the past which means that its forces were primarily for defence only. I am hopeful that we would pierce into their defence from all corners" was the strategy of the Emperor after getting information from the spies.

Now chief of the Kalinga army, *Mahasenani* Beeraprasastha appeared along with a tall robust person and introduced him as *Singhanandana* who was the Commander of South wing of Kalinga and said, "He has knowledge of military bases of the Deccan. He is well-versed in languages of south. He has a stout small sword in a scabbard on his baldric. And he has vowed to destroy Deccan hegemony."

Now the Emperor was delighted and said, "*Singhanandana*, your name meaning a cub matches perfectly with the requirement of our south expedition. Speak frankly if you need anything special for this as the Commander of the South expedition."

Singhanandana asked boldly, "Your Majesty, I need your blessings along with one hundred agile trained black robust elephants as the leading party of the expedition."

The Emperor replied, "Right, *Singhanandana*, I was thinking of the same now. We have most wild Kalinga

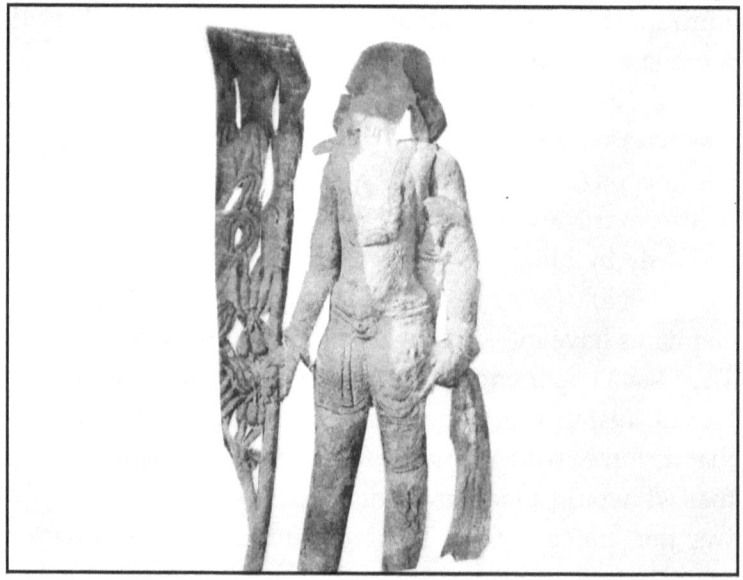

elephants trained in best possible manner by our elephant trainers with elephant goads. You select them in advance. I have something special for you in this expedition. I will give you my favourite foreign elephant, horse and chariot to use in Deccan battles. These animals from foreign lands are restless to go to war. They are intelligent enough to perceive the taste victory."

Singhanandana accepted the offer and bowed before the Emperor with gratitude. Manthanadakshya, the Naval Chief present there also expressed his happiness.

After a brief silence the Emperor said, "Listen, this is a secret, it should not reach our enemy. We have three aims, not one: defeat of Tamil Mela is our primary concern. We may win or lose, our very attack will unite them. So we should attack the individual partners in such manner, they will suspect one another for the attack and that will bring an end to thirteen hundred years of their unity. Thirdly, we have to free the Kalinga Sea from piracy. Our alliance with Tamraparni should not create any trouble for the latter."

The *Mahasenani* of Kalinga was delighted with the proposal and asked, "Excellent strategy, Your Majesty. But is it possible to break thirteen hundred years of Tamil unity?"

The Emperor replied, "Wait and watch, whether they stand united or get divided to be allies of Kalinga."

The *Mahasenani* was astonished. He dared not express his doubt which would mean his inability to act. The Emperor changed the topic and suggested Singhanandana, "You impose a three-pronged attack on Tamil Mela. Manthanadakshya would stage one vicious coastal attack on Pandya and Chola deploying all the fleets of our navy. In case some more are needed, recruit new vessels of Paloura or Tamralipti to be with them. You will get alliance of some Tamraparni bases all of a sudden from south. The Tamils will get no other way than to surrender. In case they withstand this damage their fleets and sink them into bottomless depths of the sea, You have my orders.

"Singhanandana, you enter Cheru with your agile elephant forces from western coast. Our eastern troops will tear into Chola from the east coast. I will be following the eastern group. I expect a positive result from the dynamics of our plan. Let us wait and see what time has in store for us."

The noisy departure of Chaturanga was audible from the background of the threatre platform. It was the march of Kalinga against Tamil Mela.

A floating cloud could hide the moon and the *Dishidharikas* too dimmed their lamps. A patch of darkness prevailed over the hills.

Puspita addressed, "This shade by the cloud is meant for a mystical scene. It brings about temporary intermission to indicate the war. The outcome of this long expedition will be projected shortly after this intermission. This is the mystery of Kumarigiri, granted by Adijina since the golden era of Kalinga. You will see the arrival of the victorious Kalinga party from south."

The wind dispelled the cloud to the north. The sky was clear and hill got lighted again. There was dissonant noise with victorious drums of Kalinga. The three parties from different directions were approaching the site. But the Emperor of Kalinga was seriously gazing at south west direction,. His eyes still searching some faces. His alarmed mind was eagerly expecting some important arrivals.

The *Dishidharikas* had illuminated the ground very well.

Kalinga has succeeded in the war in all three directions. The Tamil navy had surrendered. The eastern troops had glorious victory due to surrender of the Pandya which automatically confirmed victory of Kalinga over Cheru and Keralaputra. Strangely, Chola, Cheru and Keralaputra are blaming the Pandya king for their defeat. The confederacy collapsed, it repented for its enmity with Kalinga for so long.

But Kalingadhipati was sad and tearyeyed. He was searching for some one in the crowd. Nobody dared console him. He had heard from Kalinga spies Singhanandana had bravely occupied Cheru and Keralaputra from west coast but he lost his way and never returned. He was lost with the valuable elephants, horses and chariots given to him by the Emperor. The Emperor wanted him back, not the animals and the wooden chariot.

Manthanadakshya, the Naval Chief had sunk to fathomless sea along with the strongest security vessel of Kalinga. The Emperor was repenting for the loss of two brave warriors. He did not enjoy the victory at all. He was still optimistic about their safe return. They must have been stuck up somewhere and out of his intense love for them he never believed that they had died in the war.

The Pandya king had approached the Emperor to permit him to enter Kalinga. He was permitted after his surrender. He could conceive the grief of the Emperor and had consoled him with words that the land area where Singhanandana was lost, in fact was a prohibited area for human entry. Pandya had lost huge number of travellers and warriors in that trap. Again the place of the sea where the fleet was submerged was notorious for huge whirlpools that drag ships by strong current of water which trespass the alarming red floatings. Accidentally the naval chief's vessel had ventured into that danger area. Emperor should grant posthumous bravery awards and compensate the families of the two patriots and should celebrate its hard earned victory.

There was brief celebration of victory of Kalinga. At the outset, everybody present mourned the loss of two dedicated Generals and the Emperor spoke in a melancholic voice, "Kalinga is proud of our two departed Generals. Bloodshed is an outcome of war no doubt, but my Generals had disappeared in mysterious circumstances. Kalinga had learnt to win wars at the cost of blood shed. It had never depressed our march." The Emperor had dedicated all glory and achievements of Kalinga to the patriots of the kingdom.

The problem with *Tamil Mela* was solved. In history, there was no chance of Kalinga to come in contact with Pandya. This war brought an end to the enmity in land and sea and Pandya king became close to Kalinga's royal family. He volunteered to donate ship loads of precious stones for construction of new palace in Kumarigiri for academic research on all religions of India.

Pandyan, the king of Pandya liked the principles of Jainism and was a *Digambara* Jain. He intimately surveyed the *Yapannapak Jain* monks of the twin hills and was moved with the affairs of the religious background of the hill. He declared unlimited gift for the monks. He got a chance to declare his offer for Kalinga and Kumarigiri.

Here in eastern sky, the Morning Star was eager to see a bit of achievements of Kalinga. But alas! Each one of the hill disappeared at once. The celestial body considered itself as being cursed by Adijina to be deprived of the story of a golden land.

The three companions rushed back to the village.

Chapter-14

The Taksasila University

M agha Purnima came in the month of February. Puspita guided the guests to reach the Queen's Palace. The midnight environment over the hill was casting a different picture compared to the past occasions. The enchanting hour was quiet, the leaves and branches of the trees were as motionless and shadows of the tree were more prominent than the trees themselves. The desperate song of a nocturnal bird from the distance was faint but reverberating. The intermittent hooting of an owl was making the atmosphere dreadful provoking spine-chilling fear.

Puspita whispered, "This place is deadly silent and serene but the Emperor and his spies are eagerly waiting for the arrivals from distant locations. Like the lunar cycle, the emissaries of Kalinga carry information on military potential and movements of remote kingdoms; there is centripetal messenger system with *Lehaharakas* and *Dhabakas*. The mandate of Emperor of Kalinga was special for west and North West agents to present the information on the affairs of Uttarapath, Taksasila, Gandhar, Surasena, Mathura, Magadha and Anga by physical appearance. We have to patiently wait for the arrival of intelligence agents from Gandhar and Taksasila."

Breaking silence Aparti asked Puspita, "We were

moved last time the way our Emperor was upset over the loss of his two brave Generals in war with south. How could he get himself consoled during this short period?"

Salabhanjika was beautifully dressed. Her ear ornaments were long with small ball making longer excursions of pendulous movement. A garland of fresh jasmine was tied round her hairdo fragrance of which was wafting in the moonlit hours. She thought for a while and answered, "Really it was pathetic. The Emperor refused taking food for a couple of days. There were none to console him. Queen Dhruti was busy with her baby. Queen Sindhula could console the king with her soothing words. But it took a longer time for the grief-stricken Emperor to overcome the grief."

She continued after a short pause, "Pandyan, the king of Pandya was his contemporary. The Sunga king of Magadha was confined to his receding kingdom. The Satavahana kingdom was a vassal state of Kalinga. The north India lacked bigger kingdoms, few temporary unknown kings had brief period of rule being prey to the attacking *Yavanas*. Expeditions of Kalinga was sought at this juncture to drive out the foreign intruders. Pandyan had his prestige in south India but now inclined to Kalinga after the south expedition of Kalinga. He had reached Kalinga to console Kalingadhipati and to change his mind. He had assured to donate hundreds of well trained elephants, horses compensating this unfortunate loss of Kalinga in the past war.

"The Naga king from central India had come to visit Kalinga. He was neighbour of immediate western Matsya kingdom attached to Kalinga border. The relationship of the Naga king with Kalinga was matrimonial for generations. He had come on a formal visit to Kalinga to express his allegiance to the victorious power. He consoled Kalingadhipati and presented a list of valuable gifts. He solemnly acknowledged with fidelity, the spirit of Kalinga exploring the north and south and appreciated the way of driving harmful foreign forces from north India."

Just after *Salabhanjika*'s speech, all three companions on the hill were thunder-stricken when they felt somebody running under the shade of the hanging trees. Puspita consoled them, "Never get afraid of this sight. No evil soul had ever come to this divine hill. If at all some *Yakshya* or *Vidyadhar* of ancient times appear, they as celestial creatures are harbinger of joy and peace for the humanity. Like them, a number of invisible helping hands operate over the twin hills."

She continued, "Some more time elapsed to console the Emperor after the south expedition. He recollected his words when the *Mahasenani* and the General of Kalinga appeared before him. He was reminded of the next proposal of Uttarapath and Magadha expedition. It was his promise to rescue Agrajina from Magadha and to present the deity to the Jain establishment of Kalinga in one hand and to take revenge against Magadha for the past two wars and the agony it inflicted on innocent Kalinga people."

Meanwhile Abhirama queried Puspita, "The troops of Kalinga were busy with north-south and to west but what about our north-eastern border, the Banga kingdom? Was there any relationship between Kalinga and Banga?"

Puspita replied, "Banga King was a staunch Jain. Bardhaman Mahavir preached his five principles of Jainism at a location of Banga. The site bears the name Bardhaman. Banga and Kalinga take bath in same shore of the Kalinga Sea. Many royal blood relationships had been the cause of their harmony, I suppose."

During their discussion, a row of dark horses were noticed, their skirts swashed by waves. No lancer was visible. Most possibly the Kalinga spies had clandestinely entered the cave and discussing with the Emperor. Some discussion was going on inside the cave in the presence of a torch bearer. In the mean time the Emperor, the *Mahasenani* and the General came out of the cave in the bright illumination of the torch bearer.

Puspita explained, "*Mahasenani* was waiting for final orders of the Emperor for expedition of Uttarapath on the basis of intelligence approval of the current situation prevailing in the north."

They noticed the Emperor observing one map drawn on a stony surface, the route of Kalinga expedition to the North and its safe route for the return.

Mahasenani started, "Your Majesty, we have coordinated two distinct expeditions to one. We have ascertained your expedition to far northwest you had kept pending as snowfall was a hindrance last time. Next plan was expedition to Magadha on way back home carrying back the Kalinga Jina. The temple had been well constructed and waiting for the deity to be consecrated on its sanctum sanctorum. It would be cumbersome for Chaturanga forces to conduct two expeditions. As per the information I have, a weak Magadha with its king and troops will submit to our power. I can't see any obstacle in traversing through Ujjayini, Mathura then turning west to Uttarapath Taksasila and even Gandhara. All small kings of Mahajanapadas are terrorized by the *Yavanas* and are ruling their kingdom different locations changing the location of their makeshift capitals. One aspect, I am sure there is no one in power in the north to pose a threat even to one fourth of our power."

The Emperor expressed his appreciation. He queried, "In order to save time, you must have sent half of your troops to Mathura. Is not it?"

"We have made those arrangements as per your past instructions. It will not delay any more once our troops touch Mathura. Winter must be giving way to Spring for our convenience. No more to have cold wave of the north. My lord, your visit to the much cherished Taksasila would not be a problem," was the reply of General Ranaprabara.

The Emperor was delighted. Taksasila was his dream, the largest academic institution on earth. It was the teaching field of his teachers, Gyanalokananda and others. He had heard about and remembered the mode of teaching at Taksasila University and training at Kashi. He would never forget his teacher's teaching of political economy from Arthasastra of Chanakya, the Professor of this famous university and the Prime Minister of Chandragupta Maurya.

The events that passed in the mind of the Emperor like a mountain stream was politely interrupted by *Mahasenani*. He solicited his permission on matters of the ensuing expedition.

He said, "On our return journey, we would not travel back from Mathura to Ujjayini, rather we would travel eastward to reach Magadha. We have chances to come across many kingdoms on way. We will reach through territories of Magadha and Anga and will reach Tamralipti on Banga border. The estimated duration of the expedition would be of five to six months."

The Emperor eagerly asked, "Do you have any apprehension of encountering powerful kings on the way?"

"We can't expect one quarter of our one lakh Chaturanga troops anywhere. So we do not foresee any hindrance on our way. There will be unrivalled march of Kalinga troops" replied General Ranaprabara.

The Emperor queried, "Who is now managing the Taksasila University? Native Indian or the *Yavana*? It is heard that education is the primary aim of the institution irrespective of caste, creed, nationality or economic credential of a student. Do you have the latest information of the university?"

Mahasenani, the Chief of Chaturanga informed, "Our Taksasila agent speaks of ideal management of the educational institution with help mostly from nearby Indian kings. Politics, economics, religion and applied medicine are subjects sponsored spontaneously by them. The *Yavanas* also have introduced stone architecture, Wood craft and metallurgy as study courses there. However, the institution is strictly secular. Buddhists had a curriculum there highlighting their religious supremacy, so also are the Jains. The Acharyas of Sanatan and Saiba Dharma are all along there. But there has been no religious interference. Even now Taksasila comes under the kingdom ruled by *Yavans*."

After this discussion, Kalingadhipati declared, "In one of the days following the new moon day, we shall start our expedition in an auspicious hour. This time he neither has any problem as he had in South expedition nor fear of any maritime mishap. We will complete our expedition in a cool mind. If we succeed in bringing back Kalinga Jina from Magadha, I hope we will have nothing left in India for any more expedition."

The *Mahasenani* and the *Senapati* were depressed. They could not foresee the future of Chaturanga in Kalinga without constant expeditioary movement. They felt the Emperor was lopsided in his statement. They were apprehensive of the Emperor terminating the Chaturanga structures. They suspected the military organisation of Kalinga would not survive without aggressive activity. They were apprehensive that night. There was a momentary pause on the theatre platform of Queen's cave. The light disappeared and reappeared moments later.

The waves of the marching soldiers of Kalinga was visible on the platform. There was no difficulty in identifying the commander of the expedition, he was His Highness the Emperor himself. They have traversed all their way unopposed to Taksasila.

A road was visible leading from Magadha to Puskalavati (Peshawar) just at Taksasila; few students of Taksasila University were begging something to Emperor of Kalinga. The quadruple troop of *Chaturanga* of Kalinga was proceeding with a heavy momentum chasing away the traces of military presence on the way. The Indo-Scythian Satraps and small *Yavana* rulers had fled away to west. Even Gandhara kingdom which was frequently devastated by *Yavanas* was intimidated by the imposing presence of Kalinga elephantry.

The Emperor asked the begging students, "Dear students, I can't appreciate your approach to begging after obtaining precious degrees from this august institution. I am aware that this Taksasila University produces best qualifications in different subjects. Many princes of India are trained here in combativeness, archery, practice with mace, wrestling and other war skills. Your begging belittles your education."

One interpreter was there to help the linguistic barrier. He was Jain saint Kebalakalpa. He was Professor in Jain studies. He had chance to tour all Jain pilgrimage of the country. He had been to Kumari Parvata where the wheel of Jain religion was revolved by Mahavir. The saint saluted to the Emperor for saving Jainism at Mathura and sponsoring the Jain *arhats* of Kumaragiri and Kumarigiri. This learned saint was attracted to spend long period in meditating at Kumaragiri and was well versed in Pali language of Kalinga. He spent no time to find out the source of attraction of Kalinga Emperor in Taksasila. Many a Jain king visits the place on religious grounds. There was a folklore that ten thousand years ago, the premier of all Tirthankars, Risabhanatha had his foot prints here in Taksasila. The Jain Emperors often cherished to visit this sacred site. But the Emperor of Kalinga was not orthodox at all. It is not credible that he had traversed so far for this purpose. He ascertained the prime motive of Kalinga Emperor was neither conquering a remote kingdom at opposite end of the country nor to amass wealth from treasuries of other kingdoms but certainly he must have an interior motive. He was confused and could not reach any conclusion, he paused a while before he would speak out.

"Namo Arahitanam: Namo Savasidhanam". Salutation to all saints and all the enlightened ones who have crossed the ocean of worldly existence. He recited the Jain prayer to welcome and said, "Your Majesty, these four trainees virtually belong to poor families. They belong to Kasi, Koshala and Magadha. They had spent seven years here in this premier institution and have been certified by their Acharyas to be expert in their respective subjects. They have to go back to their native places but they have to complete the rituals of offering *Guru-Dakshina* or gifts to respective teachers. No one can succeed in profession without giving this gift. This is the custom of this university."

The Emperor did not look solema any more, rather he looked curious. He asked in a lighter vein, "Who is then the ruler of this kingdom? I am a visitor to this Uttarapath.

I am a mere passerby, why do you bother me without seeking his help?"

The trainee from Magadha submitted politely, "Your Highness, Emperor of Kalinga, the whole of India praises your military power and your compassionate heart. You have the record of annual expeditions to west, north or south with your unrivalled troops. We are taught here in our institution about the importance of Kalinga from our Buddhist and Jain Acharyas. Maritime trade and sea voyage is a dream in this soil but you enjoy excellence in sea business. To face a black Kalinga elephant is a nightmare. Kalinga is unique in India, it has organised itself on your able leadership not on caste proposition but on basis of professional talent. You happen to be the custodian, secular and proud son of the soil. I beg your apology to state that we are not convinced of your statement that you are a mere visitor here!"

The Emperor felt exalted at the truth of the outspoken Magadha student but he could not believe that his name and fame had been in the curriculum of the university. He was enjoying the satiety of his soul for the glory that was accumulating for his accomplishments and the humane ways he adapted. He kept looking at Kebalakalpa in thoughtfulness.

The Jain Acharya explained to the Emperor, "Your Majesty, you must be aware of this premier educational institution. It has a great reputation since it came under the Mauryan rule. During the tenure of Maurya Emperors, native Indian language, arts and crafts, architecture and metallurgy came in contact with that of the Greek and Roman civilizations. This city bears the geographical heritage of *Ramayana*, *Mahabharata*, Jainism and Buddhism. Kunal, the son of Emperor Ashok was the

Governor of this place, there is Kunal *Stupa* in his memory. Since the advent of Mauryan administration, an autonomous education system had evolved the scholastic activities beyond the influence of politics and religion. It is funded by royal donations and the donations from the rich merchants and wealthy parents. It has notable students and teachers: King Prasenjit of Koshal, Vedic mysticUddalak Aruni and his son Svetaketu and illustrious *Acharyas* like Charak, the Ayurvedic healer, Panini, the Classical Sanskrit grammarian and Chanakya, the author of *Arthasastra*. These three *Acharyas* are accepted as part of the constellation of Great Bear of Taksasila University. Another brilliant example is set by Jeevaka, a successful Ayurvedic healer who got educated from here and was capable of healing the fatal illness of Buddha on the request of Emperor Bimbisar.

"The *Acharyas* here are above any religion and politics. Education in applied aspect is imparted to a student in practical field who had completed sixteen years education from their locality."

Emperor of Kalinga could not resist his eagerness anymore and intervened, "It seems, education on religion is not a subject of students here. It is the background of princes for learning matters of warfare or archery."

Kebalakalpa continued, "Your Majesty, I am coming to that aspect. All the religious preachers elaborate their traditions here. We Jains, speak about the arrival of Adijina Risabhanatha ten thousand years ago and establishment of his sacred wheel by his son Bahu Bali. Buddhists have their story with previous birth of Buddha; Taksha, the son of Bharat in the epic Ramayana was ruling Taksasila and Mahabharata had ample description of Parikshita, the last Pandava who died of snakebite despite all his protective measures."

"The princes have their curriculum on desired warfare or religion. But meritorious poor students read and prosper in Sanskrit, Ayurveda, Philosophy, Mathematics, Linguistics, Political Economy, Diplomacy and many other allied fields. They do not pay any fees. They are educated in the spare time of the teachers and even at night. They are also accommodated in the residential hostels and are not competitors of the princes in any case."

"Gandhara architecture was a primary subject here. It was promoted to eighteen applied professional and industrial trades. Stone masonry, rock architecture and monumental carving are popular subjects now. Many trainees from here have excelled in India. A solitary example to quote before you is the art and architecture of Sanchi and Barhut of Magadha and Nanaghat and Nasik of Satavahana. Metallurgy is also another field to shape copper, silver, gold into ornaments. So also are preparations of earthen or wooden utilities. "

The Emperor was too attentive but became inattentive with the thought of applying best of stone architecture on the virgin hill of Kumarigiri and setting up a manufacturing hub for the best of ear studs and ear ornaments of Kalinga people in general and the Kalinga theatre in particular. He also had a plan playing in his mind for shapely Kumarigiri and dancing Kalinga damsel.

He muttered, "Great Taksasila, treasure house of wisdom and science, a mine of ornaments and beauty."

Kebalakalpa concluded, "After completion of studies and certification by the Acharya, a poor scholar can't leave the university without *Gurudakshina*. The students from royal families can afford to present costly gifts but the poor ones have to confine to a pair of wooden sandal, an umbrella or a turban as a gift for his teacher.

"Your Majesty, a custom runs here, if the poor student can't arrange this small gift, they are welcome by the ruler of Taksasila for collecting small dues. This is a mark of prestige for the king, mark of prestige of education and the teaching profession. As Taksasila at present runs without a king, the transitory ruler had fled away to west fearing the onslaught of black elephants of Kalinga, you are the Emperor of this kingdom. So Your Majesty would honour the custom of Taksasila."

Kharavela was impressed by this intelligent way of presentation. He smiled at the scholars and spoke to them, "I am now aware of your situation. I honour this royal duty for education of students of Taksasila University."

He was pleased to order *Padamulika* to gift away some silver coins to each of the scholars.

The Emperor was welcomed to the premises of the university by Jain Acharya. His Highness felt elevated while walking with slow regular strides inside an enlivened environment that produces the most vibrant intuitive knowledge and wisdom in the world. He was overwhelmed with the teacher-scholar relationship and the hard task undertaken by the scholars. He was most interested in the rock art and monument carving. Education and training of language and written letters by a monument carver awakened tremendous interest in him. He aspired to immortalise his motherland, his dynasty and his personal achievements through this rock scribed art. Since the days of Ashok, rock edicts were the aspiration of the Nobles.

Kharavel thought, Kumari hill was an ideal site for stone architecture. He was dreaming of reshaping the existing caves and constructing new ones and set it with all modern stone-cut art. He forgot about his return. He spent days after days in search of knowledge base to enrich his mother soil and contacted so many Acharyas. It had added anxiety to *Mahasenani*, Beeraprasastha who could not find a way to plan a return from Taksasila. He was forced to approach Kebalakalpa to motivate the Emperor to start the return journey.

Kebalakalpa found a way to lure the Emperor for return journey. He proposed to the king, "Your Majesty, the Emperor of Kalinga! The amount of pleasure you get here from the theories of stone architecture, you will see its practical application at Sanchi and Barhut on your way back. You will appreciate how the Sungas have renovated the Mauryan stone sculpture by giving new dimensions. You will see the most beautiful *Salabhanjika* at Sanchi Stupa. She is a source of attraction to visitors standing as a symbol of prosperity of

Magadha. Her hanging down from the Sal branches has enriched the tree with greenery and productivity. This is the contribution of rock cut art to the public."

Kebalakalpa continued to motivate the Emperor engrossed with stone sculpture and with his dream to carry it to Kalinga.

"Your Highness, Jain *arhats* of Kumarigiri are waiting to meet the victorious Emperor of Kalinga. You can fulfil their three centuries' old ambition of getting Agrajina back in Kalinga. You have the chance of getting back Agrajina with the miraculous rock art into Kalinga. The empire had been enriched by you from your all round expeditions. Now you can carry home this knowledge from the greatest academic institution of the world to enrich your kingdom and make a superior Kalinga."

The Emperor, out of the long reverie took leave of Jaina Acharya and was welcomed by *Mahasenani* as all of them began their return journey back home.

Chapter-15

The Greatest Revenge

Mahasenani presented the status of the Chaturanga troops.

He informed the Emperor, "On return journey, they arrived at river Ganges close to Pataliputra, the capital of Magadha. Bruhaspati Mitra, the Magadha king is in most awkward position. He might have been frightened by the last attack a year ago, when the Gorathagiri was smashed. We may witness something strange there on our arrival.

"Let them halt at the banks of Ganges until we arrive there. Our team would be escorting you," said the *Mahasenani*.

The Kalinga military troops were waiting at the banks of Ganges for the arrival of the Emperor. An envoy of Magadha king who was searching for the Emperor of Kalinga was presented before him.

He bowed down in Jain way. Prayed before him, "Your Majesty, Magadharaj Bruhaspati Mitra seeks your permission to present himself before you."

A flicker of sarcastic smile lighted the face of the Emperor. 'Is he the Emperor of this Magadha, whose ancestors had wreaked havoc in Kalinga, not once but twice. Does the Emperor of that supreme seat beg permission to meet the Emperor of Kalinga? Oh eternal Time! You are great! None can beat you!' These were the thought drifting in the mind of Kalinga Emperor.

Within a short while the Emperor of Magadha arrived with his council of ministers. He got down from his horse and bowed at the feet of the Kalingadhipati.

The inaudible voice of Kharavel was clearly audible to Magadha king and his ministers, "Can Magadha take

such a decision to surrender before Kalinga? Kalinga had faced Magadha five times in past. Kalinga's listlessness to the threatening letter of Mahapadma Nanda had led to the indiscriminate slaughter of all its warriors. The shedding of blood resulting in mass murder of our men shamefully witnessed emergence of a *'Devanam Priyadarsi'*. Sungas had attempted to conquer Kalinga so many times; But Kalinga patriots have no equals in respect of their love and sacrifice for the motherland. They do not surrender but fight until the last drop of their blood is shed. "

Next moment Emperor of Kalinga said in a commanding voice, "It is time for the king of Magadha hto return our Kalinga Agrajina that your predecessors had illegally taken by theft from Kalinga. Both Magadha and Anga will be vassal states of Kalinga. Release our Agrajina with his crown."

Agrajina with his crown and all assets of Magadha and Anga treasuries were presented to Kalingadhipati. All the assets were loaded on hundreds of elephants on way back to Kalinga. A messenger, the *Lehaharaka* was running ahead to intimate officials in Kalinga to receive the victorious team.

Kalinganagari was preparing for a grand reception of the victorious home bound Emperor. Kalinga had excelled in heroism; it had defeated its arch rival Magadha ridiculously and had restored Kalinga Jina snatched away from here three hundred years ago. Chaturanga troops had marched through whole of Bharatavarsa unopposed and with glory. But history over Magadha creates a special feeling in the heart of each subject of Kalinga. It had revenged the massacre of Kalinga War and bloodshed and death. It assuaged heaps of hatred and anger that accumulated in the heart of each Kalingan. The Kalingan is elated that the crown of dormant and dead Magadha had fallen down. A grand arrangement is underway to celebrate the victory in a big way.

The whole episode returned to life from the rock cut art in the Queen's Palace; that rock carving shows in the most solemn way the surrender of Bruhaspati Mitra with folded hands, forehead touching the ground at his feet.

There was a huge rally in Kalinganagari, witnessed by residents of the town from multistoried complex buildings. The welcome event was beautiful with auspicious *Purna Kumbha*, water pots filled with water as a symbol of fulfilment. The Emperor was returning home with

Chaturanga as the victor of war carrying with him Kalinga Jina and possessing the sovereignty of Magadha. All the drums and trumpets were loudly sounding the glory of Kalinga. The winning team was on a march of victory around the town, would ultimately enter the temple to salute the deity.

A grand felicitation acknowledging Emperor's victory and good fortune of Kalinga, was getting ready. Entire population of Kalinganagari would glorify and honour their beloved Emperor and would express gratitude for the unprecedented achievement for the motherland. The speakers on the occasion were the Emperor himself and Aparimeyananda, the Jain saint. The overflowing crowd had participants from distant locations like Kumari Parvata, Dantapur coast, Tamralipti, Kopakataka, Paloura port, Karanjia and dozens of Kalinga hinterlands. Agrajina was back in Kalinga dispelling the gloom of three hundred years. Now their joy knew no bounds.

In his opening speech Aparimeyananda solemnly expressed his salutational recognition to the Emperor of Kalinga and also welcomed the audience and dignitaries, "His Greatness, the Chakravarti King of Kalinga and my dear residents of Kalinga, You belong to the most prosperous time of your nation. You are the example of a spiritual solidarity. Your Emperor has achieved wonders by virtue of his innate ability and perseverance. He has achieved glory not only for his state but for the mankind as a whole. We had not been promised to get back Agrajina but he had been moved by the melancholic faces of Jain monks who wanted Agrajina back. Each time he was back from an expedition, the monks would be expecting this gift from him. Day by day as he gathered his might, the monks kept dreaming of a victory over Magadha for return of Agrajina.

But today's victory celebration feels the joy of subduing Magadha for a revenge without bloodshed and death."

At the end the saint advised His Highness, "Agrajina was taken away from Pithunda, which was the then capital of Kalinga. The area and geography had developed into a more vibrant Kalinganagari. Let His Highness take a decision of reestablishing Agrajina at a place that would be the most popular and secure."

Kalingasuta Ekamrak, in charge of the victory celebration had sought permission to speak a few words. With hundreds of salutations he admired the Emperor who had converted Kalinga to a most prosperous kingdom within a decade of his reign. He is the worthy son of the soil, the founder of greater Kalinga and the profound initiator of an united Bharatavarsa integration. He will be remembered with dignity for ever in history.

His words aroused grand ovation for the Emperor with incessant loud clapping for a prolonged bout. The earth and air of Kalinganagari were reverberating with the admiration for the Emperor.

Now the turn of the Emperor. The Emperor with crown of trifoliate design on his head, with his bold and brave face looking elegantly at each corner of the audience with all of his senses experiencing the throbs of his success in life. The expectant audience knew this third generation Chedi descendant who was in the habit of speaking much less than what he performs. All the spectators were in total silence like that of a dense forest where falling of a leaf would make a noise.

There was a mark of eagerness and attention to listen to the great performer, an artist in all his spheres including his histrionic talent. Always he had been smooth-spoken in his pleasing local Pali dialect.

"My beloved countrymen," he said, "Kalinga as it stands today is the outcome of all your hard labour and dedication. First I congratulate you all the worthy children of this Kalinga mother. I am revealing the secret of my life because the time has arrived to reveal it. It is not the credential of Mahameghavahana family to announce something before it is accomplished. Since the days of my education three decades ago, I had a target in the deepest corner of my mind to rebuild Kalinga after recovering Kalinga Jina from Magadha. I am now satisfied that I have achieved my target. But still some behavioural aspects are desired from each Kalingan. A Kalingan must have utmost civic sense, self prestige and humanitarian attitude. We will get miracles out of these behavioural reflections.

"I agree with the proposal of Jain proponent, Aparimeyananda on the issue of relocation of Kalinga Jina in a safe and secure custody. Pithunda is no more a central location or secure place for Kalinga administration. I want your approval for installing it at the height of Kumari Parvata, where Bardhaman Mahavir had propagated the religious wheel."

There were a chorus of supportive voices with enormous clapping for a moment. A wave of happiness swept over the audience like a strong wave of the sea inundating the shores.

"Thank you for your unanimous consent," continued the Emperor. "Of course, Kalinga Jina's presence will require major alterations and development of the hill to a high standard tourist spot of the globe. We would develop Kumarigiri as tenderly a father would nurture his mature daughter. It will be ever attractive to tourists and saints, this mountain of moderate elevation would earn a place in the history of the country. It has its glorious magnetic forces inherited from premier religious preachers like Parsvanath and Mahavir. This attraction will continue as long as the human civilisation continues on earth."

"I must congratulate our agricultural and maritime bases for their performance. But emphasis on the worship of the tree, *Brukshya Puja* is an epitome of agricultural development. Agriculture not only feeds us, provides dress and employment, but also fills our ships with cargo bound to Far East, the *Suvarna Dvipa*.

"We must adorn our own behaviour with modesty and humanism. Long live Kalinga; God bless Kalinga."

The full moon of this month was reluctantly travelling down to horizons mesmerised by the Emperor's speech. It had never experienced such heaven sent moments on the earth before.

All the spectators were silent with thoughts filling their their minds. They saw the Emperor marching to and fro on the dais. He hails from a small state but he executes excellent plans with foresight and has immense perseverance. It would have been utterly impossible on the part of any Emperor to promote the kingdom to a golden era within twelve years as he performed with giant Kalinga Chaturanga forces crossing the rivers and mountains to traverse most of India.

The reign under Kharavel was epoch making. Agricultural production had kept pace with that of maritime export. Living in Kalinga had turned to be attractive in its beauty and bliss. Women's prosperity had enhanced equality of life in Kalinga. Peace prevailed in all spheres of Kalingan life.

Yes Kalingadhipati, you are indeed Great!

The three visitors to midnight hill felt the warmth of delight in their hearts. The meaningful speech of the

Emperor was exciting, electrifying. They were too much fascinated but finally came to their senses as the glow of the ceremony started fading away.

Salabhanjika had now gone back to her mute form.

The Morning Star on eastern horizons was indicating that night would soon dawn into the day.

Chapter-16

Rock-Artisans

*D*ola Purnima comes in *Phalguna* which is in the month of of March. It is celebrated as a *vaishnav* festival of Radha Krishna with launching of new Odia calendar. The Astrologer of the village announces the forecasting of the fortunes and misfortunes for the coming year. This village function continues up to midnight.

The three friends escaped the active commotions of the celebration in the vicinity of the village community hall and they moved towards the hill. They had forgotten the exact number of episodes gone and how many more were to come. Each one of them thought hardly one to two more must have been left and the live show of ancient history will come to an end.

Salabhanjika Puspita was waiting for the invitees. She was accompanied by *Dwarapalika* Suka Swagatika and the Ganesh cave *Dishidharika,* Jyotsna Ujjwalika. The three invitees were apprehensive as a number of ladies were waiting to welcome them. After the expeditions, Kharavela's administration would be over. The running events were focused on the last lines of Hathigumpha inscriptions.

Abhirama raised an issue, "Esteemed Puspita, we presume, the episode of Kalinga administration under Kharavela is going to an end. Kharavela had completed all his expeditions and Kalinga Jina is back from Magadha. In spite of that how come you are so enthusiastic that we will be witnessing the important events of his later period."

An uneasy Puspita said, "The golden era that ushered in the reign of Kharavel is by your time a tale of two millennia ago. No evidence of such a remote past would survive till today. But this hill throws light upon the life of the great Emperor in totality. He had completed his military expeditions by the twelfth year of his rule. Emperor Kharavela survived for long years after he relinquished the throne. He had fulfilled the desire of Sindhula, his Simhapatha queen for construction of Queen's Palace. Its location was to the east of *Arhat's* dwelling at Jaya Vijaya and Alakapuri Caves that involved a royal sanction of one lakh and five thousand silver coins. About thirty five lakh pieces of costly stones were procured from distant places. These stone pieces were set on the floor. They were in pink and royal red in colour, the favourite choice of the royal and noble women. The new construction would have a number of pillars and those would be bedecked with emerald.

"The completion of the Queen's Palace with decoration took one decade long once we consider its second storey constructed by digging masons, its stone art carved by monument carving experts and its flooring and wall finishing done by specialized floor masons. The Emperor would be guiding the royal council in charge of construction to embody real pictures from the contemporary life of people, their culture and rituals. Kalinga Royal Council took a decision to record all heroic achievements of the Emperor and make symbolic carvings on cave walls, particularly in the Queen's Palace. It would survive ages like the rise and fall of ocean waves.

"The most available scripts used since Emperor Ashok was old Brahmi script. The language spoken in Kalinga was mostly Pali by residents and sometimes Sanskrit by Brahmins and priests. The best letter carvers were dispatched by Magadha administration to Kumari Parvata. They were well versed with Prakruti script and Pali language. Newly trained Kalinga cave artisans had tremendous role in localizing the linguistic part of the inscription. The last to come was the Hathigumpha inscription which was unveiled by the Emperor on the day of Kalinga Samaroh.

"You three would wait to know why the Emperor relinquished his throne so early. It was with an intention of immortalising Kalinga and to popularize dance and drama of *tauryatrika* as engraved in the seventeenth line. Now you must be convinced that he lived his full years in fullness of life. Not only he was free from day to day administration of Kalinga but he preferred a care free way of living with religious practices."

All of them took a pause for a moment. The time sequence of the historic and the heroic past was settling into their minds with the evidences put forth by *Salabhanjika*.

Puspita continued, "The centenary of this year is the twentieth when you three are the onlookers. It is our misfortune that none in past had seen it. If your conception on any aspect goes wrong, it will be a misfortune of our mission. We are depicting his non-military life briefly, though in reality it was longer than the duration of his military expeditions. To make you feel convenienced we all have come in a group.

"Come to Kumarigiri which is illuminated as brightly as day light even at midnight. The moon and all the *Dishidharikas* extend out their fullness of light over the hill. A good crowd is visible now moving from one location to another. Not only the general public of Kalinga but the artisans, noble men, religious dignitaries, achievers of diverse fields from all over Bharatavarsa are part of the whole crowd. Kalingadhipati is generous. He is neither orthodox to confine himself to one religion, nor is he parochial in his religious fervor. He was a personality that can attract thousands of his admirers from remote areas. Artisans of different fields are busy in their activity. A number of tourists are eager to meet the Emperor to bow before him. Let us move and have glimpses of the state of affairs."

They reached the popular Jaya-Vijaya cave and found the neighbouring Alakapuri cave was under repair. The multistoried cave had a steep staircase. The age-old caves provided shelter to the *Yapannapak* arhats in their rainy season retreats. Its stair was being remodeled for easy climb up. A number of carvers were working with their chisel and hammer. It was a pleasure to look at with the chisel sound constantly hammering the ears. Visitors could make the rhythm of their mindset to the synchrony of the stone carvers. Layers of satisfaction were adding up to the contents of their imagination that Kalinga people could perform miracles on stone.

They had reasons to be elated. Emperor Kharavela had given them the entire credit for all achievements. The dedication of the people of Kalinga had been in the forefront giving their life in war and taking the risks in maritime trade. The sea might have been a graveyard for few but that could neither arouse fear nor generated willingness among Kalinga traders. This proud story of Kalinga life was articulated by the jubilant Emperor.

The *Salabhanjika* was leading them through the rock carving stage. It was next to that of Alakapuri. They were two natives talking in Pali language which was partly understood by the three guests. *Salabhanjika* was explaining them when they failed to understand. The two natives were ordinarily dressed in local attire and seemed to be the elders from neighbouring settlements. They had ample knowledge on different aspects of the state affairs. They had the capacity to evaluate the activities of administration. The level of their discussions was impressive. There was a flow of participatory wave in the public. Aged and the octogenarian people had an invisible uncertainty and gloom in their mind regarding the future of their kingdom. But the victories of Magadha expedition had elevated the status of Kalinga and dispelled their fearful anticipations.

The bald-headed man said, "Magadha was capable enough to snatch away our state deity, Kalinga Jina. Kalinga had become a pauper due to centuries of heavy Mauryan taxation. Our worthy Emperor had brought back our deity with the crown in a dignified manner. He had also recovered entire taxes that we had paid to the Mauryas. The worthy son of Mahameghavahana family had succeded in amassing huge wealth from the rulers of Bharatavarsa. *Bhandagarika,* the treasurer had no space to store the wealth gained from the vanquished. It must have been the Emperor's order to bury the treasure in secret places beyond the reach of the enemy."

The two were very generous in admiring their beloved Emperor. The older added, "Now our Emperor looks cool and contented. Rays of beauty and bliss emit from his glorious face. Years back with steadiness of mind he strengthened the stamina of Chaturanga forces. He could achieve a thousand years' glory within a short span of twelve years. He had expanded the boundary of Kalinga in all directions. His Highness also as the master of sea could patronise the maritime trade and did establish huge Kalinga colonies in *Suvarna dvipa*. The *Mahasenani* and the *Senapati* were the two noble royal officials ever ready to execute his plans of action. Due to its vastness in size and intimidating in its demeanour, the very presence of his Chaturanga military force was enough to have the hostile kingdoms surrender without any encounter resulting in victory without bloodshed and death."

The bald and the elderly said teasingly, "Do you feel the strength of the military is all that will yield a victory?"

"Certainly, here is the proof"

"No my dear, it was additional diplomacy and his intelligence accuracy that helped him win every encounter No force will work before the stubborn race of Kalinga, ready to sacrifice the last drop of blood. Had there been this glorious son of the soil during Kalinga War, blood thirsty Ashok dared not think of a war."

The three friends were unmindful and were lagging behind the *Salabhanjika* and her team, so had to take long strides to cover the distance.

They reached the site of Kalinga Jina temple under construction. The place had clear visibility under moonlight. The pieces of laterite stone were lifted by elephants and the masons were busy in constructing the walls of the temple and the prayer hall. Many carpenters were also busy in fixing the doors and windows. A middle aged person with fair complexion was guiding the construction workers. He was accompanied by a tall thin lady. They were very attentive to ensure the best out of the construction.

Puspita revealed the identity of the two persons, male and female at temple site, the male person was the Chief of Works department, *Kama* and the female was his wife. The thin lady justified her name as Khina, the slender figure. Emperor Kharavela had made it clear that in all royal and civic function an officer has to be accompanied by his spouse. This would be better considered by his subjects as auspicious. He gave importance to women and considered it as the law of nature to allow them participate so that we feel doubly satisfied by sharing our happiness with spouses.

From the construction site where Mahavir had propagated the wheel of religion, they came down through western stair case. The corridor in front of Hathigumpha was over crowded. The Emperor was busy with guest kings surrounding him. Added to the crowd were members of the Council of Ministers and the monks of Kalinga. The problems submitted by such rulers were either about the attack of the neighbour or foreign intrusions. The method for solving such problems was through small military involvements. One imperceptible team of intelligence was operative to look into such external affairs.

Kalpa Bigyani, the Chief Jain of Kumarigiri was noticed by the Emperor. The sage had congratulated the Emperor in the crowd. At once His Highness set aside all his assignments to meet him. The sage thanked the Emperor for recovery of Kalinga Jina from Magadha and his decision to construct a secure temple at Kumarigiri to install it where the Parsvanath, the twenty-third Tirthankara preached early Jainism and the religious wheel was propagated by Bardhaman Mahavir. He was hopeful that people of Kalinga were shy of publicity but the achievements of Kharavela had historical distinctions and must be carved into by the new team of sculptors from Magadha.

Kama and Khina had come down to the crowded area. They had overheard the proposals of Kalpa Bigyani. Kama lowered his head in salutation to the Emperor and felt probably he was wanted by the Emperor. He informed him that the hill had so many locations, the Hathigumpha itself, few caves of the *arhat*'s residence just below where carving would be done. Caves could be dug out of the plain heap of stones followed by engraving. Once the Emperor permits the stone cutters to make the cave structures, rock artisans from Magadha, Taksasila and Nanaghat would be indented and entrusted with carving.

Kama pledged before the Emperor, "I am waiting for the approval of the caves to be dug and the arts to be engraved narrating the achievements of Your Excellency. I promise we will set throbbing hearts and purifying souls to the art life of stones."

The Emperor gave a hearty smile, which expressed joyfulness of his heart.

With a nod he answered calmly, "Allow me some time to think about it. There are some priorities. Let the temple of Agrajina be completed with deity established inside. Some caves like Patalapuri are worn out and need instant repair. Next will be our execution of extended habitable new caves and rock art."

He continued, "Kama, you belong to works department. We all will follow slow and steady principles in our field of execution."

Kama nodded his head indicating his obedience.

In the mean time, two chariots, each carrying the royal family arrived at the hill base. In the first chariot were chief queen Dhruti with her twelve year son, Kandarpashree, the dressmaker Patar and priestess Nandika. The second queen, Sindhula got down from the second with her two maids, Sagarika and Lahari. The crowd present on the hill turned their attention to the royal family, confirmed by the flags of the chariots. Everyone was astonished when the two queens climbed up the steps leading to Hathigumpha separately, the second queen lagging behind by a hundred paces. From the corridors of Hathigumpha, the Emperor had a clear vision of their arrival. He was perturbed by their repelling attitude.

Puspita was leading her team to different locations that had turned to be noisy with monotonous sound of hammering on the chisel. Rich art on the rock was being engraved and gave the feeling as if the tune of the sound too was set into the rock-art. The hill was quite dusty and noisy with the rapid ornamentation of the bare stones. A large crowd continued to throng in front of Hathigumpha. The spectators had the chance to be closer to the Emperor and the deity at the same time.

The three mortal invitees were not lost among the crowd. They were struggling through the mess to come closer to the Emperor. Kalingadhipati had the programme of worship in the temple. The whole family bowed before Agrajina and each of the members cherished something. The will of the aspirant, it was strongly believed, gets fulfilled. When they come out of the temple, the priest informed the family, "Your Highness, as per the customs of the deity, have a short stay in the Manchapuri Cave after worship. I will be collecting a few strands of Kalpataru from the temple for you and your family."

During the short sojourn at the Manchapuri cave, the Emperor had been over enthusiastic to disclose some secrets that no one other than he could do. He approached the two queens and said, "Queen Dhruti, I am sure your wish that you begged Agrajina would be fulfilled at once but not until you disclose it to me!"

Dhruti simply looked all around, had no will to reveal her wish that she asked to the deity. But she was compelled by the approach of the Emperor.

She started in a soft voice, "I have in my mind to

dedicate the Swargapuri cave in honour of my victorious husband, the Chakravarti Monarch. The Swargapuri cave is to be completed in all respects with inscription that this aspirant is the daughter of the great Lalarka and great granddaughter of Hatisimha. This will immortalise my identity and my relationship with Kalingadhipati and the philosophy of our dynasty."

The Emperor spoke as if possessed by the soul of the deity, "Queen Dhruti, you are clearly audible to me. Your wish will be fulfilled. Be prepared to dedicate the cave to *arhats* in few months from now as it is on the verge of completion."

Then he turned towards second queen, Sindhula and asks her, "Can I know your wishes?"

Sindhula was shy to reveal her deepest wish that she aspired from the deity. She was grave and kept mum for a while.

She asked the Emperor, "It is not easy to fulfil my wishes, even then it might be possible by omnipotent

Agrajina. When Emperor himself is the caretaker, I must not be a fool to judge something impossible. My wish is the contents of my dream that I dreamt last night. I witnessed a special cave in this favourite hill that has been our cave palace. It had additional apartments as abode of the wise and religious dignitaries from all streams. I had seen this cave palace vibrant with religious and mystical discourses. To my aspirations, the pillars of the palace were dazzling with emerald and precious stones and the gem studded floor justified it as Queen's Palace with its lovely pink colour. The walls were too many and anybody taking a look at the rock cut art, the shapes would dance out of the walls into live performances. The cave palace of my dream was quite relaxing and elegantly thrilling."

The Chief Queen was stunned. She was staring at the face of Sindhula who had desire of a luxurious palace not a cave. She had no wish for her husband or the dynasty. But thought only of materialistic pleasure with wisdom, arts, crafts and gems. What a selfish creature she could be!

But the instant reply was from smart Emperor, "Sindhula, I can foresee it. Agrajina blessed you for your dream too. It will come true. In fact, it has started taking shape from last week but it would be supervised by you and shape up to your own choice. I can't tell you now how the cave palace was proposed. It will come to light only after a few days. The workforce and the rock-art specialists can reveal the true shape of this project. The Deity had blessed you with such an unmatchable palace, you would be a trend setter in planning and supervising the construction of the cave palace and get it completed."

The Queen's Palace was the dream of Sindhula. The Emperor himself wanted an ideal hermitage where the discourse for different religions would be conducted. His dynasty followed Jainism, but from the core of his heart he loved all ideal and practical elements of all religions. During the course of construction of the cave, queen Sindhula and the rock artisans would engrave all major happenings of the Emperor's life to immortalise him. The morning Sun would light up the luxurious cave and would pronounce the glory of the hill.

The queen was the advisor of the artisans from north and she had to explain to engrave the warrior appearance of the Emperor. She had seen him once leaving the palace for Uttarapatha and Magadha. The war preparation and commandership of the Emperor in any war generates hundreds of apprehensions in the mind of the queens. Sindhula was startled at the attempt of expedition to far off North West. But all her gloom melt like an icicle under the Sun when the Emperor returned with the Deity back from Magadha. Many events of Kalinga and the scemic beauty of the Kalinganagari palace were prompted by the queen to the chief artisan carving there.

All the social and festivities were engraved with accuracy but mostly it propagated a sense of war. Love scenes were desired to amuse the spectators. Sindhula could not get into depth of love scene, the lover winning the heart of his beloved by offering a bunch of mango got carved on the ground floor. It came to her mind to order the chief artisan to engrave the story of her marriage with the Emperor.

The Emperor was concerned about the decaying caves of Kumarigiri. He focused his attention to repair and restore the old and degenerated caves. He explained to the Chief architect of Kumarigiri to beautify the hill without leaving any empty surface.

The Kalingadhipati solemnly addressing the artisans

emphasized, "You must adorn this Kalinga Kumari, the daughter of Kalinga as one among the best on earth; with all venerable art and craft possible so that tourist guides would find enough material to fascinate their touring guests. Each art of yours must be attractive and lively, arouse a sense of aesthetic experience among the visitors. You have within you the vast experience. I appeal to all of you here to carve meaningful sketches that would awaken a rational meaning reverberating forever!"

The grave chief artisan was quite attentive. He politely asked, "Your Highness, kindly enlighten with a small example."

"The Kumarigiri is an ideal for its feminine elegance confirming to the ultimate standard of excellence. It must have abundant architectural features of women. The cave in forefront of the hill is *Jaya-Vijaya*. It must welcome the visitors in most refined manner. Out of the two *Dwarapalas*, you make the right one as Suka Swagatika of Chief Queen, Dhruti's choice. Suka must wear the best of Kalinga clothes, will have a parrot set on her right hand who would ever ever be chanting 'welcome my guest'. *Salabhanjika* would be the other one, who will be accompanying the new comer and impressing him with her beauty and elegance. She would continue to guide the guests in the tour and would explain in an inviting and impressive way. Also the *Dishidharikas* or lamp bearers would keep the hill ever lighted and the architectural characters would perpetuate an artistic milieu in the memory of anybody who has once visited the hill."

The requisition of the Emperor impressed both the officials in charge of construction, *Kama*, the Works Minister and *Karmakara*, the chief architect. The latter had to decide upon the size and location of the rock, keeping in mind the thematic relevance and historical significance. The glamorous women folk of the hill expected *Karmakara* to have the images of their live performance set in the art in such a manner that the echoes of their musical instruments will vibrate in the heart of the spectators. *Banshivadika*, the lady with the flute whispered to the aged artisan, "O' statue maker, don't separate my flute from me. The lion headed flute in my hand will glorify your artisanship."

"We must adequately be represented in your rock-art," uttered *Mrudalabadika*, the drummer girl and the female harper simultaneously.

"Don't forget me, dear Artisan", shouted the dancing girl. "Have our imprints in the Queen's Palace, the royal place and the theatre of Emperor's choice."

"Really, my child, you are performing wonderful dance. I shall imprint the agile dance you perform firmly on the rock so that the posterity would behold and admire both you and me."

The architect was emotionally charged to display of the contemporaty history of Kalinga. He heard the glories

of the Emperor and his compassionate attitude. He was acquainted with the manner of living of Kalinga people and the domestic animals in society.

"The greatest among the great, a pragmatic man among men the Kalinga Emperor attempted to carve royal festivities in the noblest way. Here is a king who is different from the rest. They had engraved only their personal glories. But Kharavela, the Emperor wants the whole society surrounding him to be carved out in a natural manner. He thought to himself, "The characters of the art impress me with such affection that I am emotionally moved. Now I am almost confronting a competition between the original and its cave-art form. Can I work up to that extent by which it would not be lost in the darkness of night? I must set a number of lamp bearing *Dishidharikas* to make the hill neatly lighted during night."

This impression was rolling through the mind of the architect. Years of work from a number of artisans had adorned the hill with rock-art glamour.

Padamulika whispered to the Emperor, "Your Majesty, I request your Highness to pay a visit around the art emporium of the hills and to express your impression."

The Emperor was enthusiastic to see the architecture completed in past seven years. He had no intention to disturb the concentration of the artisans at work in their final stages, as they would feel embarrassed as if they have failed to produce exact outcome. He thought it wise to pay a visit in disguise with the *Padamulika*.

A healthy brown middle aged man with typical village farmer robe with sharp eyes was moving around the hill with a similar aged man with an umbrella covering the head of the healthy man in midday sun. Eyes of artisans might be deceived by the disguise, but his walk with that lofty proud gait and its dignified impact on the hill could not hide his Highness from the hill itself. She knows by her instincts, who is moving around on her surface.

Kharavel in a farmer's disguise was at minute details, his eyes rolling everywhere and noted the subtlest chisel stroke on the rock surface. The women in the rock-art are all well dressed with thin transparent drapery with folds and designs prevalent among nobles and commoners. No woman would be carved bare in this part of the country was the principle set for the artisans. They have never gone beyond the limit. But love is natural and has its spontaneous expressions. The artisans had left no skill untouched for giving love its life to breath from the rocks.

Love is never made, it just happens. The disguised farmer thought love is not like a tree that is planted by the lovers but it is an event that happens in the usual go of life, a circumstance that spontaneously begets it. It is a child of nature, not a product of coercion. An elephant is a massive animal with grotesque features would also be possessed by love with expressions on its trunk. The artisan had reflected the love episode of an elephant couple so immaculately that the visitors would get the general feeling of ecstacy at the very first glance.

For carving human love, the artists had gone a step further. Love is not purchasable yet human expression is always care based. No lover or beloved will approach or propose without a meaningful event. The feeling gets expressed in a way the artisan has shown on the ground floor of Queen's Palace. He is offering a bunch of ripe mangoes to the beloved. The lover is psychologically expectant that the beloved would receive it at once but she becomes emotional before accepting it. It is a rare expression of the artist's idea of love.

The disguised farmer and the man accompanying him express great satisfaction. The man holding umbrella asks the disguised Emperor, "How do you appreciate the architecture of the hill?"

The Emperor has no hesitation to talk intimately to the assistant of his age who is his childhood friend and is acquainted with all his affairs. He assists rightly both at home and on expedition.

"Your Majesty has generated water lilies on rock. Drought can kill all water lilies but can't touch those of yours."

"Lily is romantic to look at. But can it glorify the hill in future? Kusuma, do you follow what do I mean?"

"I follow, Your Majesty. A written document on rock is an all time memory of your achievements for unimaginable future. We have many monument carvers literate masons. They have expertise in old Brahmi script. They are well versed in local Pali and universal Sanskrit verses. They can glorify the hill and can immortalise your achievements in rock-cut inscriptions."

"In fact the Hathigumpha is a gift of nature to us. This cave is destined to have a long inscription over its front plane that exactly faces the Dhauli hill, few *yojanas* apart, where some rock edict of Maurya administration face this side.

"We would prefer the local Pali language to Sanskrit for our local spectators who will stand below the cave and will go on reading and appreciating rather than getting baffled by the bombastic words of other languages. This work has been allotted to competent editorial board."

Both the disguised Emperor and *Padamulika* heard some conversation of a group of people. *Padamulika* could trace the voice of the chief editor of Hathigumpha inscription project, the Chief Jain Saint and two linguistic experts of the editorial board on their field survey. They were initiating the special hymn composed for Kalinga Samaroh with essence of all religions, languages and emotions of Kalinga.

The Emperor was mad for the combined voice enchanting the hymn. He rushed to the spot at once in the disguise and said, "The hero of Bharatavarsa is not proud of his achievement. Many editors would come to salute him if by chance he comes to meet an editor on his assignment."

Padamulika introduced themselves to the editorial board on spot duty.

The team was amazed. An Emperor of Kharavel's stature in the robe of a local farmer! They bowed down before him. The great Emperors of Kalinga had the habit of forgiving their worst enemy who bowed before them in reverence.

Chapter-17

The Lyrical Rock Edict

The Emperor was quite enthusiastic and he requested, "Please recite two lines of your composition."

He could hear the line,

"*Namo Arihamtanam* ||
Namo Savasidhanam ||"

"Please repeat," the Emperor urged to hear it again and again. Closing his eyes he was reminded of the vibrations of the hymn. Opening his eyes, he stared at the editorial group.

The editor looked to the slate that had the verse written in seventeen lines and cited with grandeur the first stanza of the draft. He was the pacesetter of the ensemble with Kalinga linguist, Chief vocalist and Jain architect of Kumarigiri, who all chanted synchronously,

"*Namo Arihamtanam* || *Namo Savasidhanam* ||
Airena Maharajena || *Mahameghavahanena* ||"

The atmosphere of Kumarigiri was vibrating with the '*omm*' sound of the *Namokar* chanting. The sound waves echoed back from Kumaragiri was lower in intensity but more pleasing.

The Emperor sat down, all attention to the sound. He had never looked for prestige from anywhere but there he was amidst joy. His name recited in the leaflet was going to be inscribed on rock for eternity. That was a Jaina welcome hymn. Salutation to Arhats; Salutation to all Siddhas. Arya Mahameghavahana, Maharaja Sri Kharavela.

The Emperor requested to halt for some time, "Let the reciters of the hymn allow a moment's pause during recital. The resonance of your anthem echoing from the other hill is melodious, euphoric, and harmonic. A moment's pause would produce a pleasing duet by the twin hills, Kumarigiri as trend setter, Kumaragiri, as the follower to enrich the sky and the earth with its abundant soothing power. The mind freshens at once and the soul becomes blissful."

"*Namo Arihamtanam* || *Namo Savasidhanam* ||"
"*Airena Maharajena* || *Mahameghavahanena* ||"
Chetaraja vansh vardhanena||
Prasastha subha lakhanena ||"
Chaturanga gunthan gunamaten ||
Kalingadhipatina Sri Kharavelena ||"
Panchadasa varsa Sri kahara ||
Kiridanti Kumara kridara||"

The singers paused for the Emperor to comment. They also explained the contents of the lyric to him, the jewel of Chedi dynasty with all auspicious signs around him and natural brown complexion, Prince Sri Kharavela spent his time in sports and games until he was fifteen years old.

The Emperor expressed his happiness, "What a meaningful and befitting composition! Our monument script carvers must have carved the rock one finger deep in order to make the inscription durable in future. It is written in simple Pali spoken by common people of Kalinga. It bears all the charm of our colloquial language.

"Look at Sauravagiri, the Dhauli. It has the oldest inscription made by Ashok wherein he addressed them as his offspring. Oh! It is not the affectionate words of a father to his children, but a stern order and collection of rules imposed by Authority binding upon Kalinga society. How can a floral and spontaneous lyric flow from the man who had beheaded thousands of innocent people! Forget it, not a matter worth discussing. This is because we dreaded the remembrance of a river of blood which was shed in order to ruthlessly suppress the fearfully obstinate resistance of Kalinga. Each Kalingan had to be mutilated limb by limb, and finger by finger, but in spite of it none of them yielded."

In a state of ecstacy the Emperor remarked, "I am enchanted by the proposed composition of the inscription. You continue the chant until the last stanza. I find pleasure in concentrating on the lyric echoing from the other hill that is more soothing and musical."

The editorial unit was continuing the script description,

"Panchadasa varsa Sri Kahara | |
Kiridanti Kumara kridara | |"
"Kalinga rajavase purisa yuge | |
Maharaja bhisechanam papunati | |"
"Rajasi vasukula vinisito | |
Mahavijayo raja Kharavela siri | |"

The composition of the stanzas is appealing, it will impress the readers and with its rhythm and lyricism it will touch their heart and soul. Its contents are not limited only to the thirteen years of excellent reign of Kalinga, but stretches over millennia before. It speaks of the heritage of the land, it lauds the powerful expeditions of the Emperor and hints at minute details of the glorious social life of the common man during the period of the Emperor's golden rule.

The Emperor is in a state of bliss on listening to that sweet composition. The lyric enters his soul at once and overwhelms the entire soul and makes each listener dance to its tune. It wipes out sorrow, elevates every Kalingan with self esteem for being a Kalingan.

"It is that mountain stream, which with its rhythmical music can percolate into the soul of anyone." This was the afterthought of the Emperor, like any of Lord Buddha's conjectures on the future of his preaching.

The chanting scenario switched over to the next phase.

x x x x

The scene of rock inscription on the facade of Hathigumpha cave is about to start. On the advice of his Highness this Editorial Board had prepared this composed script and had got the Emperor's approval to etch it into the rock surface. The Queen's Palace had been successfully completed and Queen Sindhula has an extra duty to look after the inscription.

"We will involve all the royal officers in this inscription. It is an attempt of the Kalinga administration to project the state of Kalinga with its thirteen glorious years of well being under Emperor Kharavela. It also looks at the past years as much as the period known and calculated by our Jain Monks. At least few of the wise men are quite capable of citing the temporal sequence of events like the Nanda attack and Kalinga War." The queen articulated authoritatively.

Padamulika Kusuma took care to invite all the ministers, secretaries, Jain religious authorities with the editorial board to guide the inscription.

"The script must be flawless", declared *Kama*, the Works Minister. He proposed the inscription of Time in bright sunlight letter by letter, word by word and sentence by sentence with verification by Editorial Board.

"It is easy to inscribe with this draft containing lyrical text, that is singing itself in the mind of the monument carver," said the artisan digging the Brahmi letters half inch deep on the sandstone facade of the cave.

"Look down to the letters of next word to be inscribed from the guiding platform below made of white lime and black ashes. Remain unmindful to the piercing noise of the chisel and hammer," asked the Jain Member of the Editorial Board to the memorial carving masons.

"We salute for your preparedness for the inscription carving," replied the veteran letter carver. "Rarely had I seen so much vigilance and prompt guidance over the job by the host party in Magadha and Nanaghat. As per your instruction, we have hammered the writing surface plain and white washed it with lime. Word by word we will write first for the editor to declare it right. Each letter that we are going to dig by chisel and hammer would be equal depth which will be filled with black ashes to look distinctly to the proof reader. We have plenty of time at our hand before the scheduled inauguration ceremony. Slow and steady in our attempt will assure a durable inscription."

"We assure you a faultless inscription due to your unprecedented support to our work by making a grand scaffolding that makes our workplace in this height as safe as working on the ground." The aged architect commented from top of the tall four legged ladder-chair.

Kama, the Works Minister of Kalinga would look deep into things to ensure that each letter is carved in its desired place. He would look to the letter in the platform below and one written as pre-carving mark on rock wall undisturbed by hammer sound.

The execution of the letter digging on rock had created an academic milieu not only among the saints and the related authorities of the Emperor's work force but also among the students on research and general people of interest who formed a small fair in Kumarigiri. It would create and display a learning ambience akin to Taksasila in attracting the learned and erudite scholars with reputation of arts and crafts and a famous theatre party in the country by the time carving of letters were completed. It took almost a decade from the day the Emperor relinquished the throne.

Salabhanjika, who was expressing everything uninterrupted to the three invitees, looked up and was silent for a moment. She had noticed Queen Sindhula on the roof of the Hathigumpha observing the carving work. She had undertaken the task of preparing the hill for inaugural ceremony to be held a few months after.

One of the candle bearing *Dishidharika* on the carving platform at a height beckoned Puspita to climb up to the stage to help her.

The three friends had some time to come to reality and corrected their impression to realise the truth that each trace of art or carving must have involved immense effort of the artisan encouraged by the Emperor.

A voluminous dark cloud moving from south to north covered the full moon to bring an interval of darkness on the hill. The chisel sound ceased and the conversing friends became silent. In the absence of *Salabhanjika* they were helpless until the moon freed herself from the trespassing clouds.

Chapter-18

The Grand Celebration

The rock-inscription work got disrupted by the darkness that came to prevail for some time. Puspita appeared the moment the moon made the landscape of hill open to easy view.

Looking at the trio she said, "Are you scared of the darkness? This light and darkness are the themes of erudite Emperor Kharavela participating in different plays, folk dances and dancing songs in social movements. Play of light has tremendous impact on each of the theatrical events as much as the dialogue itself. The Emperor is well versed in each of the sixty four elements of *Atharva Veda* with chapters on dance and designates himself as a connoisseur of theatrical texts."

Now the clouds have travelled far off to the northern sky. Moon is speading silvery pearls on surface of the earth. Some colourful events are visible at some distance in the plain land in front of Kumarigiri.

"Let us proceed to that area at once." She invited them with tempting allurement.

A vast area in front of Hathigumpha was covered with tent and was beautifully decorated with green flooring. It was clear sky of March. The Moon had overwhelmed the stars with its soothing beams. Numerous decorated lights, candles and *mashals* illuminate the area under the tent.

Salabhanjika while making a short introduction of contemporary happenings in the kingdom said, "Kalinga is a dominant and established part of the country with its capital at Kalinganagari. It attracts kings, emperors and the chiefs of small kingdoms to this capital town to sort out many local and national issues. Kalinga follows its principle of natural economy. Its ministerial council acts according to the law of nature. Kalinga had experience and had adopted some principles in foreign affairs. The state exchequer earns good revenue from incoming trading vessels. Kalinga with its huge sea trade is flourishing since the day of victory over south and elimination of piracy in *Mahodadhi*, the Kaling sea."

"Agriculture not only meets the hunger of its masses, it is prosperous with irrigation and yields of cash crops and materials suitable for export. We are proud of our Emperor when during his tenure he made agricultural production tax free in order to boost exports. Kalinga is a developed region on the east coast of the country and stands as an example of prosperity and success."

She now led them to the festival ground descending the wide steps of the hill. The friends were so much dazed with the pomp and grandeur of the show that it was exactly a dream for them. She explains them that the bare area existing at present was the venue of Kalinga Samaroh that had transformed to its original form as it were during the reign of Emperor Kharavela.

Salabhanjika ecstatically proclaimed, "You look to the great gathering of the Royal and the Noble invited from the whole of Bharatavarsa. Let me introduce them to you. The prominent personality dressed in Kalinga design with a dazzling necklace and pendulous kundals is none other than Kharavela. Just to the right in the row is Pandyan, the

Emperor of Pandya, the closest friend of Kalinga and a staunch Jain. To his right is the Chola king, Uttiyachera and also the king of Keralaputra. To the extreme right is Ranachakra, the king of Tamraparni. He happens to be a glorious son in law of this state linked through matrimonial relationship with the dynasty of queen Sindhula. He is accompanied by his defence ministers, Ranatunga and Ranavairaba. The latter two are non-resident Kalingans.

"Just to the left of Kalingadhipati is the Emperor Nagaswarupa with Empress Malli Mahadevi from central India. The Empress is of Kalinga origin, daughter of Rajpur dynasty. A number of princes of blood royals occupy the unending left row consisting of Princes of Mathura, Magadha, Anga, Banga, Rathika, Bhojaka and many others. They are invitees of Kalinga Samaroh and many have been allured to the spot of religious wheel propagated by Mahavir."

There were few agenda of the festival. Kalingadhipati, the reverential host and all the invitees sat down for the proceeding of the conference. The main theme was a religious discourse on merger of the two wings of Jainism the *Svetambara* and the *Digambara* sects. The great Jainism had split into twofold from the time of Chandragupta Maurya during the decade the long absence of Vadrabahu, the great Jain preacher who left for the Deccan. On his return his orthodox disciple Atinistha joined Digambara sect of the main Jain stream. It had its ill effects throughout the country with competitive and rival dimensions. A consensus on this issue was expected from Kalinga Samaroh.

During an intermission, *Salabhanjika* led the three invitees to visit different stalls erected by kings and religious dignitaries. The Kumarigiri was no longer a Jain pilgrimage, but a place of all religions, a site with multiple banners of the Hindu Rushis, the Buddhist Sages in addition to the Jain sect. Local villages specifically the Jagamada had participated in the *Yagna* ceremony of Hindus. The environment of the Samaroh was noisy in the presence of all religions which was the ultimate objective of the Emperor of Kalinga.

The *Salabhanjika* led them still to south of the fair with huge extension to south and east.

Discourse of the erudite scholars gathered from all principal cities of India was about to start. Teachers from diverse fields were preparing to present their best way of teaching linguistics and were discussing the harmony of different regional languages as an aid to national tourism and trade. These teachers and trainees were hailed from Kashi, Magadha, Nasik, Pandya and Sarabhanga Ashram. The Jain Sage, *Acharya* Kebalakalpa also came with his scholars from Taksasila University.

They went to the west extension of the industrial exhibition housing the stalls of small scale and the cottage industries. Excellent display of their domestic and agricultural products with method of production was demonstrated. From wood to stone, from metal to ivory were the materials that were used in cottage industry to yield finished products. There was a large crowd at the jewellery stall of gold, silver and bronze. Tourists and delegates from far off places were lured to the ear ornaments and *kundals* of various shapes and sizes used in Kalinga as a sign of prosperity. The preferred high selling ear ornamentation and ear studs were made of gold, silver and bronze.

The *Salabhanjika* again changed her direction back to the northern extension of the exhibition to front area of the hills from where a road went to Kalinganagari. The city was far to the east, not visible due to gardens of flower and medicinal plants with water reservoirs constructed by the administration. There were deep wells with water lifting apparatus.

Kalinga Maritime fare was in the eastern end of the exhibition with display of some ships, medium size vessels, boats and maritime equipments. The place was crowded by central Indian people who had been deprived of seeing the sea and the ship.

The *Salabhanjika* led them back to Kalinga theatre platform at Queen's Palace where there was demonstration of varieties of special Kalinga dances performed by beautiful Kalinga *Kanyas*. The youthful daughters of the land were performing dance with movement of entire body in *tribhangi* style in the tune to the harmonious melody of the mrudala and the accompanying harp. Some girls were performing dance at each nook and corner of the exhibition chanting,

"*Namo Arihamtanam* || *Namo Savasidhanam* ||"

This music was continuously resounding in the mind of all the participants of the Samaroh. Music and dance were entirely monopolised by women folks.

The Asika Vijay episode was enacted by heavy beating of the mrudala as war music that warms up the blood of the spectators. The sound increases in intensity when the Rathikas and Bhojakas surrender. Mrudala of Kalinga sounds so loudly that the spectators have to close their ears with their palms. It was the epic on destruction of Gorathagiri, attack on Magadha and chasing of the Demetrius *Yavana*. All the expeditions of the Emperor were being displayed sequentially with a tamed war elephant on the theatre platform. The glorious procession of Chaturanga military forces with a blood warming war song on Magadha victory was the special attraction for the participants.

"You feel the essence of these dances and songs being performed by the Kalinga Kanya with tremendous talents in them. The rhythmical steps of the dancer in tune with the music and concert were ultimately to express the entire theme of dance through body movements."

"My dear Avi, Aparti and Prana, I must communicate my personal experiences which I had not yet disclosed to avoid diversion from the main theme of the centenary." Listen... ..

"I was only fifteen when I was with my parents in Kalinganagari and had completed my formal education and my hobby in Kalinga dance. My father was a royal employee of the palace. We were having our residence inside the city. But my father was one of the confidential officers of Kalingadhipati and was years older than the Emperor. We had a family chariot driven by four horses. I was a student of the *Tauryatrika* School in Sisupalagada in my teen age. I knew the school was established by Kharavel as he loved dance, drama and music. He had established this school as these native cultures of Kalinga were on the decline during Mauryan administration."

"My performances in dance and drama were rated high by my teachers and spectators. I was also the best student of Dancing Academy in Central Street of Toshali located at the western limits of Kalinganagari. The Academy, named as Cheti Nrutyalaya was funded by the Royal family."

"I had completed my dance course the year in which the Emperor relinquished his throne. He opted for his residence in this Kumarigiri hill. He formed a higher *Tauryatrika* School here with a number of versatile dance, drama and song teachers. We all know the Emperor accomplished whatever he cherished in his life. His love for the divine art of *tauryatrika* was one of the factors for his remaining away from the rapid active commotion of the state administration."

"I am not proud of my career, but opted as a scholar in the dance school of Kumarigiri. Our life in such a residential school was as pure as Jainism itself and the cadre of Kalinga in dance and music were incomparable in Bharatavarsa as a whole."

"Cave expansion and rock-art were a bold steps taken by the Emperor on the twin hills. Many expert masons, carvers and monument writers from famous fields of the country were indented for the work. Many turned up from Barhut, Sanchi, Magadha, Nasik, Nanaghat and even the Arts and Crafts department of Taksasila. The Emperor and the Empress wanted to have two symbolic characters at the entrance of Jaya-Vijaya cave as one typical Kalinga beauty receiving the guest and the second a damsel with refined quality and good taste as a guide."

"The Emperor called upon the chief monument carver to carve out one Swagatika as *Dwarapalika* of left door and a *Salabhanjika* in flying pose above the former. Karmapani, the chief monument carver wanted two models for those ideal carvings. He requested the Emperor to choose two maidens with noble hearts and pure souls, ever joyful and gracious. The chief said that the rock art figures built with these angelic virtues in mind will have its blissful impact on the onlookers.

"Who would be the two fortunate fairies among the damsels of Kalinga, the resident girls on Kumarigiri and from outside Kalinganagari? The King and Karmapani selected two lucky models from among the row of expectant maidens each one appeared dressed in silk, gold and precious stones like princess."

"Two of them could be butterflies sporting in the sun, glad to say that I was chosen for *Salabhanjika* and Sweta for *Dwarapalika Swagatika*. I can't tell the story of Sweta, who was a jewel in the song section of the school, but I felt as though I could fly on the wings of my delight."

"We had to sit as models in Jaya-Vijaya cave for seven sittings and Karmapani with his escorts was transforming the rock wall with our exact postures. It was not comfortable at all to serve as models in the dusty atmosphere created by the chisel work, but our idea of getting into an immortal shape on the wall made us ignore the discomfort."

"I had reserved my story to make you bear in your mind this tale of my heart. Ages pass by, the sun and the moon took uncountable turns but the heart and soul of the model adheres to the sculpture forever. I continue as the ancient Puspita of Kalinganagari when I get back to life on the days of centenary celebration by grace of Agrajina."

The *Salabhanjika* completed her personal story as an obligatory addition to the episode.

She was emotional and tears welled up in her eyes. She felt restless with the memory was recalled in that stance, and her joyful face turned to be melancholic. She sobbed inconsolably. The memory of the past and present events overwhelmed her. Her only consolation was that she was not that butterfly Puspita of hoary past, but a *Salabhanjika* blessed by the Almighty to be part of the grand celebration of a great soul of Kalinga for twelve full moon nights and thereafter a lifeless rock in the shape of a girl in the cave.

Three friends had a chance to console her and express gratitude for the great responsibility she had been carrying on. They wished a flow of happy feeling in her veins.

The *Salabhanjika* repented for revealing her heart and soul from her ethereal form merely on emotional human feelings. Human values are brilliant in the atoms or *panchabhuta* of Vedic concepts so long as they roll on earth.

She came to her senses and said, "I hope I have not spoiled your tour by my story. You know everything is composed of heterogenous elements gathered into a mass. We have come almost to the end of the story and barely one full moon maybe there which would present the decisive movement of conglomeration of sorrows and remorse weighing equal to the victories and cheers of the Emperor.

Now I should not disturb you anymore. The valedictory address of the Emperor is about to start, let us walk to be among the crowd in the conference hall at Tangarapada."

The three mortals had been tuned to the events of past and as if they were subjects of Kalinga empire under Kharavela. They could apprehend the end was not far off to take farewell from *Salabhanjika* with a feeling of emotional outburst. The eyes were wet and they could partially listen to what the Emperor was speaking in his slow but steady voice.

"The growth and development of Kalinga is not a story of a day or a decade. It has achieved the targets of many centuries. Neither I myself nor the present Council of Ministers would exist tomorrow. It will go to Prince Kandarpashree or his son Vaduka. My body and soul is on the verge of final minute of my life and would be extinguished soon. I should bid farewell to my motherland."

The entire audience felt as if the earth under their feet creaked and cracked vigorously before the melancholy pathos of the Emperor's speech. Pandyan, the king of

Pandya rushed to the podium, where Kharavela was standing speechless.

The east indicated the arrival of the dawn and disappearance of the live show. The hill was as still as it should be washing away the events as a heavy wind sweeps away the fallen leaves on the ground. The *Salabhanjika* was no more, nor were the flicker of the light of *Dishidharikas*, With heavy hearts the three friends departed.

Chapter-19

Saint Emperor

Chaitra Purnima was the next to arrive, the full moon thatwould include the centenary celebration. The events that were being celebrated for last one year would end at the end of the night. The three nocturnal visitors were obsessed with such apprehension. They had been so habituated with the prevailing supernatural events that their end would naturally bring discomfort to them.

They had reached the foothill too early to lose even a moment of the event. The hills were motionless and still as they were expected to be. "The moon was inching to reach the centre of the sky. "We are a bit early," whispered one of them.

The hill had transformed itself to its ancientness in physical appearance. *Salabhanjika* was descending the stairway of Kumarigiri. She arrived in a state of gloom with her unkempt appearance. Probably she had a convulsive sob and had not wiped out her tears. Her eyes were swollen and red. The folds of her drapery were loose ahd her gait had no rightliness, no zest.

She received the guests as usual. A wistful smile on her lips, she said, "Henceforth we will look to the events of Kumaragiri, not Kumarigiri. Coming period is the events of sorrow and pity. The Emperor Kharavela has confined himself to a cave preferring solitude. It had been seventeen years since Kandarpashree, his son had ascended the throne. But *Kalinga Samaroh* had been over a year before his ascent to the throne. Emperor Kharavela had strictly secluded himself from administrative affairs of the land. He was neither an advisor nor he had any need from the royal treasury."

The *Salabhanjika* was too gloomy to narrate the lonely period of an elderly Kharavela. In the absence of their beloved Emperor the emotions experienced by the people were mournful in nature. The Emperor had completed the pattern of caves and the rock-cut architecture; reached the summit of Kalingan dance and drama and created a living pattern on the residential Kumarigiri hill. He was accommodative for his age, had left the Kumarigiri and had taken shelter in Kumaragiri where only the accomplished and the meditating sages lived.

Emperor Kharavela had retired from his active life. He would no more look either to the *tauryatrika* or the architecture. He was indifferent to the dignitaries on their way to Kalinga. He was no more a visitor to Kalinganagari since his day he relinquished the throne. But his dwelling in Kumarigiri was terminated from the day of *Kalinga Samaroh*. After his farewell speech he did not return to the Queen's Palace but stayed in Kumaragiri, the abode of meditation and rigorous yogic practices.

He had realised that a function always comes to an end. He knew how to conquer an unconquerable kingdom but could not visualise what would happen after conquering. Now he was pretty sure, life of any man or animal had to extinguish at some time. He had seen the *Dishidharika* and the torch flame she used but was never aware that the flame would extinguish at the end. The lamp of his royal life had limits, so also his life with arts and crafts in Kumarigiri.

Any function is a replica of the flame in *Dishidharika*'s lamp. He should not feel sorry to adopt the life of an ascetic. It is the law of nature and no life is an exception. Realisation of the realities of life is the greatest achievement of the wise.

Once during his busy days of expeditions, he had come across a simple puzzle in human life: the body and the mind. He could not then think further with elevated consciousness whether mind is born with body and dies with the body. The burden of this puzzle had continued to stay in the innermost corner of his mind. This quest of Truth reached a peak in course of time. Truth is manifest always but people, poor souls, find it only to be mysteriously invisible. But the reality is: some can't see it, some don't want to see it. Anyway, we humans are familiar with the only truth – Death. The truth is perfectly intelligible and never contested.

However, much discipline and spirituality you may adopt, your life will end one day or the other as an insignificant event to get buried in the oblivion of the past forever. Life is a mirage. The living is allured by a set of illusions without feeling the reality that death is unavoidable. Everyday man sees that people are dying including his friends and relatives. He knows that he will die one day. But he behaves as if he is going to live for ever.

"The valediction in Kalinga Samaroh is akin to putting out the light of an era."

His search enters the revolving idea of perpetuation. He was very generous for the *arhats* and the rigorous *Yapannapak* saints. He had arranged for making caves and providing attire for them. That was a mirage for him and for the saints. The mirage bypasses the reality of life, the coordination of body and mind. Body is the visible part of the lamp, the oil and the wick that burns. The visible parts are the elements of *Panchabhuta,* the constituents of a lamp. When it is lighted, the flame becomes the life of the lamp. Flame can be extinguished and not the constituent lamp; so is the mind. This is the story of the body and the mind.

He fails to understand his own self. Whether he himself is a role model in the display of life or his military expeditions are the acts of giving a false appearance. Building up Kalinga Empire is nothing but a mirage? Life is something of passive will and performance of an individual is prewritten and man is merely an actor in the theatre of life.

Nay! Nay! Life can't be like an extinguishable flame of a lamp. Human life has inherent value. Man has got the feeling of emotions and objective of his achievements. He has some set goals to attain. Human life is invaluable. It can't be assessed by a few parameters of philosophy. His thoughts pertaining to human life and values continued to get interpreted in every aspect of his life. He is in mental agony and was moving around in search of truth.

His residence in Kumarigiri had been historically significant. He was intimately connected with Kumarigiri with all its material glories, architectural beauty and the excellence in the field of dance and drama. It was hard to lead a life of dedication as a saint at this place of material abundance. He couldn't give up the attractions of the Queen's Palace theatre platform or the expansion of construction and rock-art in Kumarigiri. Now he was determined to go for meditation. He was proud of his heritage in which his ancestor Rajarsi Vasu had become a saint from being a king and so undoubtedly established the fact that a king could also be a perfect saint. He had neither been possessive of throne nor felt materially attracted to Kumarigiri. But his only weakness was

Padamulika Kusuma, his personal assistant. He was indispensable and he could not live without him.

Kusuma, the *Padamulika* prayed the Emperor to take rest in the cave meant for his meditation in Kumaragiri. It has auspicious architectural carvings of large garlands of local flowers and that of parrot. There are many carvings of forest animals with figures of his and Chief Queen and Sindhula. It is only habitable cave specially carved and designed for shelter of His Highness.

Kusuma spoke politely, "As your *Padamulika*, I will be at your feet to serve you as you meditate and lead the life of an *arhat*." In that critical hour of the Emperor's sudden outburst, Kusuma had immense courage to stand as a great pillar of support. He had enough of foresight to take up the construction of this special cave with the help of the rock-diggers and the best monument carvers of Kalinga, while the Kumarigiri rock works were going on the other side. He had been accustomed to the whims and impulses of his master since childhood. He could foresee the desires of the Emperor to adopt the ideals of his ancestor particularly Rajarsi Vasu. So he could visualize a space for meditation in the hill.

Knowing that the king would be too lonely being away from the near and dear ones he had requested the rock-carvers to have symbolic architecture of the Emperor's family. The royal couple in jubilant mood would look as dancers on a ceremonial appearance and the tree would represent the royal umbrella above them. The meditating Emperor would not cherish to see himself with crown any more but would not keep his eyes away from the dancing couple, displaying liveliness.

The Emperor voluntarily had chosen his ascetic life by giving up all his worldly pleasures. He was away from royal life since relinquishing administration and now further away as a Jain ascetic with rigorous routine in food and meditation.

"How many mendicants are busy in their meditation on the hill now?" asked the aged Emperor with an inquisitional tone.

"More than twenty monks are in deep meditation on this Kumaragiri in appearance of *arhats, munis and sadhus.*"

"I must tell you the theme of my meditation; it is on body and mind and their coordination in the living."

"Very intriguing aspect, My Lord, a great matter of philosophy and meditation."

"Can I find a spiritual guide in this aspect? Can any saint on this meditational field would guide me to proceed on?"

The *Padamulika* paused for a while; moved his index finger in the air pointing to east and west, north and south as if counting the meditating monks on the hill and nodded his head as he could trace the desired one and spoke solemnly, "Flesh and blood of the Jain mendicant flow in the gravity of meditation. We have a great soul concentrating on body and mind. He had been meditating on corporeal control of the mind, the relationship between body and mind. Padmanandin Digambara from south Sarabhanga Ashram had achieved excellence in this field and is now designated with title of Acharya Kundkund. He is very much present in this hill now. His abode is quite close by. Let me invite him to this place."

"No, no Kusuma, no. Don't call him here. As a beginner in meditation I must go and meet him as a polite gesture and respectful act."

"Your Majesty, *Acharya* knows you and your ideals. He has immense faith and respect for an Emperor as you are and the compassionate heart you have. He will be glad to meet you", instantly replied Kusuma.

Acharya had arrived at the cave. Kusuma introduced him to the Emperor. He might be omniscient would know the discussion between the Emperor and his *Padamulika*. His Godly appearance speaks of his identity and achievements. He was gifted with a smiling face and charming composure. He had least interest in the material world. He had already spent few months here at Kumaragiri. He is an *Acharya* of Digambara sect reluctant to have any attire. He is simple and pristine. He had neither longing in life nor fearful of death.

His main attractions were the suitable meditational environment of Kumaragiri. It is the sacred location which attracted Parsvanath and Mahavir. Blessings of the two Jain leaders, the Tirthankars had brought immense glory to the holy shrine. Initially he entered the place anonymously as a *Yapannapak* monk. He had met the Emperor many times to ask something for the *Yapannapak* community of saints. He had meditated initially in Yoganadi Tapovana, north of Kumarigiri and subsequently moved to Kumaragiri.

He was always in dailogue with himself, mazed with the conundrums of life and soul. He found a new way of astral projections in which the soul can temporarily leave the body and later can be willed to enter it. He is an *Acharya* with unlimited treasure of research!

Emperor Kharavela was staring at *Acharya*.

"Have you found something out of your curiosity; any meditation on your theme of mind and soul" asked the Acharya inquisitively.

"This ascetic life would analyze itself the bondage between life and soul. Material life is like a flame, but it does not vanish after end of its fire. It exists forever and would transform to life again to burn into flame again and again. It is not a fact to infer that life ends by the process called 'release' in principles of many religions" explained the Emperor.

"Honourable Emperor Kharavela, you are quite justified in stating that man is selfish by nature. He can't survive without self-care and selfishness. He had to be as mean as possible for survival. He can go to any extent to immortalise his body and soul", interpreted the *Acharya*.

The Emperor considered himself fortunate enough to have the great *Acharya* meditating in Kumaragiri. To express his genuine reverence he said, "I consider myself and the whole of Kalinga very fortunate to have you amongst us. With your presence, we feel the presence of Mahavir amongst us by which the whole kingdom has got elevated in beauty and bliss."

In response to the Kharavela *Acharya* said, "Mahameghavahana Kharavela is most successful as an Emperor and knows the knowing as a seeker of truth."

Chapter-20

A Tearful Salabhanjika

*A*charya Kundkund had departed after leave-taking from the Emperor. Kharavela had realised many stages of life as it really is during meditation. He had evaluated his life and achievements on a newer dimension in the light of his own philosophy. As a Jain he was neither belonging to *Suklambara* nor *Digambara*; but he was a practitioner of Jainism in its simpleness and purity. He had followed the principles of idolatry, worshipping of trees, respecting the Sun, the Moon and value of meditation. The administration of Kalinga under Kandarpashree had also followed his ideology.

The *Salabhanjika* with the three invitees was descending down to Queen's Palace to see the Conference by women of Kalinga when she noticed aged queen Dhruti is racing breathlessly to *Deba Sabha*, the site of Meeting of the Deities on hilltop of Kumaragiri. She was followed by Queen Sindhula, Members of the royal employees, the royal family and all the participants of women's conference. Even the Moon in the sky was pale and feeble looking at the saddest event on the earth.

Puspita was in a state of gloom with streams of tears rolling down from her eyes. Her long hair fell dishevelled over her face. She spoke incoherently, "Let us move to *Deba Sabha* ground. Merciless event is going to explode there.

With the sunrise, *Kali Yuga*, the worst period will enter Kalinga. Wait for the proceedings of the *Deba Sabha*."

Aparti whispered, "Puspita was quite aware of the sequence of the happenings of the centenary celebration. Sincerely she had managed in getting the best time for us. Past eleven episodes had revealed her power of retaining and recalling past experiences in logical sequence. Her appearance and gestures are befitting to the situations. But today she looks apprehensive and is confused in her speech. She probably hesitates to carry us to the main site of grief. When everyone here rushes to the top of Kumaragiri she stays behind! She avoids the scene going to reel off. The sky and the earth are weeping over this event. But she might move on with the gloom of the situation."

The rhythm of the grief was visible in the eyes of sorrowful Puspita. She was not bothered to arrange her unkempt hair. The unfortunate circumstances made her disoriented as to time, space and personal identity.

"Pity on me! My God, the great Emperor Kharavel is departing. A heart breaking event. This event is unbearable with your presence my revered guests. Your patience and inquisitiveness had very much impressed me and I am sad beyond comforting but I shall not deprive you of the most melancholic chapter of Kalinga history. Let us move."

Kumaragiri was overcrowded; there was difficulty in ascending to the hilltop in the mad rush. She preferred to take an alternative route in the south. They reached the top plateau where the crowd was settling. They were at some distance from the centre of the *Deba Sabha*.

Puspita looked at them in a melancholy gesture and said, "Good bye, Guests of twentieth centenary function!"

She went through the crowd to the centre which had

few people there. She had no chance to look back to them anymore. There were so many people in the gathering but their faces could be identified in the dim light of the distant moon. *Suka Swagatika* was there with *Dishidharikas, Dwarapala* and *Banshivadika*. Almost all of the participants of the hills were in the western row. In the crowd of northern stand were the bereaved royal family: Queen Dhruti and Sindhula, Kandarpashree and Vaduka including many royal employees. The south row was occupied by the locals and many from Kalinganagari.

Padamulika Kusuma was the first to break silence and said, "With a heavy heart I would inform you that last night the emperor completed his evening prayer and called me to his side to say that he was unable to carry on his daily activities due to senility of old age. He refused to follow *Salehan,* a Jain method of accepting death by fasting indefinitely. The local people of Kalinga prefer a natural death to that of the Jain saints who go to a distant location and die there after weeks of fasting which is quite unnatural. Nature which has created this life has its natural way of destroying it. His conscience did not allow this suicidal way of departing. The Emperor also promised to disclose any serious bodily pain that would come.

"In fact, the Emperor had expressed his personal disinclination for *Salehan.* He had looked down upon this suicidal way of dying as worse than the arbitrary division of Jainism into *Svetambara* and *Digambara.* He had some unique attributes as a Jain. He was a Jain king with vigorous expeditions in life. He had not severed his life style away from society but was strong leader in social and cultural development. He had his own distinct identity of respecting all religions and was in favour of worshipping natural deities like the tree and the Nature. His ideal was ancestor Rajarsi Vasu who had proved to be an ideal ruler, able administrator and coordinator of Kalinga. He was too broad minded and did not confine himself to his native state of Kalinga. He was against the invaders of India and had a march through the whole country with his Chaturanga military forces.

"Hours later he insisted to move to the plain land on hilltop to get over his breathing difficulty with cool mountain breeze. He was assisted by Kusuma and many Jain saints and mendicants to the hilltop. Moments after his movement, he was breathless with eyes wide open with broken fragments of a word emerging, 'Ka....li....nga', 'Ka....li....nga', 'Ka....li....nga'.

On receipt of the message of his illness, the whole royal family rushed to the spot. The benevolent public was puzzled spectators of the grave situation. They only saw him on the hilltop repeating the name of his beloved kingdom in an incoherent manner, 'Ka....li....nga'."

Kusuma reached the northern crowd and invited the ruler of Kalinga, Mahameghavahana Kandarpashree for the last *darshan* of his father. Kandarpashree came with tearful eyes and knelt down beside his departing father who cited with a voice incoherent with grief, "Oh the God of benevolence, thou have initiated all welfare of life on earth. All your education, accomplishments and expeditions are meant for welfare. You throb in the heart of all your subjects. You are the great achiever of *tauryatrika*, promoter of industries. I am proud to be your son." He started crying loudly and was about to faint. Kusuma helped him back to his place.

Then Queen Dhruti ran madly to the centre and stood at the feet of the Emperor. She gasped convulsively while weeping. She uttered, "Oh Emperor of wealth and grandeur, your heart is as large as the ocean and your soul is big as the sky. You are the proud son of Kalinga. You had dedicated yourself and your family in making of a powerful and prosperous Kalinga. You had stood as the commander in chief in all your expeditions. You are the great Emperor of wealth. Why do you leave me alone to bear such intense sorrow my heart is breaking?"

She whispered in pain and sat beside the death bed inconsolable benumbed.

Queen Sindhula could not control her emotion and tears. She came to the other side of the bed and wept, "Oh Victorious Emperor, Descendant of the clan of Rajarsi Vasu, your death has broken every heart with devastating sorrow and despair. Death did not show mercy for your ideals, humanity, conscience and religiousness. You dedicated your life for welfare of your people. You did give your entire wealth as alms and even opt yourself to be an ascetic. Oh Compassionate Heart, My savior, my ideal deity. I beg your longer life at the cost of mine own!"

She was too weak to be on her feet. She dropped down on her knees on to lie on the other side of the Emperor.

There was silence for a while.

The *Padamulika* Kusuma was choked with emotions. Looking down to the ground he uttered incoherently, "Oh Great Soul, The custodian of truth and law, for me you had descended from heaven. The kingdom will be blinded by your absence"

The *Padamulika* could not utter anymore. He sat down yearning for the soul departed for a country from where nobody returns.

Puspita emerged from the crowd of western row. She suddenly appeared in the front and said, "The

Emperor had the tremendous capacity to know and comprehend the nature of problems and decides which benefits one and all. He had dreamt of building a prosperous Kalinga with an insignia of portraying an image of *Salabhanjika* in Kumarigiri. I happen to be one among the three *Salabhanjikas* carved representing the symbol of prosperity. Ony those emperors who have the aspiration to build a fertile, powerful and prospering kingdom use this rock-art symbol His intention of carving me has been fulfilled. I have served as the harbinger of golden era into the kingdom of Kalinga."

Her speech created an upsurge of emotion among the audience. Her dishevelled hair covering her face could not hide her sorrow laden tears. In the midst of so much commotion, the presence of so namy looking lifeless, one could never miss. The noisy emotional outbursts prevailed for some time making everyone dormant and lifeless.

There was recitation of continuous hymns from Hathigumpha inscription, *"Kheemaraja, Bhikhuraja, Dhamaraja pasamto sunamto anubhavanto...."* Which was echoed from the sacred Gupta Ganga cave nearby. The mountain's gentle breeze was giving consolation to the inconsolable gathering.

The three invited guests could not hold back their tears. They believed for sure that the *Salabhanjika* would come no more for explaining.

Precisely at dawn, one could see the space that had re-lived two thousand years of history minutes before. The mourning crowd had been replaced by the shrub of *Nirash* plants which justifiably means the plants of despair. Every time they came here, every time raised the height of this deity by putting stones upon stone. They were astonished to know that it was the same place of *Deba Sabha* where the Emperor Kharavela breathed his last two thousand years ago .

With gloomy face and tearful eyes, they climbed down the hill. Their heart was heavy with the thought that they had no more full moons left to enjoy and no more sweet Puspita to receive them.

Aparti suggested to move to Jaya Vijaya cave to take leave of stone version of *Salabhanjika*.

"Farewell Puspita", uttered the three friends to the flying *Salabhanjika* when they noticed tear drops in the eyes of her stone form. Her human heart, exquisitely chiseled into her stone form, suffused the visitors' soul with the pain of lost love, a sweetness of that loving memory could dwarf and defeat the entire gamut of human glossary whenever man attempted to paint in words its essence in fullness.

Publisher's Note

Since childhood, the author was attracted by Khandagiri and Udayagiri, the two popular hills near his village. The intensity of such attraction grew with becoming an adult. The history behind them mesmerizes him today. The hills with their beautiful stone caves, their enduring steps and tasty blue berries of autumn had the uncanny ability of attracting him and his mates from the days they learnt walking. Subsequently they served as a good ground for playing hide-and-seek with a scope to explore their interior. When escorting maternal grandparents and other guests as a guide to the hills was entrusted to him by his family, it became his favourite pastime to accumulate enough curiosity and endless inspiration to fulfil the aspirations as the writer of this book.

When he became aware of the sanctity of the place popularly believed to be a seat of spiritual attainment, mendicants sitting in deep meditation flew as a wave into his perception. Pages of ancient history inscribed on the cave walls manifest the existence of golden days and the pace of religious flowering The fading illegible alphabets no doubt are attempts of a great leader who believed in the worth of the inscription that had been deciphered partly and synchronized greatly.

The local villagers' own perception of the hills, a lot of folklore and legends surrounding their past history impressed him deeply. A belief goes that a flying snake lives in these hills with the capability of envenoming any one to instant death with a single bite. The other strong belief is about Suna Jakha a rolling golden ball that appears in the dead of night that may be trapped and owned. Chances of finding gold and silver coins buried somewhere in or around the hills by a powerful and wealthy Emperor had created unprecedented desire among the villagers to be rich overnight with hidden treasure. It is also assumed by the locals here that the saints in meditation are alive and can be seen in that pose within and without the caves. As an author, he does not confine himself to any limits while searching the footsteps of the great Emperor.

The author has felt that someone is continuously whispering him the story, re-opening the rolled up events in the continuum of history. The text of Salabhanjika, the Midnight Cave-Damsel is based on folklore and archaeological evidences in existence today.

BLACK EAGLE BOOKS

www.blackeaglebooks.org
info@blackeaglebooks.org

Black Eagle Books, an independent publisher, was founded as a nonprofit organization in April, 2019. It is our mission to connect and engage the Indian diaspora and the world at large with the best of works of world literature published on a collaborative platform, with special emphasis on foregrounding Contemporary Classics and New Writing.

www.ingramcontent.com/pod-product-compliance
Lightning Source LLC
Chambersburg PA
CBHW050307110726
47899CB00007B/2144